I0553548

HOW *NOT* TO SURVIVE THE HOLIDAYS

Also available from DS Publishing

Sisters in Crime Desert Sleuths Sisters in Crime
Chapter Anthologies:

SoWest: So Deadly
SoWest: Crime Time
SoWest: Desert Justice
SoWest: So Wild
How NOT to Survive a Vacation

HOW *NOT* TO SURVIVE THE HOLIDAYS

Seventeen Original Southwestern Tales
from authors of the
Sisters in Crime Desert Sleuths Chapter

DS Publishing
Scottsdale, Arizona

DS Publishing
How NOT to Survive the Holidays
Copyright © 2009 Sisters in Crime Desert Sleuths Chapter, Inc.
DS Publishing. All rights reserved. No part of this book may be used or reproduced in any manner whatsoever without written permission of both the copyright owner and the publisher except in the case of brief quotations embodied in critical articles and reviews.

Copyright Acknowledgments

"A Christmas Tail," Copyright © 2009 by Deborah J Ledford
"There's A Dead Elf in Santa's Workshop,"
          Copyright © 2009 by Constance K. Flynn
"The Red Journal," Copyright © 2009 by Susan Budavari
"The Customer," Copyright © 2009 by CR Bolinski
"Baby, It's Cold Outside," Copyright © 2009 by Chantelle Osman
"Yule Night," Copyright © 2009 by Merle McCann
"The Night Before Christmas," Copyright © 2009 by Jean Steffens
"Relativity," Copyright © 2009 by Roni Olson
"A Christmas Stalking," Copyright © 2009 by Judy Starbuck
"Christmas Lights," Copyright © 2009 by Sarah Parkin
"The Gift," Copyright © 2009 by JoAnne Zeterberg
"The Price of Diamonds," Copyright © 2009 by Ann Ciemnoczolowski
"The Twelve Days of Christmas," Copyright © 2009 by Suzanne Flaig
"A Horse of Her Own," Copyright © 2009 by Mary E. Burt
"Christmas Came Late," Copyright © 2009 by Howard B. Carron
"The Last Resort," Copyright © 2009 by Nancy Nielson Redd
"New Year's Eve Surprise," Copyright © 2009 by Kris Neri

This is a work of fiction. All the characters, places, and events portrayed in these short stories are either fictitious or are used fictitiously.

Cover Layout: Kästle Olson
Cover Artist: © Jeff Cameron Collingwood
Interior Design and Formatting: Deborah J Ledford

ISBN: 978-0-9828774-5-6

DEDICATION

Dedicated to
New voices waiting to be heard

The passion of writing

The joy of reading

ACKNOWLEDGMENTS

The Desert Sleuths Chapter of Sisters in Crime would like to acknowledge and thank our editors who worked tirelessly and devoted many hours in order to create a finished product in which all Sisters can take pride. Thank you editors, Susan Budavari, Sue Flaig, Merle McCann and Chantelle Osman for a job well done. We send additional thanks to Jean Steffens and Roni Olson for their administrative assistance; and to all of the contributing authors who helped make this memorable book happen.

TABLE OF CONTENTS

TABLE OF CONTENTS

A CHRISTMAS TAIL
DEBORAH J LEDFORD

CLUTCHING a two-foot tall Christmas tree decorated with small silver ornaments in one hand, a paper cup of coffee in the other, Salvatore Fortino walked along the garbage-strewn Manhattan alley. Fat flakes of snow whirled around him and not a single person entered the dawn's dull light. He picked up his pace, catching sight of a woman lying next to the row of dumpsters, wrapped in her customary tent of newspapers and garbage bags. Sal patted the woman's shoulder and set the cup of steaming coffee close to her grimy face. "Merry Christmas, Lucy," he said. She mumbled her thanks, but didn't stir.

Turning up the collar of his overcoat, he approached the nondescript rear door to the Fortino Feast restaurant. Unlocking the deadbolt, he felt a warm nudge at his calf. A smile swept below Sal's grey handlebar moustache as he glanced down to see the long haired, caramel-colored cat that had appeared ten days ago and had welcomed Sal every morning since.

"Step aside, Scampi," Sal said, nudging the cat with his polished wing tip. The cat padded clear of the door. Sal lowered the measly tree so that Scampi could take in the sharp evergreen scent. The cat's tail flicked, whiskers bobbed, he closed both of his brown eyes for a moment, as if replaying a cherished memory. Sal chuckled.

He lowered his bulk and glanced around the alley to make sure no one watched, then whispered, "Merry Christmas, Giuseppe."

Struggling to stand upright, he then headed through the door to disarm the alarm. He glanced back at the cat that waited in the same spot. "Okay, come in, but be quiet. No one must know our little secret."

Favoring his back right leg, Scampi bolted over the threshold, then performed a figure eight around Sal's legs, nearly causing him to lose his balance. "Stop that. You're getting hair all over my Armani." Scampi nodded and limped ahead.

Sal walked along the cold corridor lit by bare, low voltage bulbs hanging from the ceiling every few feet to where Scampi waited atop the third step in front of another closed door. The cat meowed, paw raised, batting the air.

"Yes, yes. Your treats are in there. Be patient. We must find a place for the tree first."

Sal unlocked the door and stepped inside, but Scampi only took a few steps, then he sat, licking his lips, knowing the rules. "Good kitty, kitty," Sal said, flipping on the light switch. Florescent tubes flickered and hummed and after a moment, blue light bathed the kitchen lined with stainless steel everything.

He shrugged off his coat, draped it on the chair tucked under a built-in desk, and set the Christmas tree beside the reservation pad. Plugging in the single strand of lights, random colors of red, green and blue blinked on and off. Sal turned his satisfied smile to Scampi. "Pretty, yes?" Scampi grunted. "I know," Sal responded. "It's not much, but all that Gino will allow."

Sal went to the Sub-Zero refrigerator, reached inside for a white wrapped package, then laid it on the gleaming eight foot long prep counter. He reached for a long carving knife and tapped the tip of the blade against the bottom of one of the pots and iron skillets hanging from a rack above the counter. Scampi wailed with anticipation at the *tinking* rhythm.

"How does Christmas duck sound, Scampi? Okay with you?"

The cat purred his approval.

Taking a heavy skillet from the rack, Sal lit one of the stove burners and drizzled olive oil into the warming pan. He reached into a bin, selected a head of garlic, peeled off a section, smashed it with the butt of the knife, and added the

2

clove to the oil. Turning back to the counter, he unwrapped the paper, then sliced a hunk of meat from the duck's breast. The oil popped when the fatty skin hit the sizzling oil. Man and cat closed their eyes and raised their heads, inhaling the rich aroma.

"If Enrico finds that cat in here, he'll cook it up for this evening's special," a voice boomed, reverberating against the hard surfaces of the room.

Sal whirled, his heart thudding in his chest. He let out a relieved sigh seeing only his brother, Gino, standing at the swinging double doors that led to the dining room of the twelve table restaurant. "Merry Christmas, Gino."

"It'll be our last one if Enrico walks in here and sees it in his kitchen."

"Scampi is not an 'it'," Sal said. "Have some respect."

"Respect?" Gino asked, looking more perturbed than amused. "For a cat? What's it—*he* doing here?"

"I've named him so that people don't think I've gone *pazzo*."

"I already think you're crazy, Salvatore. Why do you call him Scampi?"

"Don't you get it?" Sal beamed an amused smile. "He's a restaurant cat."

"Only you would think of that," Gino muttered.

"Listen, I've been thinking real hard and..." Sal thinned his eyes, wondering how much he should say.

"Don't hurt yourself," Gino kidded.

"I think he's Uncle Giuseppe."

Gino stared at Sal, stunned. "I knew this day was coming. Today, it is official, you've finally lost your mind, brother."

"No, it's true. Look into his eyes." Sal speared the meat in the skillet with the knife, took it to the counter, and settled it onto a plate. "Every cat I've ever seen has green eyes. His are brown. The hair too, it's the same color. Exactly like Uncle Giuseppe's. And Uncle Giuseppe had a bum knee. Scampi walks with a limp, too. Look at him. *Really* look."

Gino crossed the room and bent down in front of the cat. "What'd'ya say, cat, are you Uncle Giuseppe?"

Scampi kept his eyes trained on Sal's every move as he cut

3

bits of the dark meat into tiny bites.

"He's ignoring me," Gino said. "Maybe it *is* Uncle Giuseppe. He always liked you better than me."

Sal laughed, taking the plate to the cat. He knelt beside his brother and they watched Scampi eat.

"Wolfs down food like Uncle Giuseppe," Gino mumbled. "He looks well cared for. Must belong to someone around here."

"Uncle Giuseppe was always impeccably groomed."

Gino rolled his eyes. "That cat is not Uncle Giuseppe!" He raised up, taking Sal's arm to help him stand upright. "Not that I want to encourage you, but why do you think he's our uncle?"

"Remember back when Uncle Giuseppe disappeared?"

"Not really." Gino sounded disinterested. He flicked a non-existent speck off his tailored suit jacket.

"It was ten days before Christmas. His body turned up Christmas day, but he was missing for ten days."

"That was thirty years ago, Sal," Gino said. "Where are you going with this?"

"Scampi, here, showed up ten days ago. He meets me at the door every morning. I think he's been trying to tell me something."

"What?"

"Who killed him."

"The Sarducci brothers killed him," Gino said.

"Maybe not."

"They're still doing time at Rikers Island for it."

"They're up for parole, did you know that?"

"Nope." Gino crossed his arms against his chest. "Don't care, either."

"I don't think the Sarduccis killed Uncle Giuseppe."

"You never did."

"No, and I'm not the only one. Officer Mahoney didn't think so, and neither does Scampi." Sal turned to the cat. "Right?"

Scampi let out a blood curdling yowl, spun three times, and then sat, staring up at them.

"See?" Sal gave Gino a satisfied nod. "The Sarduccis

never killed anyone before."

"They always carried guns," Gino reminded.

"Yes, but only to scare people. They were scrawny kids— everybody picked on them, remember? They never carried knives. Uncle Giuseppe was stabbed."

Gino lowered himself onto his haunches. Scampi nudged his head against Gino's knee. "Thirty times," he mumbled, his eyes locking to the cat's. "Officer Mahoney told me that."

"I still remember that night, Uncle Giuseppe sitting at his favorite table at the front window, eating lasagna."

"Yep, like he did every night. The big mooch."

"Then the next day, *poof*, he was gone."

"Why, after thirty years, would Uncle Giuseppe suddenly reappear?" Gino asked.

"Maybe it took him that long to find us."

"We've lived in the same neighborhood all our lives. This restaurant has been in Papa's family for generations." Gino stood up, a frown creasing his brow. "What's to find?"

"Maybe he got lost."

"Maybe it took that long to dig up from Hell." Gino laughed.

Scampi raised his head and focused his glassy eyes on Gino. The cat's ears reared back and a guttural growl rolled from deep within. Gino reared back, the amusement evaporated from his face.

"You've made him mad," Sal said, shaking his head.

The front door to the restaurant slammed shut. The brothers swung their heads toward one another. The sound of a man whistling an uneven tune in the dining area grew louder.

"Enrico," they both muttered in unison.

"He'll skin us all," Sal said, raising his eyebrows. "We've got to get rid of—"

The swinging doors burst open and the chef entered, dressed head to toe in immaculate white, an apron strained over his bulging mid-section. Enrico glowered at the brothers. "What are you doing in my kitchen?"

Sal looped his arm through Gino's and tugged him closer, hiding the cat behind them. Although Enrico was not a member of the Fortino family, both were terrified of the petulant chef who had ruled the restaurant and all of its employees for thirty-two years. Neither could speak.

Panic clutched Sal's chest as Enrico approached the prep counter.

"You've ruined my Christmas duck," Enrico roared, taking up and waving the desecrated carcass at the brothers.

"I only needed a little slice," Sal muttered.

"You eat after the customers," Enrico said, his cheeks blooming red. "How many times must I tell you this, *è idiota*."

"It's not for me." Sal realized his blunder and clamped his hand over his mouth.

"If not for you, then who?" Enrico zeroed his glare on Gino who opened and closed his mouth, but no words escaped his lips. Enrico snatched the knife from the counter and pointed it at Sal. "Who?"

Sal and Gino stepped aside, revealing Scampi.

"*Madon!* What is this?" Enrico screamed. "Who let a filthy cat in my kitchen?" Knife in hand, he slowly stalked toward Scampi.

The cat growled and hissed, the hair rising on his back in spikes.

"No! Stop!" Sal grabbed Enrico's arm. "It's Uncle Giuseppe."

Enrico stopped, the blade wavering in his grasp. The color drained from his face. "That's insane. You really are *un idiota*."

"Stop saying that," Gino snapped. "My brother is not an idiot." The cat yowled and spit. Gino stood tall and proud, but Sal knew his brother's knees were shaking as badly as his own. "Sal's kind and thoughtful, and—"

"Delusional," Enrico said, a self-satisfied look on his face.

"I am not," Sal muttered. "He's Uncle Giuseppe. Just look at him."

Enrico looked down at the cat, the knife trained on him. The cat craned his neck and stared the chef down, continuing his upset, froth foaming at his mouth.

"Get it out of here," Enrico stuttered, never taking his eyes off the beast.

"Sal thinks the cat knows who killed him...I mean, Uncle Giuseppe." Gino offered.

"The Sarducci brothers killed your uncle," Enrico said, his voice quavering.

"No, they didn't," Sal said in a defiant tone, his hands clenched into tight fists.

"Well, if the Sarduccis didn't kill Giuseppe, who did?" Enrico challenged.

The cat sprung into the air and flung himself against Enrico's massive belly. Enrico slashed with the long blade, his howls mimicking the cat's. The chef stomped and flailed his body in an attempt to dislodge the claws of the suddenly feral feline.

"Oh my! Oh my!" Gino cried out, dancing about, not daring to step into the fray.

Sal grabbed one of the iron skillets from the rack, closed his eyes, and swung. The pan made contact against something solid with a *thunk*. Enrico dropped to the floor. The cat popped atop Enrico's back, spun a tight circle and emitted a howl.

The brothers stared at each other, their eyes wide as the realization set in.

"Enrico killed you, didn't he, Uncle Giuseppe?" Sal asked the cat, bending down to rub his head.

The cat jumped off Enrico, sat, then tipped his head, first at Sal, then to Gino.

Gino took a step back and tapped the sign of the cross on his chest. "Uncle Giuseppe!" He clamped his hands together, holding them close to his heart. "It *is* you."

"The Sarducci brothers are innocent!" Sal said.

"You're right, Salvatore. Enrico always hated Uncle Giuseppe."

"He never thought Enrico used enough oregano in his sauce."

Gino shook his head. "Well, that, and the fact that Uncle Giuseppe was bedding Enrico's wife."

Sal's mouth dropped open as he turned to his brother. "No. Really?"

"You're not an idiot, Sal, but you are a little dense

7

sometimes."

Sal shrugged and then pointed to Enrico's motionless body. "Did I kill him?"

Gino lowered himself and carefully placed his ear close to Enrico's mouth. "He's still breathing. We need to get Officer Mahoney over here."

"What if Enrico doesn't tell him he killed Uncle Giuseppe."

Gino righted himself, scowled and slapped a fist into his palm. "Oh, he'll tell." Then his menacing expression faded. "But until he gets here, you better keep that skillet handy."

Sal clamped the pan's handle with both hands and took a batters stance. "What do we do now?"

Gino stood there, hands on his hips. "Warm up last night's lasagna. I'll call Officer Mahoney. But first..." Gino crossed the room, opened one of the swinging doors and turned to the cat. Gino took on his most professional waiter pose, bowing at the waist, sweeping his arm toward the door. "Welcome back, Uncle Giuseppe. Your favorite table is waiting for you."

The cat lifted his head in an arrogant pose and strode into the dining area, knowing exactly where to go.

DEBORAH J LEDFORD is the award-winning author of the Inola Walela and Steven Hawk suspense series. Three-time nominee for the Pushcart Prize, her short stories appear in the print publications *Arizona Literary Magazine, Forge Journal* literary magazine, *Twisted Dreams Magazine, AnthologyBuilder,* and other Sisters in Crime anthologies to name a few. Deborah invites you to visit her website for a complete listing of credits: DeborahJLedford.com.

THERE'S A DEAD ELF IN SANTA'S WORKSHOP
CONNIE FLYNN

"DEREK..."

I set my water bottle down on my cluttered desk and looked up. Maureen's ashen face peered over the cubicle wall. Today she had hollow eyes, making her pallor seem even worse, but since she always looked colorless, I paid it little mind. "Yes?"

"There's a dead elf in Santa's workshop." Her tone was hushed, horrified. The words were silly. I laughed.

"A dead elf? Riiight. Good one, Maureen."

"I'm not joking."

I shoulda figured. She wasn't known for her sense of humor. A grim little woman with those marionette lines going all the way to her chin. Still, she was a damn good book-keeper and Santa thought well of her. But a dead person? In Christmasland? Sure it was only fifty miles from Vegas, the sin capital of the world, but it was still The Place Where Dreams Come True. Oh, come on.

"You mean he's unproductive. You want me to talk to him? Lay him off?"

"No, Derek. A body! A dead one, real dead. I'm sure of it. I checked his pulse. Besides, there was a hole between his eyes and all this gooey stuff splattered..."

"Okay, okay." Putting my hands up to ward off the mental picture that sprouted from her words, I rose from my chair. "Did you call 911?"

"Noooooo." She shook her head like a puppy shaking off bath water. Impossibly, her tone sounded even more horrified. "Opening day's just a week away. Besides, there's another problem. A worse one."

"Worse than a murdered elf?"

"The elf's my husband."

"Oh, hell. This will be real bad for business." S.C. had fired Ron the week before and the man wasn't even supposed to be on the grounds, much less in Santa's workshop. But his death would be all over the news, S.C. would be implicated. I sounded heartless even to myself. A man was dead for God's sake, his wife had found him with his brains shot out.

I was a miserable excuse for a human being, I'll admit. But opening day was this Monday. Christmasland couldn't withstand a scandal. Murder? In Santa's workshop? If I were female, I would have swooned.

I hot-footed it from my cube to the entrance of Maureen's. "Come on, we've got to tell Santa."

"No, no. He'll blow his top, I mean..." Her grim little face crumpled. "The blood...I can't do it...pleeease, Derek, don't make me go with you."

A thin line of black mascara streaked from one hollow eye down her cheek, and she looked deeply troubled. Her husband had died in a horrible way. I admit I tried not to, but I pitied her. "One of us has to call the cops. Are you up to it?"

"Yeah. I can call."

"Okay. I'll tell S.C.

A few minutes later I dragged S.C. from his palatial office.

"If this is some kind of stale April Fool's joke," S.C. grumbled as we entered the workshop, "you're losing your Christmas bon—"

His last word got lost in retching sounds and he sank to his knees.

Never before had the workshop's polished wood and muted carpet been quite so elegantly contrasted against the image of a brain-spattered elf sprawled like a forgotten puppet on an ergonomic chair. It was art noir at its worst.

Unfortunately, this wasn't art. Ron Pasternik, husband to Maureen, former head elf of Christmasland's Premier Gifts division, was a for-real, eyes-wide-open, bullet-hole-between-them goner.

Forewarned by Maureen's gory description, I managed to

hold down my breakfast, but Samuel Claus Holiday, President of Christmasland, aka Santa Claus to hundreds of thousands of yearly visitors, rocked back and forth on his knees muttering, "Jesus, Jesus, Jesus," while spilling his guts out onto the thick Berber carpet.

I walked over to a hand-woven basket, pulled out a clean shop rag and carried it back to my partner.

The basket was uncomfortably close to Ron and his blowback, but I saw something reflect in the dawn light coming through the clerestory windows. A Razor-type cell phone.

Something I knew I should leave for the police to find, but I had a sick feeling about how this murder would affect Christmasland. This amusement park was my life. I lived for the holiday events—the raising of the thirty foot pine, the decoration ceremony with Santa and his elves, the releasing of the reindeer and the tinkling bells on their harness, the rapidly increasing balances in all our bank accounts. Yes, Christmas was a miraculous time and nothing should be allowed to interfere.

S.C. wiped his face while I mentally digressed, then offered the soiled rag back up to me for disposal. Tempted to lift my eyebrows disapprovingly, I stopped, seeing this as a perfect opportunity to get the phone without being noticed. "You owe me." I plucked the rag from his hand by a corner and carried it to the service's return bin, which was next to the basket.

It was easy enough to accidentally drop the rag, then swoop down and simultaneously pick up the phone. It was damp and had leaves and God knew what sticking to it and I had no choice but to shove it in my pocket. When I turned back I saw that my cover-up was unnecessary. S.C. was still rocking on the floor. I returned to him and extended my hand, helping him to his feet. A man's legs had to be shaky after such an intense experience. Truth was, I still felt a bit unsteady myself.

"Who could've done this, Derek?" S.C. turned away from the carnage. "Why didn't you just throw away the rag? It's covered with puke."

11

"Every missing rag costs us money."

"Crunching numbers at a time like this? Give it a rest, Derek."

"Only if you'll stop throw—" I shook my head. "Never mind. You're right. Not now."

"Damn straight. Where are those cops, anyway? I've gotta get out of here." S.C. practically broad jumped to the door and with those long legs he almost made it.

My walkie-talkie gurgled. "Shriver," I answered.

"Detective Zilog is here," Maureen said. She sounded funereal.

"I'll let him in," I told her. "Go home."

"I can't. He ordered a lockdown on Christmasland. No one in. No one out. Not until the murder weapon is found."

I frowned. "There goes the neighborhood."

FLAGPOLE, Nevada, was a small community that existed solely because of Christmasland. Detective Zilog ran the police force with an intensity of a big city Police Commissioner. He favored tailored suits in charcoal gray and shoes polished to an unfashionable gleam. Today a trench coat hung over his sloped shoulders, and he looked English, although I knew he'd grown up on the streets of Detroit. I waited on the porch as he approached. Zilog looked disappointed.

Zilog had been chomping for an excuse to prowl Christmasland's five-square miles ever since it opened five years ago. He'd sent his inappropriately copious staff out like a nasty rash spreading across the rolling landscape of the park, insanely convinced they'd apprehend a bunch of drug-dealing elves and Santa's helpers. They'd returned empty-handed.

What? No crack or speed? How could that be in this virtual opium den? Lord, the man was a paranoid sicko, who saw crime everywhere, even in places as wholesome as Christmasland.

"What's got you down, Detective?"

"No weapon, no people. Where is everyone?"

"On a needed break, resting up. We open next week you

know. Besides, it's not even eight a.m. Right now, just me, S.C., Maureen and the dead guy are here. Well, Clara, too, but she wasn't here when we discovered the body. Have you looked at it yet?"

"Got my CSI on it."

You mean your rookie cop who shot himself in the foot? Oh, how I wanted to ask—Zilog had been so proud when he'd stolen this guy from the Reno police force—but instead I probed to see what he'd learned. "You got a time of death?"

He grimaced at the clipboard he carried, and scanned a list. "Ron Pasternik. Married to Maureen."

Nope. No time of death. He wrote something on the clipboard, lifting it to see better in the muted morning light. "Maureen's the bookkeeper, is that right?"

"Yep, and you should let her go home. Or have you forgotten she just lost her husband?"

"Not at all. You think she killed him?"

He let his arm fall, the clipboard slapped dramatically against his leg. I suspected it was deliberate. I was also miffed that his question had occurred to me, too. The Pasterniks' marriage wasn't exactly made in heaven.

Zilog scanned the park again, his gaze going across the barren grounds filled with sleighs and crystal-covered buildings. Off to one side was the barn for the reindeer—a couple of them grazed in the corral. "Doesn't look like much, you know," Zilog said. "Always wondered why people'd pay so much to come here."

"For the magic of Christmas," I provided. "Why else?"

"Or to buy drugs."

"Oh, get off it, Zilog. You've been riding that horse ever since we opened Christmasland. If you had proof, you'd have made an arrest."

"Some crimes are hard to prove."

"Well, prove who murdered Ron. This is very bad for business. We open next Monday."

"So you've said."

"And for good reason. If you aren't careful, Flagpole's tax revenues won't be enough to pay your salary."

"There you go again, throwing your weight around."

13

"Can't you come up with something new, Zilog? Reagan wore that line out."

Zilog glared, reminding me that he was a lawman and I wasn't...and that a murder investigation was on the table. He cleared his throat. "I need to question everyone who was present when the body was found. Are they all here?"

I nodded.

"Including Mrs. Claus?"

"She wasn't here when we found the body." I started to remind him that the Clauses weren't really Clauses, when he said, "How 'bout that, here she comes."

I turned in the direction that drew his ogle. Yes, here she came, a vision in a winter white pantsuit, dark curls piled atop her head. She smiled, sad lines remaining around her eyes.

"Mrs. Claus," Zilog said, extending his hand to her.

"Holiday," she corrected, but her tone was courteous. "Mrs. Holiday."

"Exactly." He turned to me. "Where can we gather the persons of interest?"

"Santa's office. Where else?"

SO here we sat in S.C.'s office, Zilog staring at each of us one by one as though we were Sons of Sam, or even worse, the parents who spawned that evil killer. Zilog sat alone at one end of the table. Maureen, me, S.C. and Clara sat at the other end.

In line with the Christmasland theme, Santa's all white office was spacious and filled with clear glass furniture. Clusters of giant glittery snowflakes covered the walls. There's always snow in Christmasland was one of our promises. We made sure of that by trucking it in if nature failed to cooperate, and it made the park famous. I should know, I came up with the slogan. Yet I still held only forty-nine percent of the stock and had a cubicle in accounting, while S.C. held fifty-one percent with an office that was his version of an ice palace.

"Only fitting for Santa...and my Mrs. Claus," he'd once said, stroking Clara's sculpted arm to make sure everyone knew they were married.

14

Only fitting. Riiight! After all, the Holidays run the entertainment division of the park. I only handle operations. Who cares what my office looks like?

But we had a dead elf to contend with, so I tamped down my bitterness and let Zilog have the floor. Besides, Clara and I had plans to change a few things at Christmasland.

Zilog started with Maureen. How like the jerk to pick on the weak link. "Where were you when your husband was murdered?"

"I, uh, what?" she asked vaguely, ripping her attention from the pristine wall in front of her, which she'd been eyeing as though an angel might step out of it at any time.

"Where were you when—"

"I heard you the first time!" She shook her head. "How would I know? When did Ron die?"

Much as I disliked it, my respect for Zilog shot up. He'd worded that question beautifully and could have trapped Maureen, especially in her state of mind. But having failed, he dismissed her with a curt nod and leveled the same question at the rest of us. We shrugged almost simultaneously and Clara said, "We'll tell you when we know the time."

"Soon as I know," Zilog replied, then lobbed a packet of papers onto the table in front of Maureen. "Recognize those?"

Lips compressed, she flicked the packet, not bothering to pick it up. "Our divorce petition. Ron and I were splitting up."

"Yes!" Zilog leaned forward. "And having quite some battle over assets, I hear."

Maureen was getting a white line around her compressed lips and I didn't like Zilog's bullying ways. "What are you getting at?" I leaned aggressively forward, mirroring him.

"I think Maureen looks good for killing hubby."

Maureen gasped, swayed. I steadied her. "No, no," she intoned. "No. I didn't kill him. Not only was Ron trying to steal me blind, he was a cheat. He and Clara were fooling around. She killed him."

S.C.'s whiplash must have hurt as much as mine when we both whirled our necks to look at Clara. She'd been cheating?

15

With Ron, the head elf? The guy was a borderline creep, who deserved to be dumped by Maureen, but not for fooling around with Clara.

"Ron?" Clara clipped out. "Me and Ron? You're nuts, Maureen."

"I have proof." Maureen whipped her cell phone from her purse and flipped it open. "Right there." She pointed to a picture. "Right there. Him and Clara, embracing like lovers."

"For God's sake, it was a thank-you hug."

"For what?" S.C.'s voice held more ice than hung on the walls.

"A gift," Clara answered. "I'd asked him to make a special gift…for…for someone." She looked down and not for the first time I admired how her dark lashes curled over that perfect skin.

"I fired the bastard last week," S.C. said. "Why was he making you a gift?"

"He didn't make it here," Clara replied with forced evenness. "He was delivering it."

The family feud progressed, nothing new being added. In what seemed an attempt to distract himself, Zilog gripped the phone in Maureen's hand. "I'll take that."

She resisted his tug, then let go, apparently realizing she was an actual suspect. Just then, an officer appeared at the door.

"Sir?"

Zilog signaled him to wait.

During the pause, S.C. said to Clara, "What did you have Ron make for me?"

My God, the man was beyond arrogant. What did women see in him? That he was tall? So was I, although not as much. That he had all his hair? So did I, although not as much. That he charmed them? How? By constantly asking what they'd done for him?

"You'll like it," Clara said, still looking down.

I could stomach no more. "Detective," I asserted. "We need to establish alibis. End all this speculation and accusation. When did Ron Pasternik die?"

The uniform was still waiting at the door and Zilog shot

him a questioning glance.

"Near as they can determine, between eight and ten p.m. last night."

"That settles it," S.C. proclaimed. "Clara and I were together."

Clara's head shot up. I gave her a quick warning look.

"Is that true?" Zilog tilted his head in her direction.

She nodded.

"How about you, Mrs. Pasternik?"

"In the barn, feeding the reindeer. I talked to the handler."

He turned to me. "You got someone to vouch for you, Shriver?"

"My mom. We were on the phone." I hoped I didn't get struck by lightning. S.C. had opened a sniper's nest with his lie, one Clara had no choice but to confirm. Admitting she was with me would only make things worse.

"You got a record of that call."

I shrugged. "Probably not. I used my land line. It's a local call."

"You saying we have to take Mom's word on it?"

"Pretty much." I shrugged yet again, and Zilog didn't look worried. I knew he wouldn't. He'd already pegged this murder as domestic violence.

"Well, we're at a standstill for now." He looked at Maureen, S.C. and Clara. "You three, don't go anywhere," then at me. "You're free to go." He picked up his clipboard and prepared to stand.

"Sir?" the uniform said. "You might want to reconsider."

"Why is that?"

"We discovered the gun, sir. Uses the same caliber bullet found in the vic. Most likely the murder weapon."

"You found the gun?" S.C. sounded surprised.

"Where?" asked Zilog.

"In Derek Shriver's cubicle. Buried deep in a crammed full drawer. He did a damn fine job of hiding it."

I jumped to my feet. "That's impossible."

"You did discover the body," Zilog said.

I shook my head. "Maureen did. She asked me to tell

S.C."

"I did not!" Maureen's indignation sounded so genuine that I almost laughed.

S. C. eyes bored into me. "You're the one who came to get me."

Clara said nothing.

I glanced around the table at each and every one, and in that moment the good news was that I was sure S.C. killed the elf. The bad news was that Zilog's officer found Ron's phone in my pocket. He confiscated it along with my phone and the walkie-talkie, then made a show of cuffing me. I stayed silent, aware that no one would believe a word I said.

Except Clara.

I hoped.

MAKE yourself comfortable, Mr. Shriver." Officer Found-the-Gun, currently warden pro temp of the Flagpole City jail, ushered me into what he called a cell. "This is almost like one of those grand hotels. Not like any jail I ever seen." And not like any grand hotel I'd ever seen. Officer Found-the-Gun apparently hadn't traveled much. But I thanked him anyway and looked around, as he locked the door with parting words that I could expect dinner soon.

I was actually quite familiar with this room—I slept in it when I was a kid. My mom and I had lived in this bungalow for nearly three years while my dad was off fighting the first Gulf war, followed by a stay in Afghanistan. The minute the officer walked me in I checked all the visible locks and saw that they'd never been changed. Not that Flagpole needed a lockdown facility. Mostly they used the four small rooms to house drunks while they slept off benders. Still, you'd think they would have updated the hardware.

My good luck. As soon as I finished off the chicken fried steak from the local diner, I lounged on the soft bed until Officer Found-the-Gun settled in for the night.

It wouldn't take me long after that to gather proof of my innocence. And, hopefully, Clara's. When they booked me into the jail, I watched them log in the gun and the phones, including mine and Maureen's, place them in a plastic bin, and store them behind a door that also had a flimsy lock.

My guard was a nice enough guy, but no match for my Special Forces training if he caught me. And adding to my luck was that Detective Zilog was more interested in proving that opium and demon weed grew in Christmasland's back forty. So while he was spinning his wheels, I'd prove that S.C. killed Ron.

I'd be out of here by morning.

AFTER lights out, the bungalow fell as quiet as the night before Christmas. I followed my plan, did some skulking and some simple lock jiggling and soon carried the plastic container back to my room.

Maureen's phone first. After putting on the latex gloves that were part of the evidence room's supplies, I went straight to the phone's picture files, interested in seeing if there were any other cozy shots of Clara and Ron I should know about. There was just the one, and things were starting to go downhill for Maureen. She'd implied she snapped the picture just before Ron was killed, but the timestamp showed it was taken several weeks before. I'd love to get a peek at S.C.'s phone. Had she sent it to him? Not unlikely. But my suspicious mind doubted she'd taken the pic as a prelude to murder. Ron's shooting wasn't premeditated. No one in their right mind would sully Santa's workshop with blood and brains.

So I moved on to Maureen's text messages. There were a couple in the box from her service provider and she'd erased some recently. I hit the undo feature.

The phone beeped as loud as a Chinese gong and went on as long. My heart pounding just as loud, I dropped the phone back into the lockup container, dragged it with me under the covers and waited. My good luck saved me again. Several minutes passed and Officer Found-the-Gun didn't show up. Must be a heavy sleeper.

When my heart finally stilled, I threw back the spread. Maureen's phone glared up at me, its screen filled with a long list of messages.

Over half were from S.C. I skimmed them and while

some were strangely cryptic, others were shockingly direct and revealed an affair. *Last night was heaven on earth; Your lips taste like wine* — that from Maureen. *Your body feels like silk beneath my hands.* Yuk! Double yuk. I'd been right! S.C. had murdered Ron. But not once had I considered that it wasn't about Clara. It was about Maureen. The idiot had cheated on Clara! Outraged as I was, I couldn't ignore the irony. Santa Claus trading his Beauty for a woman who was definitely Cinderella before the ball? But so much the better for me, although I was trying not to think that way. Yes, Clara could be mine, but first I had to clear myself of murder.

I was about to put the phone back in the container when I saw one message had a picture attachment. A click on the icon opened it. Odd thing to send to a mistress, I thought, viewing what looked like a plant nursery. With a shrug, I turned off the phone and picked up Ron's phone.

I was hoping for more evidence of infidelity and runaway passion, but when I opened the phone, I found a small damp leaf stuck to the screen. A quick tour through the photos revealed that Ron had snapped a mother lode of incriminating evidence.

And now I knew why he'd been murdered.

Taking my own cell phone out of the bin, I phoned Zilog, who barked, upon answering, "How'd you get a phone, Shriver?"

"You won't care," I told him, "because I'm about to give you the best Christmas present ever."

A week later, Santa and Mrs. Claus stood by Christmasland's main gate, greeting visitors on opening day. Only this time I wore the Santa getup and for the umpteenth time wondered how any disguise could hide Clara's curvy figure.

And now she was my Mrs. Claus. Once more my luck astounded me.

I'd met Zilog that night at the reindeer barn. Everyone thought Maureen frequented the barn because she loved the animals, never suspecting the marijuana farm in a secret basement. But all the proof was in Ron's phone. He'd tried to blackmail Maureen and S.C. Neither had been charged yet, because they each blamed the murder on the other and fingerprints had been wiped from the gun. I liked to think it was an accident, but dead is dead and eventually one or both of them would face the music. Ron got the last laugh. His pictures would send them both away on drug charges.

It still troubled me that S.C. would jeopardize Christmasland for a few bucks and also that Zilog was proved right. But at least Clara and I were fully cleared and free to plan our future. We knew nothing about the under-barn marijuana factory, and Zilog soon became convinced.

The silver lining was that the press went crazy about the marijuana factory and it totally eclipsed news of Ron's murder —may he rest in peace. And for some perverse twenty-first century reason, people were coming to tour the nursery, which we'd already adapted for growing poinsettias and other Christmas plants.

"Santa." A boy about seven tugged on my jacket. "Jeremy Carson told me you sold drugs. I told him he was a dweeb, Santa'd never sell drugs."

"You were right," I assured the worried boy. "That Santa was an imposter. I only sell healthy junk food."

The kid stared up at me. "Oh sure," he sniped. "Jeremy said you're all imposters."

I wasn't yet an experienced Santa and the remark left me speechless.

"Well," he asked. "Is that true?"

Clara touched his shoulder. "Do you want Santa to be real?"

His head went up and down like a bobble elf.

"Then believe it, kid," she said. "Remember, this is Christmasland, the place where dreams come true."

✝ ✝ ✝

CONNIE FLYNN, best known for her paranormal romantic thrillers from Penguin Publishing, *Shadow on the Moon* and *The Dragon Hour*, among others, has switched to writing suspense novels. Her first ever short story, *Old Bones*, appeared in *Map of Murder* (Red Coyote Press). She claims writing short was the hardest thing she's ever done and says "I'm pleased 'There's a Dead Elf in Santa's Workshop' is part of our chapter's first anthology. Writing it was pure fun." Connie lives in Arizona, teaches creative writing at Phoenix College, and is co-owner of Bootcamp for Novelists Online, a web-based novel writing school. ConnieFlynn.com

THE RED JOURNAL
SUSAN BUDAVARI

"IT'S a pile of money, Aunt Carolyn," the five-year-old insisted.

"How do you know, Sammy?" Carolyn Baxter asked her brother Jim's son.

"The lady in the picture told me."

"Sweetie, what are you talking about? What lady?"

"Her." He pointed to a photograph on the desk next to them in the family room.

"You mean your Aunt Valerie?" She touched the framed photo of her late sister who had died of leukemia on Christmas morning six years earlier.

He nodded, his lips puckered.

"Are you joking with me?" The precocious little boy sometimes liked to tease her.

"No, Aunt Carolyn. She told me." He brushed his left eyelid with the back of his hand. "It's true. She talks to me."

Carolyn wondered why Sammy would say he could talk to an aunt who'd died before he was born. Taking the parental approach, she knelt down, placed her hands on his waist, and looked into his eyes. "Sweetie, do you know what fibbing is?"

"Uh-huh. Telling a lie."

"What's a lie?"

"You make up something. That's not true."

"Like saying you spoke to your Aunt Valerie?" She held the photo in front of him.

"No. Really. She told me she wrote in her umm...*journey*...where she put the money. She hid the...journey in the fireplace." His eyes sparkled, a look of absolute innocence and honesty on his face.

"Her *journal*? She hid her journal in the fireplace?"

"Yeah," he said. "She said that. I just forgot the word." He giggled.

"Why would a grown lady talk to you about her journal?"

He shrugged. "I don't know. She just does."

"Do you talk to her, too?"

"Only a little. I listen, mostly."

Carolyn wondered what to ask him next. Then, Stacy, her sister-in-law, walked into the room.

"It looks like the two of you are having a nice visit." Stacy turned her attention to her son. "Sammy, please go wash your hands for dinner."

Once Sammy left the room, Stacy said, "Jim just called that he's stuck late at work. So it'll just be the three of us for dinner."

Carolyn nodded. "Sammy claims Val talks to him."

Stacy waved her hand. "Yeah. He's told us that, too. We didn't pay much attention to it. When I was his age I had a secret friend."

"Did your secret friend write in her journal where she stashed a ton of money, and then hide her journal in *your* fireplace?"

With a straight face, Stacy shot back, "A *ton* of money? And where in the fireplace did she hide it?"

Carolyn rolled her eyes. "I didn't ask Sammy for specifics."

"Dinner can wait. Let's take a look."

"You're putting me on, right?"

"What have we got to lose?" Stacy shrugged. "Money couldn't come at a better time with me out of work and Christmas just days away."

Carolyn threw up her hands and laughed. "I don't believe this."

"Look, anything's possible. Val spent a lot of time here right before she died and she always had a pen and pad in hand." Stacy nodded. "And with her weird sense of humor, she could've hidden something in the fireplace."

"I doubt Val communicated from the Hereafter about anything," Carolyn mumbled, as she followed Stacy into the living room to check out the fireplace. Sammy was a very bright boy for his age, but psychic? It would take an awful lot to convince her of that.

Failing to find the journal stuck in the crevices of the fireplace, the two women were still on their knees when Sammy came into the room carrying a toy airplane and an army tank.

Stacy asked her son, "Where in the fireplace did your Aunt Valerie say she hid her journal?"

"Huh?" was his only response. He dropped his toys on the floor and began pulling an ornament off the Christmas tree.

"Sammy, leave that alone," she scolded.

Carolyn crawled over to him, took a porcelain angel from his hands, and hung it back on the tree. In her kindest voice she said, "Sammy, please look at me. Honey, you said the lady *told* you she hid her journal in the fireplace."

"Oh, the lady's *journal*," he recited. He pointed to the bottom row of fireplace bricks. "Behind there."

While Stacy stood with her arms folded, Carolyn inched back to the fireplace and began jiggling bricks in the bottom row. The only thing she dislodged was an acrylic fingernail. She complained to Sammy, "There's nothing here."

The boy walked over to the fireplace. "The lady said to kick the bricks. I'll show you."

Sammy began kicking. His mom joined in. Suddenly, one of the center bricks moved a tiny bit. The women tried to wiggle it free, but weren't able to.

"I'll get something to pry it out," Stacy said.

In a few minutes she returned, face flushed, carrying an iron chisel and hammer. After a few well-placed taps, she eased the brick out and reached inside. "I found it!" When she took her hand out, she held a thin red leather notebook.

Carolyn pressed her hand against her chest, barely able to contain her excitement. She blurted, "Let me see, too."

While the women huddled, Sammy, no longer interested in the whole matter, picked up his toy airplane and ran around the room waving it in the air.

After flipping through some of the pages, Stacy looked at Carolyn with a dismayed expression on her face. "I can't make head or tail of what Val wrote here."

"Give it to me." Carolyn took a long look. "It's some sort of code. Val liked to play tricks on everyone. I'm not surprised she'd make it difficult for us."

"So what are we going to do?" Stacy pleaded.

"Try and figure it out. *Duh!*"

Carolyn searched her memory. Did Val have a secret code when they were kids? While the notion seemed familiar, she couldn't remember anything specific. She had no idea what to do next. So she asked her nephew.

Reaching for his hands, Carolyn said, "Sammy, honey, stay still for a moment. Did Aunt Valerie, the lady, tell you how to read her journal?"

He giggled. "You're silly, Aunt Carolyn. She knows I can't read."

"Well, I *can* read, but I *can't* read the journal." Carolyn wondered if she really expected a sensible answer from a five-year-old kid—albeit a possibly psychic one. "How are we supposed to find out what she wrote?" Her question was directed at Stacy, but Sammy responded.

"You're 'posed to go to a mirror," he said.

The two women looked at each other, shrugged, then rushed to a nearby mirror.

After several minutes of detective work, they'd deciphered the name of a bank. What they needed to do next was to go to a local branch of the bank named in Valerie's journal.

ARMED with Valerie's death certificate and her will, Carolyn, Stacy and Jim Baxter sat nervously waiting until a bank clerk in a crisp navy suit and a Santa hat introduced herself and escorted them over to her desk.

"Happy holidays, folks," the perky twenty-something-year-old said, as she offered them some foil-wrapped holiday chocolates. "How may I help you?"

Carolyn introduced herself and spoke for the group. "I'm the executor of the estate of our late sister and sister-in-law, Valerie Lindsey, and we've just found out she had an account at this bank at the time she died."

"May I see your papers and ID?

Carolyn handed them to the clerk who inspected them, then asked, "Do you have your sister's social security number?"

Carolyn read the number out loud.

The clerk keyed the information into her computer, glanced at a card on her desk, pressed a few more keys then announced, "I'll need to check with my manager. Be back in a minute." She took Carolyn's paperwork with her.

While they waited, Jim said, "I just had a thought. Maybe Val used Baxter, not Lindsey. Especially if she opened the account before 2000, then didn't change the name on it when she married Drew Lindsey." He chuckled. "I bet she knew something—that she wouldn't stay married to him for very long."

"There you go again, Jim," Stacy protested, "you never liked Drew. You were delighted when they split."

"That aside, I could be right," Jim countered.

"Okay, guys," Carolyn said, "hold that thought until you get home."

"In a way, I feel a little foolish sitting here six years after Val's death," Stacy said to Carolyn. "If I were to tell anyone that my five-year-old son talked to his dead aunt and that's how we found out about this account, they'd think I'm crazy."

"We'll have time to figure that one out," Jim said. "We have to get the money first. It could still turn out to be a wild goose chase. I kinda doubt any son of mine has a sixth sense." He snickered. "Wouldn't it be great, though, if he did?"

Carolyn nodded. "I hate to admit it, but I'm starting to feel Sammy's on to something. We've gotten this far and I think we're going to find Val's money."

"The whole thing doesn't make much sense to me," Jim said. "Then again, Val was always unpredictable and she loved giving people gifts, especially for Christmas."

The clerk reappeared with a printout in her hand. "Well, there's an account connected with that social security number under the name, Valerie *Baxter*."

Jim smirked and patted himself on the shoulder.

The clerk said to Carolyn, "You'll need to fill out some forms to get the funds released. It shouldn't take very long to process the documents."

"Could you tell us how much is in the account?" Jim asked, his hands trembling.

The woman glanced at the printout. "Just under forty-five thousand dollars."

Carolyn's mouth fell open and Jim's eyes glazed over. Stacy looked upward and mouthed, "Thank you, Val."

ON the drive back to Stacy and Jim's house, Carolyn spoke from the back seat, "I still can't figure it out. Could it really be that Val talked to Sammy?"

Stacy looked back at Carolyn. "I can't believe it. People don't talk from the Hereafter, especially to a kid they've never known. Why pick Sammy, and not you, Carolyn, or Jim, or even me? There has to be another explanation."

Without taking his eyes off the road, Jim mumbled, "I'll talk to Sammy and find out what's really going on. But, who knows? Maybe the kid is psychic. We've got to keep an open mind about this."

Both women said in unison, "Yeah, right."

A door slammed and Jim Baxter stomped into the living room where Carolyn and Stacy sat chatting.

"That kid's stubborn. He still insists Val talked to him. I had to leave his room before I lost my temper." Jim shook his head. "Even after I threatened he wouldn't get any Christmas presents if he didn't tell me the truth, he didn't change his story."

Stacy looked from Jim to Carolyn. "How could it be true?"

"Why don't you and Jim go to the kitchen for a cup of coffee and let me try to find out some more," Carolyn offered. "Sometimes kids respond better to somebody other than a parent."

She knocked on Sammy's door. "It's Aunt Carolyn. Can we talk a little bit?"

The door opened. "Hi Aunt Carolyn."

"What are you doing?"

"Watching a movie." He sat down on his little red chair facing the TV screen.

"Which movie?"

"*Rudolph the Red-Nosed Reindeer.* It's my super favorite."

"I like it too."

"Mom recorded it for me from TV."

"Could you please pause it, so we can talk just a little?"

"A-huh." Sammy clicked the remote.

Carolyn sat down on the floor next to the boy's chair. "I wanted to ask you again about your talk with Aunt Valerie, the lady in the photo."

"Okay."

"Well, you were right. We found the journal in the fireplace and then we went to the bank where Aunt Valerie kept her money."

Sammy smiled. "I know, Daddy said. But he didn't believe Aunt Valerie told me."

"I'd like to believe you, Sammy."

"I wasn't lying." He shook his head and puckered his lower lip.

"I know you said that Aunt Valerie told you. But she died a long time ago. Do you know what that means?"

"She went away and she's never coming back."

"Yes. That's why we wonder how you could talk to her."

"She talks to me a lot."

"Okay, she talks to you. But I don't understand *how* she does that."

"Oh." His face lit up in a big smile. "I'll show you." He flicked the remote to continue the movie.

"Sammy, please stop the video. We haven't finished talking."

The little boy made a face. "I'm gonna show you." He focused on the movie.

Losing patience, Carolyn said, "You can watch the movie later, Sammy. You said you were going to show me."

"You have to look at the movie."

Trying to control her voice, Carolyn said, "Sweetheart, it's not very nice of you to do this. You're making me wait while you watch a movie."

"You have to wait until the movie is *over*."

She stood. "No, Sammy, I won't wait. You need to show me *now*."

"I don't know how."

"What do you mean?"

"Can you make the movie go to the end?"

"Fast forward it?"

"Yeah, that's it."

She took the remote from him and pressed the button. When the movie ended there were some outdoor scenes at the seashore. Then an interior image came on the screen. Carolyn watched it for a few moments then froze the frame, rushed to the door, and called out to Stacy and Jim. "Guys, come in here. There's something you have to see!"

While waiting for them, Carolyn played the video to the end then rewound it to just past the final credits of the movie.

When Sammy's parents entered the room, Carolyn pointed to the TV and pressed play.

Valerie appeared on the screen. Her complexion was pale and she had dark rings under her eyes. "Now that you've probably had your fill of all my favorite home movies," she said in a strong voice, "I'm going to get to the good part." Her face cracked a broad smile. "I've squirreled away a pile of money." She held up a red notebook and waved it in the air. "I've written in here, where I put the money. I know my days are numbered and when you listen to this, I won't be around. I had planned to take a cruise around the world. That's not going to happen." She paused for a moment then spread out her arms. "So, my dear family, check out my journal, then claim the money and have a very merry Christmas. My last gift to you."

"Omigod!" Stacy cried out. She rushed to the VCR, removed the tape and inspected the casing. "I didn't notice this earlier, but Val's initials and the year code are etched in the corner: *VB 2K3*. This is from 2003, the year she died." Stacy started shaking. "I must have recorded *Rudolph* over her home movies." She shrugged. "I found the tape in the family room and assumed it was blank." After catching her breath, she added, "I guess it wasn't. I'm really sorry."

Jim heaved a sigh of relief. "At least, now we know the source of Sammy's *psychic* ability." He bent down to give his son a quick hug, then stood and put his arm around his wife, drawing her close to him.

"Not so fast," Carolyn exclaimed. "I watched that video to the very end. Val never said *where* she hid her journal."

All eyes turned to Sammy.

The little boy sat facing the TV, his eyes glued to the screen, silently moving his lips.

SUSAN BUDAVARI has written two psychological suspense novels, several award-winning short stories and co-edited and contributed to three mystery anthologies for Red Coyote Press, the most recent, *Medium of Murder* (2008). Prior to that she worked in scientific information management and chemical research in the pharmaceutical industry and was editor of *The Merck Index*, a best-selling encyclopedia of chemicals, drugs and biologicals. She is an avid portrait painter and photographer of desert landscape.

THE CUSTOMER
CR BOLINSKI

ERIN weaseled over to me, pushed my coat open and pointed to my suit. It was 100% wool, purchased as is and on sale.

"Good taste," the sarcasm in her words had a bite. We were wearing the same outfit. Only mine had a hole under the right armpit.

"Humph," I responded, and walked in the opposite direction. As if I really cared—she had the bigger hips.

It was winter, no doubt about it. The frosty December mornings in northern Arizona were quite different from Phoenix. Everyone was bundled in wool coats, scarves and gloves.

While we waited outside in the snow and ice for our manager to let us into the clothing store, I looked at the lighted reindeers that hung rigid against the outdoor mall lights. They circled the shopping center's Christmas tree which was an Arizona spruce this year. Its many decorations were donated by the small businesses in the mall.

Damn. My heel caught in a metal grate even though ice covered most of the sidewalk. It probably served me right for thinking bad thoughts about Erin's hips. Carefully I pulled my heel loose and joined the other employees, all of whom chose to wear boots because of the snow. I was determined to wear my designer shoes, bad weather or not.

When Toni, our boss, appeared at the door, I should have interpreted her red eyes as an omen. She jammed the key in the front lock, pried it loose, than tried again. Finally, she managed to open it and greeted us with a big smile. The smile was unusual and I became suspicious that something was going down. We marched through, pushing our way in, out of the weather.

"Girls, we're going to try something new today!" Toni's enthusiasm should have awakened us. "You'll be given an assigned position and I want you to stay in it–all day." That was a surprise. Toni previously told us we would never have to be in a specified area for more than two hours at a time. I wondered why she changed her mind. It may have had something to do with the jeans she purchased on a 40% discount, and were much too tight on her.

Toni and I were friends since high school. She bubbled with personality. It was easy for her to whisk away old friends from their other professions to work for her. We all enjoyed being around her. But Toni was boss, and whatever direction she gave, we listened–usually. I wanted to ask her about the red eyes, but thought that should wait for another time.

She pulled me aside, "We've got to do better. Our sales have really been down."

There were five of us in attendance. Toni, of course. Erin, my bigger outfitted twin. Katia, who usually worked in the stockroom, and Rena, also a floor person like me. Our actual titles, *sales consultants*, were plastered on our name tags, although sometimes we were clothes coordinators or clothing specialists. We needed to be clothing connoisseurs, or at least, well informed amateurs. And that was me, a clothing amateur.

We had an hour before the store opened. My early morning task began with vacuuming the front section. After locating an outlet and nearly tripping on the mannequin that greeted customers by the front door, I begrudgingly pushed and pulled the electric machine along the tiled and carpeted floor. I suppose I could say that vacuuming was part of my job responsibilities and add that to my resume.

Erin retrieved some racks of new synthetic suits and rolled them onto the floor where the other daily specials were being offered. They had arrived the day before and were going to be part of the day's sale items. She lingered over the suits, probably deciding which one to buy with her store discount.

I finished cleaning just as Toni shoved the welcome signs out, and pulled in, literally, those few customers that stood frozen by the glass windows outside. We were officially open.

34

One of the frozen-looking customers was a medium-sized man, dark curly hair, as thick as this season's new mohair sweaters. His clean shaven face radiated against his black leather jacket and black pants. Apparently he didn't know it was too late in the season to wear leather. He smiled when he caught me looking him over, but stayed in the front and seemed to be searching for someone. Then he vanished into the early morning crowd, probably on his way for coffee. Too bad I couldn't have been his personal shopper. But I was sure there were other late-in-the-season dressers I could nab.

I was ready at the first of four cash registers, when a tall slender woman entered the store. She removed her leather gloves and hurried to the polyesters where she proceeded to finger each pants suit on display, as if inspecting for sewing defects. As I bent to retrieve my glasses which had slid onto the floor, I considered rushing over to stop her peculiar scrutiny of the non-porous materials. When I looked up I was face-to-face with the same woman, whose fingers anxiously tapped on the counter.

My upper lip puckered into a smile. "May I help you?"

"I hope so." She appeared out of breath, which seemed odd. All I saw her do was leave her fingerprints all over our daily specials.

"Were you looking for anything in particular? A pair of pants? Something on sale?"

"No. Nothing." She tapped more frantically on the counter.

It's a clothing store. What else could she possibly want? "Well. Is there anything else I can do for you?"

"That man outside. Do you see him?" She raised her eyebrows. "He's been following me." She bit her bottom lip.

I looked toward the door but the mannequin was in the way, today dressed in a purple tencel jacket, with a long patterned skirt and high black boots.

"No. I don't see anyone."

She stretched her long lean neck over the aisles of clothing, over the metal roadrunner that hung on the wall, and over the beaded necklaces scrunched together, hanging from a jewelry tray near the front doors.

35

"He was right there, by the entrance," and pointed her finger toward the front of the store.

I stared out front and may have seen a flash of something dark fleeting across the street, toward the bookstore.

Please the customer, I thought, although I wasn't sure whether to believe her. It was still pretty early and we weren't that crowded. What the heck.

"Let me run out there and take a look. I'll be right back." The woman was obviously shaken up about something.

I grabbed the big sweater jacket I kept under the register and ran out the door. A figure in black pants and leather jacket turned the corner, and immediately I recognized him as the man who was in our store before the lady entered. I wondered if I should let her know, but didn't want to scare her any more than she seemed to be. After all, I wasn't sure about the intentions of someone who obviously wore the wrong fabrics during winter.

She was waiting for me when I returned.

"Did you see him?"

"I'm not sure. Maybe." I breathed into my hands to start some circulation. "Was he wearing a black leather jacket?"

She nodded and clasped her hands together. "Yes!"

"And you're sure that was him?"

"Of course."

She seemed glad I saw her guy. *But now what?*

I asked, "Why are you so afraid of him? He looks so, so last year."

The woman whispered, "I got here early this morning hoping to buy some synthetics for a trip I'm planning. So I started window shopping, you know, at that other store near here."

That *other* store was our competitor, at the end of the block.

She looked around our counter then back at me. "I saw him reflected in the window display while I was looking at a coat. I continued walking down the block and caught a glimpse of his face in every store's window. I heard footsteps and it sounded like they were running toward me. I dashed into the shop next to yours just as they opened and ran to the back. He chased me in there, and when he wasn't looking, I slipped out and came in here." Perspiration seeped from her forehead. "Please help me."

Her plea for assistance came at a bad time. Toni was adamant about her girls staying in one place today. Of course I felt for the woman. "Do you want me to get my manager, or have her call the police?"

The woman answered rapidly, "No! No police. Just let me stay here a while. Maybe he gave up. We could watch and see if he comes back.

I wasn't a good baby-sitter, I knew for sure I wasn't a good adult-sitter, but what else could I do. Of course I would try to guard her from harm; it was a woman's thing. At least until the store got busier.

Three customers were rummaging through items at a nearby table. The sales area looked like a mess. I told the lady to stay close to me, and headed toward the middle of the store where the sale items were about to drop on the floor.

I turned toward her and asked, "Is he someone you know?"

"Never saw him before in my life." She hesitated, "I'm carrying a great deal of cash."

"Perhaps you'd like to go into one of the dressing rooms and hide your money," I offered. "Put it in your shoe or bra. May make you feel a little safer." I remembered seeing that in a movie. But she didn't appear interested in taking my advice.

THE colored piles of 100% cotton shirts were jumbled together. They were one of the day's store specials, and immediately drew attention. Casually I refolded a ¾ sleeve maroon tee, using the plastic folding board we hid under the table. I looked up at the woman when I heard her breathing become more rapid.

"Can I get you a cup of water?"

She turned away, looked at the front of the store, and held her neck.

"If not water, maybe something else? I think there's a can of cold soda in the back." I waited but got no response from her. "Miss."

Her back was to me. I started to pick up another shirt, turquoise with a bell shaped logo on the pocket. When the lady didn't respond, I dropped the shirt.

"Miss, can I...?" I watched her fall on the floor like a dishrag. "Oh no!" Her hand dropped by my foot. I screamed out, "Oh, my God!" and stared down at the woman.

Toni who was speaking to another customer nearby, heard me and quickly came over.

"Toni..." I pointed to the woman's head. "She thought someone was after her, turned toward the door, then collapsed. Can you tell if she's all right?"

I was glad to have another person handle the comatose body. My boss and friend, and evidently master of many talents, including CPR, knew that when she couldn't get a pulse or hear her breathe, the woman was dead.

It surprised me that the customers, who walked into the store, didn't even notice the body. Perhaps it was the daily specials, but none of the potential buyers were looking at the floor, or at any of the sales associates who gathered near the victim.

I helped Toni push four clothes racks together, forming a square around the woman. Of course we used those racks that had the long dangling, wide-leg, 95% polyester pants. Our woman now hid inside black and brown dress slacks, the ones that were $10 cheaper if you bought two.

Together we headed toward the stockroom, in the back of the store. We had an emergency situation here, and she needed to call 911 right away.

The stockroom also contained Toni's office—a small opened closet that now housed a computer desk. Toni nearly tripped over my feet when I bumped against some boxes in our back room.

"Why didn't you stay in your station?" she asked. "I told everyone to stay in their assigned positions today."

"Why was that so important?"

"An order from the owners. They insisted we try this new floor plan. They thought if our sales associates stay put, the customers will be able to rely on having the same person to answer their questions. They said they wanted *stability* on the floor." Our eyes locked, the red in hers seemed to intensify. "I can't believe this happened. Not today." She walked to her office and reached for the phone.

There was no place to sit. I held onto a nearby clothes rack, filled with tan woolen pants about to be steamed. When I leaned further into the rack, Katia, who was scheduled as the day's steamer, grabbed its silver rods and took off with it. I was left standing, holding onto air.

I wondered if wearing the same outfit as Erin today was bad luck.

"They're on their way," Toni announced. Impatience spilled into her voice. "I was told to close the doors, explain to the customers what happened, and ask them to stay, at least until the police arrived. Just let me…" She sat down at her computer, ran a tally of the morning's sales. Her tight jeans ripped into her waist causing some exposed skin to roll out of her sweater.

I reminded her, "Toni, the lady." My voice felt like an article of clothing that had been tried on too many times.

Her red eyes bulging, she snapped, "I'm so stressed out. The owners are very upset about our sales figures. And last night," she paused, "Pete and I had it out about money again. I can't lose this job!"

She regained her composure, and looked my way, "But you're right. There's time for that later."

Toni closed the computer program and grabbed me by the hand, pulling me along as we left the stockroom. She then rushed outside and put a big "temporarily closed" sign on both glass doors, and told the remaining customers what happened. Their facial expressions showed concern and I concluded they'd decided to stay. Toni stood by the front to inform any new clientele who hadn't noticed the signs, that the store was closed. She continued to wait there for the police or medical people, whoever showed up first.

Within fifteen minutes sirens screamed outside the store. An ambulance pulled into an emergency space right in front. Toni responded quickly and immediately opened the doors. Two EMTs pushed their way through carrying a stretcher. Three police officers followed.

Two of the officers traded places with Toni, as she handed the keys to one of them. While that officer locked the doors, the other asked the waiting customers questions. I wondered how often the police departments changed their style of uniforms. How many professionals specialized in designing police clothing? I'd have to add that to my career opportunities list.

Toni ran over to the EMTs and pointed to the racks of clothing that neatly tucked the woman away. We were told to move the pant specials immediately. The third officer followed the emergency medical men. A few minutes later, Toni introduced him as Officer Styles. "I'm a homicide detective," he announced.

Detective Styles carried yellow tape in his hand. Our comfy retail store had just turned into a crime scene.

My adrenalin was pumping overtime and my face, for sure, must have been as red as the latest sweat suit that hung in the *new arrivals* area in the back.

"Suppose the woman only had a heart attack?" I asked anyone who happened to be around.

Officer Styles overheard my comment. "It's just a precaution, Miss. We always bring tape."

I looked down at the strange woman, turned away abruptly and hoped the cause of her death was simple, like the new synthetics that didn't need ironing.

I noticed the police officer's clothes were wrinkled and moist. His boots needed polishing; scuffed soles and black marks ran down the heels of his shoes. He certainly could have used an appointment with our personal shopper.

Rena was getting ready to take cartons to the compactor outside. Another duty tacked onto her sales associate status, which she seemed to enjoy. We'd nicknamed her *garbage gal*. Rena also made soap, an interesting hobby for someone who liked garbage.

She parked her dolly by the front and took out a key from her pocket. One of the two officers stopped her from reopening the doors.

"Hey. Lady! Not now. No one is to leave this store until we say so." Her tiny figure was wrapped into a white fake fur coat, ready to brave the snow.

Her cart, loaded with the yesterday's packing materials, shimmied and swayed as Rena reversed her destination and headed toward the back. The officer stayed close by her.

Officer Styles called my name. "Your boss tells me you're the one who talked to the deceased woman." He took out a pen and pad from his shirt pocket. "I want to know everything that happened, from the time you first saw her."

I told him about the woman's heavy breathing before her fall, and the stranger dressed in black pants and leather jacket. I mentioned to him that leather was an already outdated winter material, but some people loved to play with the clothing seasons.

Erin interrupted, "Look at that rug!"

The EMTs had taken the lady away and what remained were body stains on the carpet—a medium-grade Berber, the industrial kind.

Toni told Erin to hide the area again with clothing racks and that we'd shampoo that portion of the rug later in the day when it wasn't as hectic.

Officer Styles didn't have any more questions for me and informed Toni he was going to be in the store for awhile.

"I better call the owners," Tony said, and submissively headed back to her office. There was only one officer left in front questioning customers. He unlocked the doors and let them go, one-by-one. I tried to lip-read but even with my glasses on, I couldn't understand anything he asked. I just stood there watching, my good heels glued to the floor. The officer was on his last customer when Toni rejoined me. She didn't look too good.

"The owners are very upset. They said I better listen to the cops and do everything they say." She stood thoughtful for a moment, "I can't believe what my sales figures are going to look like when this week is over."

Toni stormed over to Officer Styles and at first looked as if she was begging. Her hands were pleading for him to do something. Then I caught her thanking the officer, shaking his hand. I didn't know how she did it, but the store was reopened to customers. Toni took the sign off the front doors and swung them open, not caring that our heat was escaping into the lunchtime crowd of shoppers. I wondered if any new customers would enter since Officer Styles and the other two officers still remained in the store.

Erin pushed me toward a cash register. She suggested I get back to work; it would take my mind off the lady.

After ringing up three two-hundred dollar sales, I looked toward the front and watched as the next few customers entered. Then I saw him again, the man in black! His leather jacket shone like this year's newly polished pearls. Its folds looked soft and smooth. I wasn't sure how to feel, afraid or delighted. The man was a looker.

He approached the counter.

I managed to say, "Yes?" and glanced around for Officer Styles, who was busy wrapping the yellow caution tape around the clothes racks. I got his attention and waved him over.

The cleft in the man's chin seemed to move as he spoke, "I'm looking for a tall woman, thin. Wearing a navy blue suit under a heavy beige jacket." He pointed to his ear lobes. "Long gold earrings. I thought I saw her coming into this store." He smiled. "I've been waiting for her outside, but had to run a quick errand and may have missed her. It's pretty important."

His grin melted away any initial fear. His memory of clothing was so refreshing and I was feeling comfortable with him, like wearing Egyptian cotton over a sun burn. How would I be able to tell him that the woman he was looking for was dead?

The officer got there before I could say anything, and suggested the man move to the corner with him. I took off my sweater. Even with the doors wide open, it was getting a little warm.

My attention shifted to Erin. She was busy arguing with a customer who didn't like the ensemble she'd suggested. It looked great, but the woman thought the orange color clashed with her red hair.

"It's all in the material," Erin said, trying to convince the lady that the better quality clothing naturally improved one's looks.

"But it doesn't fit," the bifocaled woman said. "It's too tight here." She pulled out the waistband that hugged her hips, then pointed to her thighs, "and too loose there."

The police detective and leather man were speaking by the travel knits; the police officer looked as though he were asking a question. The man nodded and pointed outside.

Evidence? I wondered.

Toni came over to tell me, "He didn't do anything. He was just trying to return a gold bracelet he thought belonged to the woman. It must have fallen off her wrist."

Nice to know that not everyone who wears leather too late in the season is a potential killer. But what did happen to the woman?

I doubted she was here long enough to leave behind any clues.

Did anything look out of place? I'll admit the store moved its merchandise around so often it became difficult to find anything in the same place twice. Everyone tried to blame the visual supervisor, the person responsible for the store's appearance.

I looked at the clothes racks in front of the cash area. Knit pants hung folded by their side creases on special pant hangers; nearby jeans were opened to the front. Everything had a particular way to be folded and hung. How could I tell if something were disturbed?

The foot traffic had quieted down and the cashier area was slow. I walked away from the cashier's register, to the front, following the woman's trail before she got my attention. I cruised past each clothes display—the spandex pants, nylon jackets, polyester skirts, searching through the front garment on every clothes stand for something that looked flawed, even a thread that didn't seem to belong. But everything, including the acrylic blouses, draped neatly from their hangers. No daggers, knives or pins stuck out of anything that I could find.

Toni crept up behind me, reminding me why I was there. "You're supposed to be checking out customers, not making them wait to purchase our merchandise." She pointed to the waiting line in front of the cash enclosure.

"Yes. Right away." It helps to be good friends with your boss...sometimes.

I scooted behind the nearest register. "Next!"

One of the women in line noted to another, "Love that synthetic fiber. Polyester has changed so much. Feels just like rayon. Actually, I can't tell the difference."

The owner of the new clothing agreed.

When it was her turn to hand me her purchases, I informed her that synthetics were easy to clean and very cost effective.

It was then I realized out of all the clothing fibers that the store offered, it was only the synthetic materials that the dead woman passed through and touched. They were being offered as a store special because we needed more space for the winter wools and heavier cottons. Although synthetics were durable, they were loaded with chemicals. Maybe I should mention that to Officer Styles.

The casher's area was at a lull again. Officer Styles had seen the man off and remained inside the store. Toni, Erin and Rena crowded around him. He blocked my view of any incoming patrons, so I joined the group just as the officer told them that the EMTs had questioned the color on the woman's hands. In their investigation they found a residue, which they've sent to the lab for identification. They were now considering the possibility that the woman may have been poisoned by something she touched.

"Touched? As in fabric?"

Everyone looked at me, as if I actually knew clothing.

"Well..." The officer cleared his throat. "That could be possible."

Toni's attention was on me. "What are you suggesting?"

"Could be something in the material." I offered.

"An unknown substance?" Officer Styles rattled off.

"Remember that formaldehyde scare last year?" Boy was I feeling like a real clothes connoisseur. "About too much being found in children's clothing? There's a lot of information out there," I pointed to the sky referring to the information highway, "Some countries even put limits on how much chemicals can be used in certain clothing items." I had everyone's attention now. "Synthetics particularly use a lot. Even natural fibers, think about it, are sprayed with pesticides."

Officer Styles met with his other two officers and our next instructions from him were to leave everything as it was, the store was closed for the rest of the day.

Toni looked like she feared this would be her last day as our supervisor. She pleaded with the officer, overlooking the danger that could be present in the store. But Officer Styles didn't budge. He was adamant that it was too much of a risk.

Toni finally submitted to his orders.

I reassured her that the store's sales figures would get better because of all the specials and holidays.

Rena wanted to know, "What about our hours?"

"You'll be paid whatever you were scheduled for," Toni answered and promised to clock us out.

We retrieved our stuff from the stockroom. Toni hugged me and said not to worry, we'd pull through this and that she'd be okay. I saw a bottle of eye drops in her hand.

"Thought I better give my eyes a good rinse, in case I touched something," she explained. "No one knows, not even you, and definitely not the owners, but I'm allergic to polyester. And today, I certainly don't want my eyes to get any redder." Her confession made sense to me now.

On our way out the door, she yelled she'd call as soon as she found out anything. I took one last look over the synthetics; my fingers throbbed with the notion that I could have easily touched a contaminated fabric. I walked through the door and turned my head in the direction of the front mannequin. An inside label on her jacket, clearly in view, popped open, *Made in China.*

I couldn't wait to get home and scrub my hands.

✝ ✝ ✝

CR BOLINSKI has published poetry, flash fiction and short stories. She writes in many genres and recently completed a poetry collection with her brother, *Along the Way*. One of her mystery stories appears in *Medley of Murder* (Red Coyote Press, 2005). CR presently lives in northern Arizona.

BABY, IT'S COLD OUTSIDE
CHANTELLE AIMÉE OSMAN

THE cabin stood just above the rise of the hill. Inside, a fire blazed a warm welcome, while outside the world was a frozen holiday postcard. A sprinkling of freshly fallen snow covered the trees and the ground. A lone herd of deer drank from the partially frozen lake just beyond.

Then the noise began. One by one, the deer raised their heads as the rumbling grew louder and closer. The trees shook; snow fell from the boughs onto the ground below, and the spooked deer ran for the safety of the forest.

The powder blue Cadillac convertible roared around the curve and came to a stop in front of the cabin door. Inside the car, the driver reapplied her lipstick, positioned her long blonde hair so the wave parted to reveal one shockingly blue eye, and adjusted the cloche hat on her head. With a snap, she shut the visor mirror, and exited the car. Dressed as if for a cocktail party in a gold lame V-neck sheath covered by a black trench-coat, she picked her way across the icy driveway and up the stairs. Halfway to the door, she hesitated, car keys in hand, and turned back to look at the Cadillac. Taking a deep breath, she dropped the keys into her pocketbook, and knocked.

The door was opened by a tall, handsome man with dark, wavy hair. He wore a black turtleneck sweater under a red checkered flannel shirt. His clothes and demeanor gave him the air of a man of leisure, equally at home on the tennis court or in the woods.

He smiled seductively. "Baby, come in, it's cold outside."

As the cabin door closed behind her, she tossed one last look at the car. "I really can't stay," she said, as he went to take her coat. She glanced haltingly around the cozy cabin, as if the speed of her examination would make her departure all the sooner.

"But baby, it's cold outside."

Resigning herself, she sat on the overstuffed brown leather sofa facing the fire. "I've got to go," said the blonde, her mouth set in a thin line of determination. She gauged his reaction from under lidded eyes, as her hands fingered the clasp of the pocketbook in her lap.

"It's freezing out there," he reiterated.

She got up and walked to the fireplace, where she stood staring contemplatively into the flames. "God, what an evening. Pretending everything is normal, being nice to all those horrid people, smiling while they sang inane Christmas carols."

"I was hoping you'd drop by, I'd almost given up on you." He crossed the expanse of the living room and joined her. The fresh scent of her hair, mingled with the heady, spicier aroma of her perfume seemed to intoxicate him. He took her hands in his. "Your hands are just like ice," he said as he gently kissed them. "I'm sorry darling, I wish I could have been at the party with you tonight." She pulled her hands away, and opened her mouth to protest, but he continued before she could. "I know it's too soon for us to be together, but just to be in the same room with you, to let you know I was there." He sighed, his breath ruffling her hair. "Soon. Soon this will all be over."

"No," she corrected. "I need to go away. I can't keep up this façade much longer. My parents have started to worry about me. Mother's a wreck, and I woke up in the middle of the night and found Dad nervously pacing the floor of his study. I just can't keep this up any longer." The fireplace popped and the flames rose higher, which seemed to shake her out of her daze. She turned and started back to the sofa where her purse still lay. "I should really get back to them before they notice I'm gone."

He intercepted her, grabbing her hand just as it clasped over her pocketbook. "No, stay. What's your hurry? An hour more won't make any difference. There are some things we really should discuss. Let me put on some coffee, you're freezing."

She nodded, "All right, but just half a cup."

As he pushed open the door to the kitchen, he paused. "By the way, you look beautiful."

When the door swung closed, she relaxed. Now moving with swift assurance rather than nervous energy, she walked to the radio cabinet by the kitchen door, and tuned the dial until she found a big band station, then raised the volume until it was loud enough for him to hear clearly.

"Good idea, put some music on while I make the coffee," came the muffled voice from the kitchen.

She quickly crossed the room to the built-in bar in the corner and sat down on the last stool. She set her pocketbook down on the counter, slid the telephone over, and dialed. She spoke quickly and kept her voice low. The conversation was inaudible from the kitchen.

"I was thinking of something a little more relaxing," he called again.

She hung up the phone, grabbed her purse, and darted over to the radio, where she toyed with the dial until it rested on a man crooning a sentimental ballad. She flipped open her purse, and out of habit checked her lipstick in the mirror on the inside flap. Then she removed something from the inside pocket, and snapped the purse closed.

She was drawing the curtains across the window, when he reentered the room carrying two mugs of steaming coffee.

"Worried what the neighbors might think?" he asked, laughing as he handed her a mug. "We're out in the middle of nowhere." She raised the mug and was about to take a sip, when she hesitated and looked at it in revulsion.

"Say, what's in this? You know I like it black."

"I'd forgotten. Let me get you another cup," he said, taking hers and going back into the kitchen.

She claimed her previous place on the sofa and fidgeted in her seat. She adjusted her neckline then reached over his coffee mug to the stack of newspapers that sat there. She picked them up and began to flip through them. Other than a small column dedicated to the ongoing cab drivers' strike, the headlines all screamed of a missing local businessman. A photo of a handsome smiling man in a suit accompanied them. She put the papers down in disgust. She was more than tired of hearing the speculation and gossip about what had happened to him, it was the only topic people at the party discussed.

He brought in another cup of coffee, and sat down next to her on the sofa.

"Honestly, I'm at the end of my rope," she blurted, cupping her mug with both hands. "I feel like everything has just spiraled out of control." Her eyes blazed in indignation. "I just wish I knew what to do, how to break this spell."

"It's going to be fine, trust me," he said. "Here, let me take your hat; drink your coffee, and relax a little."

She handed him her hat and shook out her long blonde hair. He stared at the shimmering golden waves.

"I ought to have just said no when my parents asked me to go to that party tonight." She sniffled. He moved in closer to her and put his arm around her shoulders. She shied away.

"It's fine for you, you get to sit out here in the woods where there are no prying eyes to glare at you whenever you leave the house." She slammed her coffee cup down on the table. "I'm the one that's had to keep a smile on my face while people whisper behind my back. At least I'm going to say that I tried, that I was doing my part, not hiding away."

"Gee, what's the sense in hurting my pride? Do you think I like sitting out here alone, waiting helpless, while you have to face everyone?"

Slightly shocked at his passionate outburst, she stared at him for a moment then stood. "I simply have to go."

"Oh, but it's so cold out, just look out the window at that storm coming in. I think we're in for a white Christmas."

"I think my sister has started to be suspicious. When I came home from Christmas shopping earlier in the week, she and my brother were waiting for me. They're starting to ask questions." She gnawed nervously at her lower lip.

"I'm not worried about your brother. He's spent so much

time in Palm Beach his head is filled with waves," he replied, his eyes focused on her mouth,

"It's my aunt we really need to worry about," she said, removing a pack of cigarettes from her purse.

"That old biddy doesn't bother me either." He glanced at the cigarettes, "I thought you quit."

She eyed the pack guiltily. "I guess it's been all this stress. I needed something to do with my hands, so I started back up again."

He took the pack away from her, walked to the nearest waste basket, and tossed it in. She raised an eyebrow, then shrugged as she sat and continued.

"Anyway, I think we should worry about her. She's got a vicious mind and loves spreading even the tiniest morsel of gossip—particularly to my brother and sister, who are her favorite listeners. She never married and has no life of her own so she's always sticking her nose in other people's business."

"Think logically," he replied from behind the bar where he had gone to add something a bit stronger to his coffee. "She can talk to everyone we know until she's blue in the face. It's not like she's got anything on us." He hit the bar with his fist to emphasize this last point. The force of his blow bounced the handset off the telephone. He quickly grabbed it before it could fall off the bar, and set it back on the cradle. A look of confusion crossed his face. "Did you make a phone call?"

"No!" Her hands resumed their frenetic playing with her purse strap. "Who would I call? No one should know I'm here, let alone with you." She glanced at her watch and stood abruptly. "I've got to go home."

She turned her back to him, and glanced at her reflection in the mirror above the fireplace. She patted her hair, which had fallen ever so slightly out of place when she removed her hat. "Say, lend me a comb," she tossed casually over her shoulder as she continued to primp with shaky hands.

Out of the corner of her eye she watched him come from behind the bar and cross the room. Then she heard the scraping sound of a drawer opening and closing. Her previously stiff shoulders relaxed, and she turned to him, her hand reaching out expectantly for the comb.

Her blue eyes widened in surprise and fear. He stood before her holding, not a comb, but a pistol.

She took a deep breath, and stepped toward him. "I don't think I'll be needing a gun, do you? I mean, people are starting to suspect, but I don't think things have gone quite that far yet," she stammered, hoping her innocent act, and his obvious attraction to her, would be enough to distract him.

He smiled but this time it was a feral, wicked grin. Not taking his eyes off of her, he backed slowly to the window, and pushed the curtain aside with the nose of the gun. "It's up to your knees out there."

"You've really been grand tonight, listening to me talk, keeping me warm," she said, continuing her act. Slowly she sat back down on the sofa. "You know, I haven't really been gone that long. I should have time for one more cup of coffee."

"I think we've had enough coffee." He walked over to her. His free hand brushed the strands of flaxen hair behind her ear, exposing both of her eyes. With almost a caress, he lifted her chin. "Your eyes are like starlight. I used to dream of staring into them for the rest of my life."

"I don't understand, what's wrong? What are you saying? You said yourself we would be together soon!" she cried, clasping the hand that held her chin.

He flicked her hand away and stepped back, shaking his head as if to clear it. "No. I thought we could but I fooled myself. The moment I first saw you, I knew I'd do anything to have you, no matter what. I thought I would be saving you, my angel."

He wavered a bit as he spoke, and grasped the mantle of the fireplace to steady himself. "But now, for the first time I see you clearly. You've been using me as a puppet, your toy. You never loved me at all. You promised if I did what you asked we'd be together, but you've given me nothing, not even a kiss, and you shy away from my touch. Then this strange act of yours tonight, coming all the way up here to see me, playing nervous and scared. Now, why don't you tell me who you phoned?"

She noted his unsteadiness, and suddenly all the innocence dropped away from her wide blue eyes, leaving them hard and cold. No longer afraid, she sat up straighter.

"My husband."

He laughed awkwardly, and rubbed his eyes. "The truth, if you please." He raised the gun with a shaking hand and pointed it at her.

"But don't you see? I am telling you the truth."

"I killed him—I watched the life slowly ebb away from his body, then left him in the woods just like we planned!"

She smirked at him. "You did leave him in the woods, but you didn't kill him. The drug we used just weakened him— and, stupidly, you didn't check to see if he was really dead. The drug wore off after about an hour, and he's been in hiding ever since."

"How could you do this to me? Why would you do this?" he cried, as the gun fell on the floor and he collapsed onto his knees.

As she bent to remove the gun from his reach, a small vial fell from the neck of her dress and onto the floor. Casually, she picked them both up and placed them on the coffee table. "Tomorrow, I'm going to say that I can't handle the pressure anymore and have decided to go away for the holidays, maybe to Paris to see some old school friends. There's bound to be talk, but they'll assume it's my way of dealing with the grief. The only person who will know the truth—that I've taken the insurance money and gone to meet my husband in the Bahamas—will be, well, indisposed." She nodded squarely in his direction.

They were momentarily quiet as he digested her words. Then he raised his head, eyes wide with fear, as the silence was broken by a heavy rapping on the cabin door.

She quickly ran to throw open the door.

"Hello, darling!" She exclaimed and plunged into her husband's outstretched arms. They held each other as lovers who have endured a long absence. When they finished their embrace, he continued to hold her close, with her head tucked under his chin, while he surveyed the situation.

"You came at the perfect time," she muttered into his chest. "The drug only started to kick in a few minutes ago, but it was just at the right moment; he was starting to put two and two together." She gestured at the gun on the table.

He released her and looked into her face with a mixture of concern and growing fury. "Did he threaten you?"

She glanced at the man sprawled on the floor. He was staring at her imploringly. She turned back to her husband. "Not really." She grabbed her husband's arm as he made for the prone man. "It doesn't matter now, anyway."

"You're right, of course. How much have you told him?"

"Well, he knows you're alive," she said, beaming at her husband. "And I think he's probably figured out by now that I drugged his coffee."

Her husband knelt in front of the man, "The drug makes you feel warm and comfortable, doesn't it? At least that's what I felt at the time—but then I wasn't fighting for my life. In a moment, I'm going to carry you outside and throw you in the lake. Your system is numb, so you won't feel much cold, but you won't be able to swim either. You're lucky you didn't touch a hair on my wife's head, or I would have made sure you had a life of pain and sorrow, not a quick death."

The man on the floor moaned.

"Now," the husband said rising. "Let's have a look at that note before the drug really kicks in, and he's useless to us."

She pulled an envelope addressed to the police out of her purse, and handed it to her husband. The note inside was short and typewritten; it read: I saw her photo and had to have her. So he had to die. I can no longer live with the guilt.

"Very nice, darling, at least there's plenty implied," he said. "The case will stay closed. They won't even begin to know where to look for a body. And his fixation for you from afar was quite the clever touch. That way you can claim ignorance, but any items linking him to you would be explained as mementos of his manic obsession. Once we add his signature it will be perfect."

He picked up the gun from the table and held it to the man's head, then set the letter on the floor, and put a pen in his hand. "Sign it."

Shock and the drug had combined to turn the man into a quivering mass, but he mustered his dwindling strength to shake his head no.

Her husband sighed. "She wanted me to make your death as painless as possible, but if you don't sign, I guarantee you will suffer."

"I've changed my mind," she said. "He deserves to suffer." The bite to her words was more devastating than her husband's outright threat.

The man seemed stunned by the cold promise in the words. His eyes squinted in an apparent attempt to focus. Then he signed.

Her husband put the letter back into the envelope and tucked it in his pocket along with the gun that he would bury in the forest at a distance from the cabin. Then he picked up the weakened man like a sack of potatoes and carried him effortlessly out into the cold night.

As she watched from the doorway, the sounds of the man's feeble struggles drifted back to her, and she heard her husband grunt as he repositioned him over his shoulder.

"I hope you both catch pneumonia and die," muttered the man in a thickened voice.

"Quit being such a hold-out, struggling will only make it worse for you," her husband replied curtly.

Not wanting to hear any more, she shut the door, and poured herself a stiff drink from the bar and stood staring into the fire, sipping her drink slowly as the minutes ticked by.

She heard her husband's footsteps crunching in the snow, and momentarily he appeared in the doorway, where he shook the flakes off of his jacket and shoes.

"It's done."

"Where's the note?" she asked.

He reached into his pocket and handed it to her. She took

it and walked over to the coffee table where she thumbed through the stack of newspapers, and eventually selected the one she was looking for. It bore the headline Missing Man Declared Dead, but the photo accompanying this article was different from all the others. This time the missing man was smiling at a sultry blonde by his side. The caption underneath identified her as the grieving widow. She put the newspaper in a noticeable position by the telephone, and set the note directly on top of the photo of the couple.

Calmly, she walked to the mirror and delicately positioned her hat on her head. Meanwhile, her husband collected her coat from the hook by the door, and held it out for her expectantly. She slipped it on and tightly knotted the belt. Sighing deeply, she took a long last look around the room. Her husband put his arm around her and together they exited the cabin. As they walked down the steps to the car, a shiver ran through her and she nuzzled closer to him.

"Baby, it sure is cold outside."

CHANTELLE AIMÉE OSMAN has worked in the fields of art, politics and entertainment. She recently returned to her hometown of Scottsdale and started her own company, A Twist of Karma Entertainment (twistofkarma.com). Chantelle also speaks on film and screenplay writing at conferences across the country. She is currently working on two mysteries.

YULE NIGHT
MERLE MCCANN

December 21st, 1902
Aspen Wells, Colorado

IN the early evening darkness Deputy Bill Hicks bolted from his saddle, darted up the steps of Sheriff Andy Olsen's front porch, and pounded on his door. Bill had news, important and shocking, and he was eager to see the sheriff's face when he told him.

Bill tightened the knot in his muffler and raised his sheepskin collar. The thermometer at the jail read thirty above when he left and it was droppin' like a stone.

To his recollection, there'd never been a murder in Aspen Wells and this one would raise eyebrows. Anything that happened up at Kendall Hall provoked gossip, but the townsfolk will buzz for days over this. He wouldn't be surprised if the *Denver Post* carried the story.

Bill banged again on the door then turned away from the bitter wind that blew sleet sideways into his face. He shifted his weight from foot to icy foot and clamped a hand on his wide brimmed hat to save it from the wind.

He was about to knock once more when Sheriff Olsen opened his door. "What's all the ruckus?" he barked.

"There's been a murder up to Kendall Hall! We gotta go right now."

Olsen's eyebrows shot toward his hairline. "Who got killed?"

"The butler," Bill said, his voice tinged with excitement. "That young fella, Tony somebody, who sees to Ryan, telephoned the jail—said Jeffries was dead. I came to fetcha fast as I could. They found the old coot lying face down in one of the gardens." Bill took time to inhale. "If you had a telephone I could've called you from the jail."

The sheriff scowled. "It'll be a cold day in Haiti 'fore I get a telephone. Same goes for electricity." He frowned at the weather. "Head over to the livery and get a buckboard. We'll be bringing the body to Doc Scranton's." He turned from the door. "I'll see to my gas lamps and be ready when you get back."

Bill dashed for his horse. Twenty minutes later, he returned to the sheriff's house, driving an open wagon, and found him waiting on the porch with a rolled buffalo hide under each arm. *They'd need 'em on a night like this.*

Sheriff Olsen handed Bill one of the hides. "Wrap this around yourself. Ain't no time to fall sick—not with a murder on our hands." Olsen climbed onto the wooden seat and Bill snapped the reins. The horse trudged into the muddy and deeply rutted road.

Cloaked in his buffalo skin, Olsen reached into his Mackinaw for a cheroot. "Did the kid say how the family's doing? Mrs. Kendall ain't gonna handle this well. She's a flighty one."

"I didn't ask. The fella said they were at her Yule Night ritual when they heard a woman scream from down near the house. Mrs. Kendall chose the top of the ridge, just above the manor, for her bonfire this year, probably to get closer to the stars. Tony and Mr. K raced down to the house—found the body in the kitchen garden."

Bill steered the horse to the left where the road climbed all the way to Kendall Ridge, the name given the location of the new manor house. "Isn't Yule Night the same as winter solstice?" Bill asked, as the buckboard lurched out of a pothole.

"Yup, longest night of the year. You know Mrs. Kendall goes for all that metaphysical mumbo jumbo."

"My mom, too. Some years back, a rumor went 'round that Mrs. K could cast evil spells to make ya do her bidding."

"Silly women." Olsen sighed. "I expect she'll have their house decorated with all manner of herbs and doodads to ward off evil spirits, especially now that Jeffries got hisself killed. By tomorrow, they'll all be wearin' amulets under their shirts and studyin' astrology charts."

Surprised at Olsen's comments, Bill didn't respond. He knew the sheriff's late wife had practiced metaphysics. She, Mrs. Kendall, and his mom used to share garden herbs for their potions and spells.

Personally, he didn't place much stock in spirits and omens but he admired Mrs. Kendall. She was a kind Christian lady. If she also believed in magic, so be it. He recalled the day she drove her sleigh with her high steppin' trotter to deliver a doll buggy to his little sister for Christmas. The gift came from Europe where Mrs. Kendall, Lady Bountiful to the children, went every summer searching for gifts for the miners' little ones. He'd felt grateful to the lady and her husband ever since, like the rest of the villagers. If it weren't for the Kendalls, residents wouldn't have the mines, their jobs, the company homes, the town, or the school. If the lady believed in metaphysics or the man in the moon, it was fine by him. America was a free country.

"Bill, what do you know about the crew up at the Hall?"

"Not much. I see the housekeeper, Miss Wren, at Mass on Sundays. She's always very tidy and buzzes around like she's out of time. And Jeffries—he enjoyed a regular game of billiards at the men's club. I heard he enjoyed his rum and gum, too."

"Rum in maple syrup? Yikes!"

Bill laughed. "He liked beer, too." Bill flicked a rein. "I saw Ryan Kendall at the men's club a while back. Tony, his companion, was helping him play pool. The men gathered 'round to see a blind man shoot pool. Surprizin' how good he did."

THE rain stopped by the time they arrived at Kendall Hall. The mansion's garland-trimmed windows glowed with candles. Decorating the two tall entry doors were wreaths made of evergreens, holly, and mistletoe and tied with red ribbon bows.

The sheriff climbed down from the wagon and approached the house while Bill maneuvered the rig to a hitching ring imbedded in the high walls surrounding the cobblestone courtyard. He had just secured the horse when he heard the groan of a hinge and hurried to Olsen's side.

Matilda Wren opened the door. Her immaculate gray dress bore a white Eton collar with matching cuffs. Her hair was pulled into a knot at the back of her neck, and she carried a clipboard in the crook of her arm. When she saw them, she stepped aside. "The family's in the great hall," she said with haughty crispness.

"And the staff?" Olsen asked.

She gestured for them to follow her. "All but cook; she's locked in her room, quite overcome it seems."

"I see," the sheriff muttered as they crossed the gleaming hardwood and entered the huge, two-story room in the center of the house.

The family sat clustered on couches near the wide fireplace where a welcoming fire burned. The mantle held pine boughs, sprigs of dried anise, mistletoe, and long sticks of cinnamon, exactly what one would expect in the home of a metaphysical maven. Amongst the boughs, tall, thick, lighted candles infused the air with the scent of bayberry. To the side of the fireplace two young women in starched aprons stood staring at the lawmen. Miss Wren joined them. Across the room, in a broad bay window, an exquisitely adorned Christmas tree reached nearly to the ceiling, its many small candles ready for Christmas Eve.

As they approached the family, Mr. Kendall stood, offering his hand to each of the lawmen. "I think you know my family, Sheriff. Allow me to introduce my son's companion, Mr. Tony Lyndon." Kendall gestured to the serving girls and said, "Annette and Jane."

Bill sized up Lyndon who stood behind the sofa, his hand resting next to Ryan's shoulder. Then Bill turned his attention to Mrs. Kendall. She appeared distraught as she sat, head bowed, holding a small, wadded linen handkerchief to her reddened nose. Her son, Ryan sat next to her with his face turned in the direction of the sheriff's voice. She gripped his hand.

The sheriff cleared his throat. "First, I'd like to see the

body."

Kendall grimaced. "Tony and I carried him into the servants' dining room and placed him on the table. I'll take you."

"Good. We can talk while we're at it. Could someone assist my deputy in bringing the buckboard to the door closest to the body? We'll be taking the deceased to Doc Scranton's when we're done here."

"Of course," Mr. Kendall replied. "Miss Wren, would you please show Mr. Hicks around to the side entrance?"

Miss Wren retrieved her coat from a nearby closet and left the house with Bill. The cloudy night felt icy and the moon provided barely enough light to steer the horse and wagon between the hedgerows to the kitchen garden. Bill helped Miss Wren down from the wagon and followed her along the cobblestone path, past the garden to the side door of the servants' wing.

Miss Wren avoided the staff's dining room, disappearing instead down a back hall. As Bill entered the room, the sheriff glanced up from the body which was half covered in a white sheet. "Have a look, Bill. You can see by the head wound's shape it was probably made by a large tool—I'm guessin' it's the edge of a shovel blade since he was in the garden."

The moon emerged from a cloud as the lawmen laid Jeffries in the buckboard and covered him with a tarp. As they headed for the door, the sheriff said, "Look there, Bill, amidst the raspberry canes. Ain't that a shovel handle?"

Bill circled the garden. "Sure enough, Sheriff," Bill said as he pulled it free. "I'll put it in the buckboard. We'll have a good look at it tomorrow."

After returning to the great hall, Sheriff Olsen explained that he and Deputy Hicks would speak with each staff member privately in the library.

"Mr. Kendall and I've talked already." He looked at Ryan and his mother. "I don't need to talk to you tonight. I'll start with Mr. Lyndon." He glanced from face to face. "Tomorrow we'll examine the kitchen garden. Until then, I want no one going near it. Is that clear?" Everyone gave a nervous nod.

He turned to Tony. "Mr. Lyndon, will you lead the way?"

As the three men left the room, Tony asked to be called by his first name.

In the library, Tony raised the flame in the wall lamps, placed a log on the dwindling fire, and all three men sat in the leather chairs in front of the fireplace. The sheriff removed a notepad and pencil from his shirt pocket.

"Tony, how old are you?"

"Seventeen."

"You're a big fella with a mighty big job for one so young. How'd you come by it?"

"I saved Ryan's life in a bar fight. He and a coalminer were mixin' it up in a saloon in Georgetown when I happened in. Ryan was on the floor and the miner was comin' at him with a knife. I managed to kick the blade from the man's hand then slugged him. He fell, giving me time to get Ryan to his feet and out of there."

Entranced, Bill blurted. "Holy Moses! Did you know Ryan was blind?"

Tony nodded. "I'd seen him earlier having dinner at the Marble Café. I recognized him in the saloon by his fancy cravat. I didn't know who he was. I'd only just hit town. But, drunk as Ryan seemed, I thought I'd better take him home before anything more happened. I rented a horse and buggy and drove him here. It was late by then so Mr. Kendall insisted I stay over. Two days later, he offered me the job. It sounded better than mining coal, which was what I was aimin' to do."

The sheriff scribbled a few notes. "How'd you hear the scream from so far away?"

"I expect it carried on the breeze. The wind was comin' from the direction of the house."

How'd you get on with Jeffries?"

"Fair to middlin'. We had an understanding early on, and he never bothered me."

"How so?" the sheriff asked.

"Jeffries was in charge of the staff. He thought that made him my boss. I made him understand that I answered to Ryan and his parents and nobody else. The Kendalls agreed."

"How'd Jeffries take it?"

"Didn't like it, but there was nothin' he could do. So, we got along fine."

"Tell me about the staff."

"Don't know them well. They seem like nice folks."

"How'd they treat each other?"

"I don't cotton to gossip, Sheriff." Tony leaned his elbows onto his knees. "But I'll tell you this, Jeffries wasn't liked. He acted hateful and mean to the staff."

"Like what?" Olsen asked.

"Wren looked down her nose at him, of course, she does that to all of us. He tended to avoid her—they were known to argue some. The maids, Annette and Jane, had to put up with his nastiness or lose their jobs. He made their lives miserable. About the only one who seemed to like him was Clara, the cook. Jane thinks he and Clara were—friendly."

The sheriff made another note. "Why's that?"

"Clara defended him, made him special meals and desserts, catered to him."

The sheriff nodded. "How about the Kendalls?"

"They must have approved of him. He'd been with them a good while."

"Who all attended the Yule Night ritual?"

"Ryan, his parents and me. They include me like family."

Bill leaned forward. "Did you dance around the fire like a band of faeries? That's what I heard."

Tony laughed. "No, we circled the fire once after Mrs. Kendall's prepared greeting and explanation of the ceremony. She recited a lengthy, meaningful poem, and so did Ryan. It must have been a first for Ryan because Mrs. Kendall was very touched by it. We exchanged gifts and a few jokes—and that was when we heard the scream."

"Do you know who screamed?" Sheriff Olsen asked.

"It must've been Jane because she told us where the body was."

Bill smoothed his moustache. "Then what happened?"

"Mr. Kendall told Ryan to come down to the house with his mother—said he and I would hurry ahead to find out what happened. We never expected to find Jeffries in the garden with his head split open. Mr. Kendall seemed quite shaken. I helped him sit down on the porch steps; otherwise, he might've collapsed there in the mud. That's when I rang up your office."

Olsen stood and thanked Tony for his help. He glanced at the Regulator clock on the wall near the door. "Ask Miss Wren to come in, will you please?"

A few minutes later there was a tap on the door and Miss Wren walked primly into the library. The sheriff motioned her to sit near the fire and began his questions.

"Where were you when the family was up on the ridge for Yule Night?"

She frowned as she studied the sheriff's face. "I was arranging the dining room for the after party."

"The entire time they were out of the house?" Bill asked.

"Yes, Deputy Hicks." She glared at him. "Mrs. Kendall insists everything be just so. She'd written out instructions for decorating the table from her *Spells and Rituals Guide*. Cook placed the silver punch bowl in the middle of the table and arranged the cups in two arcs, like embracing arms. I decorated the eggnog with fresh-cut holly and lighted the frankincense and myrrh on the sideboard—such fragrant incense. I had barely enough time to arrange the gingerbread, plum pudding, and sugar cookies compatibly."

She focused on the sheriff and smiled sweetly. "I'm sorry we haven't offered you gentlemen some refreshments. I'm afraid no one is thinking of food right now, even though we worked so hard on it. The sugar cookies have anise frosting, you know. I'll prepare a box for you to take home to your family when you're finished."

"Thank you." Olsen studied her, believing she knew full well he had no family. "Where were you when you heard the scream?"

"In the dining room. I barely noticed it—the house is quite large."

Olsen paused. "What was your relationship with Jeffries?"

"We worked together for ten years. He was a dear man. He'll be missed. He and I moved to Colorado with the family when the Mister decided to go into mining. We worked well together because Jeffries knew his job and I knew mine. We were both thrilled to move into this grand house and finally have the class of home to manage for which we'd been trained. We got on wonderfully."

"What about the serving girls?"

"Annette's a good worker. Jane requires watching—little tramp's not trustworthy. Can't tell you how many times I disciplined her for—being in Master Ryan's room. Then I caught her in the barn with the stableman. He hated Jeffries. Now, it's that Tony she fancies. Fine upbringing that girl's had."

"I see. Were the Kendalls aware of Jane's habits?"

"Oh, no. The Missus would have sacked her instantly. She believes in keeping a proper home. And, I try my best."

"Tell me about the cook. Did she get on well with Jeffries?"

"Cook does a good enough job, if you like German food. She has a sour disposition, never mingles with the staff. As far as Jeffries was concerned, I couldn't say."

"Yet, she's too upset by his death to leave her quarters."

"Well, the poor dear has a tendency to overdramatize, if you know what I mean."

The sheriff thanked Miss Wren for her cooperation and asked her to send in Annette.

When Annette was seated across from them, the sheriff took the lead.

"How old are you, Annette, and how long have you worked here?"

"Twenty-two," she said softly. "I've worked for Mrs. Kendall since they moved into this house last May."

Olsen nodded. "What was it like working for Jeffries?"

Her eyes fluttered. "I was supposed to take orders from Miss Wren, but he bossed me around, too. He had a way of looking at me. I was afraid if I didn't do his bidding, I'd be sacked. I need this job."

"Did you like Jeffries, Annette?"

She quickly crossed herself. "No, sir. He was mean—he'd use his hands on us. Nobody liked him."

"Did you report him to Miss Wren or Mrs. Kendall?"

"No. It would've made it worse. Once he pushed Jane

65

down the back stairs because she complained to Wren about him coming into her room at night."

"Where are your rooms?"

"All of the staff, but Mr. Tony and Wren, have rooms on the third floor. Mr. Tony is on two next door to Mr. Ryan, and Wren has the housekeeper's apartment behind the kitchen."

"So Jeffries wouldn't likely be seen moving about in the middle of the night. Did he ever come into your room?"

She clinched her hands together in her lap. "Yes. Our doors have no locks, you see. I woke the first time he tried to come into my bed. I fought him—scratched his neck bloody. He split my lip with his fist and told Wren I scratched him for no reason so he had to hit me—to put me in my place."

"Did he come to your room after that?"

She raised her face and the firelight illuminated a look of hatred. "Twice a week, and twice a week he went to Jane's—until today. Thank God, it's over." The room went silent.

"Did you kill Jeffries, Annette?" the sheriff asked quietly.

A tear slipped onto her cheek. "No, sir. But I thank God he's dead."

Olsen stood. "That'll be all for tonight, Annette. Thank you for your help."

As Annette left the room, the sheriff handed Bill his pad and pencil. "You take the next interview; time you try your hand at the investigatin' business."

A few minutes later, Jane was seated by the fire, and Bill, sitting very erect, was poised to take notes. "How old are you?" he asked.

"Nineteen, if it matters to ya."

"How long have you worked here?"

She heaved a weary sigh. "Since June."

"How did you get on with Jeffries?"

"I got on fine with the old bugger."

Bill glanced at the sheriff. "Did he ever bother you in the night?"

"Come into my room, you mean?"

Bill nodded.

"No. I'da kicked him in the jewels, I would."

"So he never came to your room, and you never went to his?"

She glared at Bill. "Why're you askin' such questions? Did that ol' crow, Wren, say things about me? I'll blacken her eyes if she did."

"What do you think of Miss Wren?"

"She's a nag—always worried about the clock what with her minute by minute schedule on that clipboard of hers—timing everything we do." Jane's tone turned sarcastic: "Hurry up, Jane—it took you twenty minutes to iron that shirt, Jane—you should make up a bed in five minutes, Jane—nobody needs a half hour to sweep that porch, Jane." She took a deep breath. "As you might guess, I don't much care for her, but I need the work."

"How did Miss Wren get on with Jeffries?"

"Okay, I guess. Sometimes she'd make remarks like they had a future together, but he didn't like her much. I could tell."

"What was his relationship with Clara?"

She stared at Bill as if she were trying to decide what to say. "It was good. He liked Clara. 'Course she was always doin' him favors. But everybody likes Clara. She's a pet."

LATER, huddled beneath their buffalo hides and leaning into the wind, Sheriff Olsen and Bill drove out of the courtyard. When Bill turned the horse down the mountain and rested his foot on the brake handle, the sheriff asked, "Whatcha think?"

"I think we got us a passel of liars."

"Me, too. Tomorrow I'll poke around—see what I can find out about these folks." He lit a cheroot and crossed his arms over his chest. "Tony's a straight shooter. If he can handle hisself in a bar fight, he could easily intimidate Jeffries. He had no reason to kill him."

"True," Bill said. "But what about the others?"

"We pretty much know the family didn't do it—they were all up prancin' around a bonfire, unless Mrs. K cast a deadly spell, that is." He cocked an eyebrow at Bill and grinned.

Bill didn't smile. "She's not the murderin' kind; she's a

do-gooder. Besides, if she'd wanted Jeffries gone, Kendall woulda fired him."

Olsen dragged on his cheroot. "Wren is wound tight as a clock on Saturday morning; Annette was beaten into submission; and Jane? Now, there's a question. You think she's as tough as she talks?"

"I don't know. Truthfully, I think it would take the strength of a man to crease a skull the way Jeffries' head looked."

Olsen flicked his cheroot to the ground. "You know, we haven't talked to the barn man. We'll start there in the morning."

Bill nodded. "I've a feeling we're overlookin' something, but I can't put my finger on it. Maybe tomorrow it'll hit me."

THE next morning, during their examination of the shovel, Sheriff Olsen was called to investigate an attempted burglary at Rocky Mountain Mine Number Three, one of six Kendall coal mines that supported Aspen Wells. After Bill noted in the crime log the discovery of blood along the shovel blade's edge, he rode up to Kendall Ridge, stopping first to speak with the stableman.

"I'm investigating Jeffries' murder, and I hear tell you and he didn't get along."

"What? We got on fine—played chess together every Tuesday night." He pushed his hat back. "You want honest answers around here? You best talk to Annette."

Hicks rubbed his chin. "Where were you last night?"

"In town with my family celebrating my son's tenth birthday."

BILL was escorted to the library by Miss Wren, dressed in a plain, crisp brown dress. Her immaculate dark shoes were the same she'd worn last night. She carried her clipboard.

He asked Wren to fetch Annette, and when she entered the library, Annette seemed agitated. Once she was seated, Bill asked, "Did you ever hear Jeffries arguing with any of the staff?"

"No, sir," she said as she glanced at the clock. "Nobody

dared—except Wren. I think she knew he came to our rooms and didn't like it. Just last week I heard her shout at him: 'but you promised me,' real angry like. Then she scurried to her apartment. She may have been crying. Never saw her scurry before—unladylike, you know." She glanced again at the clock.

"Am I keeping you from your work?"

"Before dinner service, I must launder Miss Wren's black dress—even though laundry day isn't until Monday. She said she soiled it cutting holly for the Yule Night party. She's quite fussy, and it's her church favorite."

Having no more questions, Bill stood. "If you think of anything else, let me know." She nodded.

When he was alone, he tried to recall everything he'd heard and seen. There was something niggling his mind, but he couldn't bring it forward. His thoughts went to the waiting garden. Perhaps the fresh air would clear his mind. Donning his heavy duster, he made his way through the house.

At the garden's edge, Bill studied its perfect rows of tilled ground. Rain water still collected in some of the furrows. The rows in the area where the body had lain were obliterated; the dirt tossed about as if there'd been a fight. He saw several partial foot prints: the wide curve of a heel; the narrower curve of a boot's toe; perhaps made by Mr. Kendall and Tony when they plucked Jeffries from the mud.

Bill noticed a four-tined cultivator rake lying at the far end of the garden and wondered about it. Typically used for weeding, it should be in the tool shed this time of year. Kneeling, he spotted patches of fresh scratches in the dirt. *Had the killer searched for something lost in the scuffle?*

Excited by his potential discovery, he slogged across the garden, studying the ground closely. A few feet from the rake, he noticed a well defined shoe print the size of a child's…or a woman's.

Working quickly, he searched the soil with the rake, pulling it this way and that, turning over clods of dirt. He raked his way to where the body fell, afraid whatever was lost had already been found. Just when he was about to give up, the tines caught on something. A strand of ribbon. He plucked it from the mud, and a clear image of what happened in the garden formed in his mind. Pocketing his discovery, he dashed for his horse.

At the jail, he proudly placed his evidence on Olsen's desk. "Sheriff, it appears Wren killed Jeffries."

"No, she ain't powerful enough, and she's too prissy to step in the mud."

"She might if she were hoppin' mad. Wren craved efficiency, kept a precise schedule on her clipboard, and timed the maids' work. How do you manage that without a watch?" He picked up a small time piece dangling from the dirty ribbon. "She always wore this. But not on Yule Night. That's what I didn't see. Her watch. She even wore it to Mass. It must have been torn off when she and Jeffries scuffled in the garden. The ground is really chewed up—there's no doubt there was a scuffle."

"But she'd have dirtied her dress, and nobody mentioned it. Come to think of it, last night her dress hadn't a wrinkle in it—and after a day's work."

"Wren's apartment is behind the kitchen. She could've come in and changed her clothes without being seen." Bill raised his finger. "Wait a minute, Annette told me Wren assigned her a black dress to launder today."

Olsen raised his chin. "She had Annette clean it up? Do you think Wren would be that stupid?"

Bill shrugged. "You're always sayin' it's the stupid people who commit most crimes." He rubbed his jaw. "Let's head for Kendall Ridge—have a look in Wren's closet—talk to Annette again if necessary."

Olsen grinned. "If we find what you're thinkin', I'll arrest her on the spot."

AN hour later, with Wren looking on, they examined her closet. They found no black dress, muddy or otherwise, and there were no shoes at all. But an old faded hat box under a folded quilt in the corner caught Bill's eye. He lifted the lid.

"Sheriff?"

Olsen glanced into the box. "I'll be darned." He removed the shoes. "I'll compare 'em to that footprint in the garden.

You talk to Annette." He glared at Wren. "And you stay put!"

Bill located Annette who said she'd just finished cleaning Wren's dress. "Now I'm to fetch her shoes since Jeffries will no longer be maintaining them."

Bill shook his head. "You'll not be cleaning any shoes; but you'd best show that dress to the sheriff, pronto."

"But it's not dry!"

Bill chuckled. "Nobody'll care."

A few minutes later, when shown the evidence in Mrs. Kendall's presence, Wren broke down.

"He drove me to it!" she blurted. "For ten years he strung me along with promises we'd marry. Meanwhile, he was bedding the maids right under my nose. Then yesterday, during Yule Night," she lowered her head to hide her face, "after a rendezvous, the louse tells me he's gone and married Clara!" She sneered. "I hope he rots in purgatory 'til the end of time."

† † †

MERLE McCANN, award winning author, is best known for her Longjohners' Mystery Series for young adults, a literacy project to which she's devoted the past six years. Born in the Yukon, raised in Seattle, she traveled the United States and Europe with her husband pursuing their thirty year Arabian horse business. Before settling down to write serious fiction, McCann worked as a scenic photographer. She lives with her husband in Scottsdale, Arizona.

THE NIGHT BEFORE CHRISTMAS
JEAN STEFFENS

TAKE the fifteen hour flight from Kabul to Washington, plus a six hour debriefing in D.C., add more hours on a turbulent jet to Los Angeles, put together with the four day special ops mission in the rugged White Mountains of Afghanistan, and you could say it had definitely been a while since Jake Morgan saw any shuteye. As he admitted to his superior officer during the closing interview, "Tired? Sir, my butt's dragging so low, pretty soon they'll have to scrape me up with a shovel."

At seventeen hundred forty-five hours on Christmas Eve, he was finally home. Home. Hot water. Hot food. Clean, cool sheets. Solitude. But it wasn't half an hour before the phone rang.

"Jake?" His sister's voice was strained, wrong.

He was suddenly wide awake. "What is it, Roni?"

"It's Kelly, Jake." An aching catch and a sob broke through. "She's gone. Somebody took her."

Jake went ice cold all over. Kelly, his godchild, only niece, and the love of his life ever since he first held the tiny girl in his arms eighteen years ago couldn't be gone.

"Tell me," was all he said, the hardness he'd left behind in Afghanistan rising in him again.

Christmas break, Veronica had explained. Kelly and some of her friends from USC motored on down to San Diego. It was now two days since Kelly was last seen leaving a bar near the border with a young man none of the others knew. It didn't sound good.

"The cops, Jake," Veronica pleaded tearfully. "They won't get her back as quick as you can."

The pain in his sister's voice went straight to his heart and

73

Jake was out the door within minutes.

The cops. Veronica had worried they wouldn't find Kelly. He agreed with her and had no plans to involve them.

This won't be the first time I've worked alone. The thought didn't phase him.

Men who knew him said to his face he was dark, rebellious, and a loner. They also said there was no one they'd rather have covering their back than Jake Morgan. For this mission working alone was his preference.

From Costa Mesa he took the 405 south, then I-5 to the border town of San Ysidro, working his cell phone non-stop until he finally made a connection with an old buddy from Desert Storm.

In fifteen minutes he had his call back.

"Ramos is the guy's name," Jake's friend told him. "He's a Mexican national who's known to take young American girls from bars and other places. Stashes 'em for a while—nobody really knows where. Within three days, they say he puts them out on the street to work sleazy motels on the other side of the border. If she's gone two days already, Jake…" He didn't need to finish.

This wouldn't be easy. Morgan had no illusions about that. Ramos was smart and had a team of dangerous men watching his back. But Jake was smarter; and he was dangerous without a gang of thugs.

Jake hit the Pelican Club in San Ysidro around eight thirty that night. The place was in full swing with holiday partiers, a lot of them kids like Kelly.

He made his way to the bar, asking around some, and mixing casually with Ramos' hooligans over a few beers.

"Si, amigo. My boss has plenty of work for a guy like you." One heavyset Latino named Jorge was the most talkative. "That's him over there."

Morgan sipped his beer and watched Ramos hold court in a corner booth. Ramos was athletically built and obviously partial to flashy clothes and jewelry. He was clean-shaven and wore his thick black hair pulled back in a long ponytail.

Morgan watched his target with unflinching calm, stoically formulating a plan. He knew Ramos without thinking very hard. He'd come across that same low-life breed of bottom feeder dozens of times before.

"But you want to talk to him about work," the big man went on, "you got to do it tonight before he leaves for his place.

He's got a transport coming in around two," Jorge paused meaningfully and smirked, "so he can, you know, relocate some merchandise."

Morgan checked his watch. Two a.m.? It was after nine already. *God help me. If you can't help me, at least please look the other way.*

JAKE crossed the border at nine thirty. Tijuana. Kelly was here somewhere and he was dead set on finding her—finding her in time.

Two blocks off Constitution Avenue he found what he was looking for, Hotel Mariposa, a dreary hole in the wall with sagging beds and unidentifiable things growing in the bathrooms. A half-burned out row of Christmas lights flickered pitifully over the office door. He parked in front and got out of his Jeep. Young girls of the night called to him, but Morgan ignored them.

The Mariposa, he'd been told, was somewhat of a central station for Ramos. He trafficked drugs and stabled his young Latina talent at that location. The unwilling girls were drugged and beaten if they didn't comply.

The greasy desk clerk sauntered from the back room still chewing a mouthful of food. He wore a Santa hat so dirty Jake couldn't tell what color it was. Jake paid him in cash.

"You like the chicas really young, my friend? You've come to the best place. Young. Cute. You know?"

Jake resisted the urge to smash his fist right in the middle of the clerk's knowing leer. Instead he smiled tightly.

He stepped outside and leaned against the building, dug out a pack of smokes and lit one. A lethal calmness overtook him as he made a quick inventory of the girls out front plying their trade. Kelly wasn't there. He'd known she wouldn't be, because in just four hours she'd be on her way to only-God-knew-where, to do only-God-knew-what.

A young girl with dyed red hair strolled toward him. Her smile was beguiling in a drug induced way. She batted her eyes with false innocence. "You want a date, hombre?" she asked. Her voice sounded tired.

His gaze traveled from her stiletto sandals to her black leather mini skirt. Her skimpy halter revealed small, firm, round breasts. *Ho! Ho! Ho!* was ironically embroidered across one cup of the halter. She was too young and small for his taste, not much more than a child. Jake liked his women mature and more voluptuous. But he wasn't there for fun.

"How much for the whole night?" Morgan asked.

Her right hand rested on her hip. "Three hundred? You know, U.S.?" she said uncertainly but with a slow, seductive smile.

"Okay, I already got us a room." Morgan threw down his cigarette and ground it out.

"Wow. The whole night? Baby, it's a deal." Red waved triumphantly to a skinny, twitchy guy hanging out across the parking lot who was probably one of Ramos' watchdogs, before following Morgan to his room.

Morgan unlocked the door and led her inside, hating the musty smell that hit him in the face. He flicked on the lights, set the wheezing air conditioner to Sub-Zero, closed the blinds and turned to her. "What's your name?"

"What do you want it to be?" Red started to unbutton Morgan's denim shirt.

He stopped her. "Sit down," he commanded. "I just want some information."

Red's body stiffened in suspicion. "What is it?"

Morgan stuck his hand in his jeans pocket and pulled out several hundred dollar bills. "Here's your three." He threw a wad on the stained bedspread, but held back another three hundred for her to see. "This is extra for you if you tell me what I want to know."

Red grabbed the cash off the bed, counted it, and stuck it in her hip pocket. "What do you want?" she stammered in bewilderment.

"I'm looking for this girl." Morgan pulled a picture of Kelly from his wallet and handed it to her. "Have you seen her?"

Red narrowed her dark eyes. "Why? What did she do?"

Morgan glanced at his watch impatiently. Three and a half hours for him to get Kelly back before Ramos turned her out, or worse, sold her to white slave traders. "Have you seen her?" He ground it out one more time.

"Yes," she blurted nervously, as she eyed the cash in his hand. "She's at Ramos' place. She's his special girl now. Pobrecita." Red spoke in a weak and tremulous whisper. "But not for long. She leaves soon. That's all I know."

As she grabbed at the cash in his hand, Morgan clamped his fingers on her arm. "Listen to me. You stay here. Take the night off. The room's paid all night. You're paid all night. If you're smart, you'll take that extra cash and get as far away from this nightmare as you can." He spun and was gone, leaving her staring after him. It was ten forty-five.

RAMOS'S place was on the coast, over an hour and a half from the motel. Morgan drove it in an hour. He parked about a quarter mile away and approached on foot.

The compound looked like a highfalutin beach resort, but was monitored and armed like a down and dirty high security prison.

Morgan's backpack was light on his back and he effortlessly climbed a tree, dropped down onto the fence and lowered himself onto the soft green lawn. The landscaping was lush and elaborate—a wide, perfectly manicured grassy area, groves of huge palm trees. Pathways lined by color coordinated flower beds lead to a flagstone terrace that stretched all the way across the back of the impressive house.

Crouching behind one of the trees, Jake watched two security men on night watch amble toward each other. His searching gaze left nothing to chance.

The two guards nodded to each other, then moved on, obviously not expecting any trouble.

Morgan waited patiently as the first guard rounded the corner of the house and moved out of sight, but the second man planted himself on the terrace. His back to Morgan, he bent his head to light a smoke.

Jake was running out of time. The first guard would be coming back around any minute. Quick as a high-speed download, Jake altered his original plan to avoid confrontation. He had to do what he had to do. After first making sure he'd be out of range of the motion detectors, he sprinted cat-like to the edge of the terrace behind the guard. Before the man could even turn, Jake snapped his neck, letting him drop at his feet. With skills honed from years of practiced killing, he located two more guards and ended their lives just as quickly and efficiently.

Three of Ramos' henchmen lay dead. He knew there might be others. These weren't good men. Even so, maybe they didn't deserve to die. But the truth of the matter was the men didn't matter to him. Kelly did. Ramos' thugs were casualties of the war Jake was waging against the Mexican crime lord.

Morgan moved closer to the main residence where he found the security system's junction box. He slipped a small wire cutter and screwdriver from his pocket, knelt on one knee, popped the cover off the box, and went to work. The elaborate system was useless within seconds.

At ten past midnight, Jake opened the terrace door carefully and went silently inside, his gun drawn. The lights were dim throughout the place, at least as far as he could see. A Christmas carol CD was being played somewhere in the house. The cover noise made it easy to move around without being detected.

In the front hall of the huge residence, he surprised a guard whose gun came level too late. Morgan nailed him between the eyes, the spit of his silenced Glock nine millimeter no louder than the soft thud of the body hitting the carpet. Swiftly, he dragged the man inside the library and closed the door.

It occurred to him that he would never tell Kelly the cost of her Christmas vacation.

Morgan went quickly on, checking all the rooms on the first floor. From a flash of movement down a hallway and random phrases from a one-sided conversation in Spanish, Morgan knew Ramos was now in the house and was still unaware of an intruder. Jake's plan called for getting Kelly to safety before squaring off with Ramos, so he put aside the primal urge to go after the crime lord and moved warily on through the house. He would face things as they came.

His success so far had been won by the element of surprise, but that would evaporate as soon as his handiwork was discovered. Taking the stairs two at a time, he drew up sharply on the landing watching for movement or any sign his presence was known. Nothing. Cautiously, he moved ahead. He had no desire to die. He wanted this over with, but years of training and covert ops taught him patience.

Upstairs, Morgan searched several more rooms. No one, *nada.*

A closed door at the end of the hall drew his attention. He turned the knob slowly, stood to the side, pushed it open and had to resist the urge to laugh out loud with relief. There was Kelly huddled in the corner, her leg shackled to a U-bolt in the wall. She was still in what Jake guessed were the clothes she'd worn to the bar the night of her disappearance. She was tussled and maybe a little banged up; but, by God, she was alive and in pretty good shape.

"Uncle Jake. You found me." Kelly blurted, bursting into tears.

Morgan put his finger to his lips and rushed to her side. He looked around carefully before holstering his gun and went to work.

Kelly's face was pale, and she kept darting frantic glances at the closed bedroom door while Jake took a small crowbar from his bag and pried the U-bolt from the wall. When the shackle opened up, and he took it off her leg, she threw herself at him. "I thought you were Ramos. I was so scared."

His arms went around her and wanted to stay that way, shielding her, protecting her forever. Instead he pushed her gently away. "That's okay, honey. I was scared too." He looked her over. She seemed intact, unhurt, except her ankle was bruised, swollen pretty bad, and chaffed raw. "Can you walk?"

He went to the door, cracked it and took a peek. The hall was empty.

She struggled to get her emotions in check. "Yes. I can walk." She choked back a yelp when she got up off the floor, but nearly fell with her first step. "Or maybe not."

He went back, wrapped one arm around her in support and drew his gun. "Lean on me, kid. Ramos is still here somewhere so we need to get out."

They moved out into the hall. The sound of Jose Feliciano's voice floated up the stairs with the sound of clock chimes striking one.

"It's Christmas, isn't it?" She looked up at him with questioning eyes.

"Yeah," he whispered, his gaze darting everywhere. "I guess it is."

Before they'd gone even a few steps, they were stopped dead.

"What the hell!" It was Ramos, running up the stairs, gun drawn and pointed straight at them.

Morgan's gun came up in a blur as he pushed Kelly down onto the floor out of harm's way.

Ramos fired, but he was still moving up the stairs and his aim was bad.

Morgan wasn't moving and his aim was perfect. As Ramos turned at the top of the stairs, Jake shot two bullets into his heart.

The impact catapulted Ramos back down the stairs to the landing where he lay flat on his back in pain and disbelief, struggling to breathe. Blood poured from beneath him, soaking darkly into the plush carpet.

Jake went to stand over him, staring down at the man he'd grown to hate so vehemently in just a few hours.

Ramos spat feebly, whispering a curse in Spanish. His last breath wheezed from him, and he was dead.

Morgan toed him with his boot. "Seasons greetings, scum sucker." Never again would this human trash take a woman against her will and use her.

When Jake got back to Kelly, she was trembling like a leaf in the wind. "You okay?"

She nodded.

He helped her up as gently as possible. His voice husky

with pent up emotion, he said, "Let's go home."

She balanced on one foot. "Merry Christmas, Uncle Jake. Do you have plans for Christmas?"

He smiled. "I was thinking of settling down for a long winter's nap."

JEAN STEFFENS was raised in the Midwest and now lives in Scottsdale, Arizona, with her husband, Michael. Between writing spurts, she chauffeurs her two children to their many sporting events. Hiking, books, travel, and her writing keep her sane. She enjoys being an active member of Desert Sleuths Phoenix Chapter of Sisters in Crime.

RELATIVITY
R K OLSON

CLOSING the door quietly on the heat and noise inside, Corinne stepped out of her house into a world shrouded in silence by the blanket of new-fallen snow. The air felt fresh in her lungs but she did not feel the chill. Her son, Jake, had shoveled the walks earlier or she would have been up to her knees in fresh powder. Making her way around the corner of her house, she headed for cover under the pergola.

No cars drove by, unusual even for eight o'clock on Christmas Eve. The storm had ground everything to a halt. The snow plows wouldn't make it this far out until after the holiday.

Through the bay window she saw her family in the dining room laughing, faces flushed from liquor and laughter. Rob was there. Bad enough to have the ex over, but he had the new wife with him. Corinne had relented at the last minute and allowed him to join the festivities with his sons; it was Christmas after all.

He had been no great shakes as a husband or a father, but he did have an attractive lifestyle. Must be why MaryAnn had married him. Corinne laughed at herself. Why should she mock MaryAnn, after all, she had married him too.

She could see him near the hearth, drink in hand; still slender, his good looks holding up well with age. Maybe he was happy now; maybe MaryAnn met all his expectations. Or maybe he had lowered them and now accepted something less than absolute perfection. A successful business woman, MaryAnn had never borne a child. She was nearing forty and still had the firm body of youth. She had brains and beauty, Rob supplied the bucks. They had become the local power couple.

Corinne tucked her hands under her armpits. As much as she enjoyed being outside looking in, she would freeze to death if she stayed out much longer. She heard the crunch of boots on packed snow and saw her younger son come around the corner.

"There you are." Ben looked up at the sky. "It's so quiet out here, kinda nice, no traffic. Has it crossed your mind that Dad and Step-Mommie dearest may have to stay tonight? I'm thinking the roads into town may be impassable. Dad said they were pretty bad when they came out this afternoon and there must be another eight inches since then."

Corinne focused on the hazy ring around the moon, a snow moon. "And more any minute. Well, we have enough beds if you and Jake don't mind sharing your old room. Your Dad and MaryAnn can have Jake's old room; Grace and the baby have been staying in my studio."

"I'm sorry Mom. I shouldn't have asked you to let Dad come tonight. I just thought if we got the visit with Dad in, we could squeeze in a ski trip, too. But I probably won't make it before I head back to school anyway. Hundred year snowfall and I can't get to the ski area." He shook his head. "You okay with this?"

She smiled. "I'm an adult. I can handle it. Better that everyone is safe inside in this weather."

"And Dad's not really in any condition to drive. He's had several of your cosmos. MaryAnn keeps pouring and he keeps drinking. He might be a little uncomfortable with the new wife and the old wife—"

"I prefer former wife, hon, I'm a little sensitive about the word old these days and in this company."

"Awww, Mom, you're still beautiful...and *young*."

Corinne smiled at her son and looked up as an onslaught of fresh snowflakes floated around them. "Here it comes." She shivered. "Let's go in and deal with reality."

The scent of burning juniper wafted out as Corinne opened the front door. Inside, the small group had gathered around the piano, forced into singing carols by her older son Jake, who pounded the keys with gusto.

"Deck the halls with boughs of holly..."

84

The boys had arrived from college just before breakfast, and Rob and MaryAnn during the afternoon. Corinne's sister, Grace, a new single mother, had been there since June, having moved in during her eighth month of a difficult pregnancy.

"Fa lalalala lala...la...laaaaaaaaa." Jake ended with a tinkling honky-tonk flourish on the old baby grand. "Ben, we need you here bro. We're doing 'Little Drummer Boy' next...you be the drum. Come on," he teased. "You know the words, pah rum pum pum pum..."

"No time for singing, Jakie. We need to move your stuff into my room. It's snowing again. Dad, you guys are gonna have to stay until the plows make it through tomorrow."

Corinne saw a flash in MaryAnn's eyes. I'm not too crazy about the idea myself, she thought.

Rob looked confused. "Ben, we'll be okay, take it real slow," he slurred slightly. "I'll give MaryAnn the keys. She hasn't been drinking."

"Dad, you don't understand. The roads are impassable, and it's still coming down. You won't make it out of the driveway. The only option is to wait for the snowplow."

MaryAnn glared at Rob. "I told you we should have brought the Rover." Her voice was piercing. "Please excuse me," she said to everyone, heading toward the powder room. "This cannot be happening," she mumbled under her breath.

Rob looked at Ben through bloodshot eyes. "We have to leave."

"Dad there's no way. You can't drive, can't walk. It's not like you can call a cab. Look out there." Ben gestured to the front window. "It's a blizzard."

MaryAnn stuck her head out of the powder room. "Rob!"

Rob looked at the door and back to Ben. "There must be some way out of here."

Jake started singing Hendrix. "There must be some kinda way outta here, said the jok—"

"Jake!"

"Sorry Mom. Look Dad, we'll get you on your way as soon as possible, but it's not going to be tonight."

"Robert!"

Corinne watched as her ex polished off his drink, then stumbled toward the powder room. She hardly recognized the half-drunk, frightened man who had intimidated her for years.

"Honey, we hafta sh-tay." They overheard Rob, then MaryAnn's shrill voice. "The snowplows won't be here on Christmas! Are you crazy? This is our best chance to leave."

The door opened and MaryAnn flew out. She grabbed her handbag and mink coat off the entry settee and struggled to shove an arm in. "Thanks for a lovely time." She forced her other arm in the sleeve. "Sorry I can't stay."

Snow blew in as she opened the front door and her coat flew out behind her. She dropped her bag on the porch and turned with both hands to pull the door closed, hair whipping over her face, mink sweeping the boards. The latch caught, and there was relative silence, leaving the group inside staring at the puddle of melting snow.

"I'll get a towel," Ben offered.

"I'll go move my stuff." Jake walked away. "I give the Wicked Witch three minutes max out there."

"Hey don' talk about your ssshtep-mother like tha'." Rob sat heavily on the settee, eyes glazed. He looked at Corinne. "She's mad at me...not your fault. Will upset her." His head fell forward onto his chest.

"Who's Will?" Corinne asked as he began to snore.

The door flew open, and MaryAnn rushed back inside smelling of damp animal, her face flushed from exertion and exposure, wiping melted snow from her forehead. They stared as she dropped her damp coat onto Rob's lap. "Look, it's not that I'm ungrateful." She searched their faces. "You must see how difficult this is for me."

"For everyone's sake," Jake said coming down the stairs, "let's just make the best of it. Christmas spirit and all that." He rubbed his hands together. "Where are the gifts?"

Ben spoke up. "Christmas isn't about that. Well actually it isn't even about Christ; it started way before he was born. Constantine, who wasn't even a Christian wanted to get the—"

"Ben. Bro. Not the time for a history lesson, huh?" Jake

chided.

Ben, family know-it-all, frowned. "Whatever."

Jake looked at the leather satchel on MaryAnn's arm. "Shall I take your bag to your room, MaryAnn?"

"I didn't pack a bag, I wasn't planning on staying," she said sarcastically. "This is just my purse." MaryAnn glanced at Rob; a drop of drool rolled from his slack mouth. "Maybe you can help your father?" She leaned forward, inches from his face. "Robert! Time for bed!"

Jake put an arm around his father, steered him upstairs and sat him on the bed. "A little too much holiday cheer, huh, Dad?"

"Cheers!" Rob raised a fantasy glass briefly then let his hand flop back to his side.

Jake slipped his father's shoes off, and Rob laid his head on the pillow. He was snoring softly when MaryAnn came into the room.

"He's all yours," Jake said.

"Look Jake, I'm sorry. It's been a long day and I just really don't want to be here. I didn't intend to ruin anybody's Christmas."

"No worries, nothing is ruined. I'm sure it will all look better in the morning."

JAKE woke to the smell of coffee and frying bacon and headed downstairs. His mother was dressed and uncharacteristically made-up as she cooked a full breakfast.

"Mmm. You made biscuits and gravy, too. My favorite."

"Help yourself, just save some for the rest. You're the first one up. I don't feel like I even slept. Grace had a headache and Emme was fussing. I didn't want her to keep everyone else awake so I walked the halls with her down here. I guess it worked."

Grace appeared in the doorway, rubbing her temples. "Emme's out like a light now. You are so good with her. Thanks Sis."

"I don't mind. I love having a baby around again." Corinne handed her sister a cup of coffee.

"Merry Christmas, ho ho ho," Ben boomed as he walked

in.

"It's Christmas Day. I actually forgot." Corinne put her hand to her head.

"That's okay, Mom. It doesn't really have anything to do with Christ's birth any—"

"Ben? Can we not have a history lesson on Christmas Day? Please?"

Jake handed him a cup of coffee and a plate. "Here, dig in, and don't talk with food in your mouth." He ruffled his brother's hair.

MARYANN came down at nine o'clock. Alone in the kitchen, she looked over the last of the morning's breakfast with disgust. "No wonder these people are out of shape," she muttered under her breath as she took a spoonful of scrambled eggs and a cup of black coffee.

"Oh." Grace entered the room and stopped short when she saw MaryAnn at the table. "I didn't know you were up. How's Rob this morning?"

"Still hung-over I guess. He didn't stir when I got up."

"Well, he got pretty hammered last night. I think he felt a little awkward."

"Didn't we all…I'm sorry. I do appreciate your sister's hospitality, it's just…"

"Uncomfortable?" Grace suggested.

"Exactly. Not to mention, I've been in these clothes for twenty-four hours."

Grace looked MaryAnn up and down and shrugged. "Just tell me what you need. I thought Corinne had some things set out."

"Oh she did. I'm just not comfortable in someone else's clothes. But it was very thoughtful of her. And thank you for checking on Rob last night. I know you both are trying to make this…situation less awkward."

"No problem. We are sort of related, after all."

"Yes, sort of." MaryAnn sniffed, turning back to her plate.

ALONE upstairs, Corinne sipped coffee and tried to get a handle on how to feed and entertain the group the rest of the day. MaryAnn did not seem to eat much. She was thin and fit, with a face that had the drawn look of someone who avoids fat at all costs.

Meow. Jealous of the new wife? thought Corinne. No. But she resented the fact that MaryAnn was reaping the ever-increasing financial rewards that should have been hers. She was sorry for her children, and wished they had experienced a more caring, nurturing, well...interested father. He had never been home, never made it to a soccer game, school program. He had provided well materially, and there were worse fathers out there, but to her he was a zero. Still, he was a zero who would need Christmas dinner.

Carrying her cup down to the kitchen, she saw MaryAnn standing at the window, staring out.

"How's Rob?"

MaryAnn jumped "Oh. Still out. Hung-over."

"Hmmm. Should I send up some coffee, or aspirin?"

"No, let's just let him sleep it off."

CORINNE was in the living room reading when Grace came down. "You okay, Grace? You look a little peaked."

"Just feeling the strain. Nothing like having the whole family for Christmas." Grace smiled weakly, dropping onto the sofa. "When did Rob start being a boozer? I thought that was one of the few vices he missed."

"I don't know. My guess is he was just tense being here last night, especially with the charming new wife, and he didn't realize how much he was drinking. He did always like my cosmos, but he never overindulged before, that I'm aware of. Not my problem, anyway. And I guess he won't be eating much dinner, which solves my other dilemma."

"Other dilemma?" Grace asked.

"How to stretch one tenderloin roast meant for four to feed six."

"Well, five you mean. The wicked stepmother doesn't eat. Haven't you noticed?"

"Maybe she's afraid I'll poison her. Maybe she thinks I want him back. If she only knew how many times I would have poisoned *him*!"

"I wish you had."

"Grace!"

"It's no secret that I never liked the man. He was so hard on you and the boys. And you would have been really well off if he had died while you were married. You would have gotten everything! Why didn't we think of that?"

"I did."

"Did what?" Ben asked, walking down the stairs.

"Ben, it was a private conversation, honey. Nothing that matters anyway. And don't be sneaking around like that."

"Not sneaking, just trying not to wake the tiny terror."

"Good boy. How's your dad?"

"Still out. MaryAnn's checking on him. Looks like they'll have to stay again tonight. Maybe the plows will get here by morning."

"Maybe. The hotline says they are working as fast as they can, but may be shorthanded due to the holiday. They appreciate our patience."

"I guess we just wait, huh?"

"Doesn't seem like a holiday though, does it honey?"

"No, it's really weird, Mom," Ben lowered his voice, "especially with MaryAnn here."

"It's hard for her too. Let's make the best of it. How about some hot chocolate with whipped cream?"

"Now that's festive. Let's have a few more calories to celebrate. Merry Christmas and Happy Birthday Jesus!" said Grace sarcastically.

"Well it's not really Jesus' birthday." Ben grinned.

Jake walked in and looked around. "Shouldn't someone check on Dad? I've never seen anyone stay down this long from a hangover. Not that I have any experience with that kind of thing." He grinned.

Corinne smiled. "MaryAnn is up with your dad now."

GRACE was the first to notice MaryAnn standing on the landing, white knuckles gripping the banister for support. "MaryAnn?" she asked. "Are you all right?"

"I can't wake him!"

"What do you mean?" Jake was on his feet, running for the stairs, followed by the others.

They rushed to Rob's bedside, staring in stunned silence at the lifeless body. As time passed, their disbelief turned into a kind of vague acceptance. Finally, Corinne put her hand on Jake's arm. "Honey, he's gone ..."

MaryAnn buried her face in her hands.

Jake leaned over and pulled the sheet over his father's head, then turned to the group. "Now what?" he asked softly.

"I'll call 911," Corinne said solemnly.

"LET'S go over this again," Jake said. The family sat around the fireplace, while MaryAnn paced in the background. Grace held Emme to her chest, listening to Jake try to make sense of his father's unexplained death. "Who was the last one to see him alive? MaryAnn?"

"I don't know! I thought he was sleeping. Don't imply that this is my fault, Jake!" MaryAnn shrieked.

"Jake," Corinne said softly, "we've gone over and over this. We'll have to wait for the authorities."

"Where will they take the body?" MaryAnn asked suddenly.

Corinne stared at her. "To the morgue, I imagine."

"Don't you watch TV?" Ben asked. "They have to do an autopsy."

"It's obvious, he drank himself to death."

"MaryAnn," Grace said, feigning patience. "He was a wealthy, high-profile man. We'd better all plan on being questioned. We'll all come under suspicion. I wouldn't have anything to gain, but you and the boys certainly benefit financially from his death." She stood. "I need to put Emme to bed."

TIDYING up several hours later, Corinne reflected on the holiday, and on her life. She had two good boys, nice home, good friends. She was happy. A happy ending was all you could hope for, right? She wondered if Rob had been happy. Her view of him had gone from controlling bully to pathetic loser in less than twenty-four hours. She had almost felt sorry for him. This was no loss for her, the man she had fallen in love with had never existed.

Pouring herself a small brandy, she sat down at the kitchen table and thought back on the evening. They had been told by the 911 operator to leave Rob undisturbed and wait for the Medical Examiner to arrive. Grace had distributed pillows and quilts as the group sprawled around the living room, everyone but Corinne eventually giving in to exhaustion. MaryAnn had finally dropped onto the large club chair in the corner, her drawn face turned toward the frosted window.

Corinne put the last of the dishes away. She was exhausted but not sleepy. Brandy in hand, she stepped out on the front porch and looked at the sky. The ring around the moon was gone, the sky was clear. No more snow. Please, no more snow.

BREAKFAST was a quiet affair. They ate in silence and listened for the sounds of the snow plow, pushing its way in, making a way out.

Corinne walked into the room and hung up the phone. "Plows are making progress. They should reach us sometime today." She looked over at MaryAnn. She was a Zombie, eating a small bowl of plain oatmeal and still in her clothes from Christmas Eve, no makeup, teased hair standing on end.

MaryAnn glared at Corinne. "He told me the vicious things you said to him over the years." She stood abruptly. "You hated him!"

Grace rolled her eyes as MaryAnn turned on her heel and said, "I have funeral arrangements to make. I'll be upstairs."

The next hours seemed interminable. Jake maintained a vigil standing at the window, while Ben lost himself on his computer. Eventually they were joined by a freshly coiffed and made up MaryAnn.

"Going somewhere?" Jake asked sarcastically.

"I certainly hope so."

"WHAT do you think?" Grace asked that afternoon, as she and Corinne moved into the kitchen to make tea. "Maybe he had a secret drinking problem or he had a bottle in his room?"

Corinne had already checked her liquor cabinet. The few bottles kept on hand stood in place, most still sealed. "All alcohol is accounted for. I would have noticed if he walked in with a bottle."

"Unless he stored some in MaryAnn's bag. She must be hiding something in there."

"Mom," Ben called softly, slipping into the kitchen. "I've been researching death from alcohol on the web. There's no way that happened. Dad walked upstairs under his own power. He couldn't have been so drunk he just didn't wake up. And I bet if you added up all the alcohol that was drunk in this house last night, it wouldn't be enough to kill a relatively healthy middle-aged man. I wish I had checked on him. Do you think he had a heart attack?"

"We'll just have to wait and see, son."

"Why don't you call the hotline again," Grace suggested. "It'll be dark soon."

Ben took the phone into the hall and came back looking disappointed. "All emergency vehicles have been redirected to a major pileup on the highway. Please call only with life-threatening emergencies." He frowned at the phone.

Grace smiled. "Call 911 and tell them I'm going to strangle MaryAnn if we don't get out of here soon."

Jake took the news of the delay with his usual composure. "Then I guess we wait." He looked around the table at his family. "Does she know yet?"

"Do I know what?" MaryAnn appeared in the doorway and stared at them. "Well?"

Grace spoke first. "Look, MaryAnn. There's been a terrible accident on the interstate. All emergency equipment is going there first. They can't spare anyone. It's possible they may not be here until morning."

MaryAnn shrieked. "Well, do any of you have a Valium or something? I cannot take another night here!"

Grace dug through her purse. "Xanax?" She handed a bottle to MaryAnn, then looked at Corinne. "I think we need to camp downstairs again tonight. I hate to be gross, but if we bring Emme's cradle down here, we can turn the heat down upstairs."

"Unhhh." Corinne sounded as if she had been punched in the stomach. "You're right, of course." She shuddered and took the childproof bottle from a frantic MaryAnn, handing it back without the lid.

AS the sky darkened into evening, everyone huddled in the kitchen except MaryAnn, who snored loudly in her reclaimed corner chair.

"Grilled cheese and tomato soup," Ben said, holding a triangle of sandwich in one hand and a mug of steaming soup in the other. "Comfort food." He looked at his mother. "I feel guilty that I'm not sadder. But, I mean, we weren't that close. I'm more creeped out than sad."

"Benjie, your feelings are what they are. No need to apologize."

"I just wish I could figure out what happened to him."

Jake looked disgusted. "I can't believe we let him lay there all day alone, dying, or maybe even dead. MaryAnn is so self-absorbed she would never have noticed. I'd love to know how many times she went in and out of that room without even looking at him."

Grace snorted. "I would have loved to have been a fly on the wall of their bedroom. I can just imagine ..." She looked at the boys and her hand flew to her mouth. "Oh, I'm so sorry. That was really in poor taste. Maybe I should take a pill too. I think all this is getting to be too much for me." She peeked into the living room. "I'm not crazy about my baby and MaryAnn being alone in the same room. Don't want to take a chance of waking up the bi...b...bereaved widow."

"No chance of that. Look at her. Wouldn't she be mortified if she knew she was drooling?" Jake laughed. "Ben, get the video camera."

"Funny." Grace sighed, rubbing her head. "I'm sorry about that remark guys. But they will be able to figure out what happened."

Corinne nodded. "Forensics these days can recreate what went on in a person's last hours, what they did, when and what they ate...it's almost like they have a movie of their actions..." She stood abruptly. "Ben, come upstairs with me."

Standing next to Rob's body, Corinne pointed to the vent above the door. "There. Can you see that? It's a camera. I had it installed before Grace came. This was supposed to be Emme's room, but she's still in with Grace. I forgot all about it. It's motion-activated, and there was no motion in this room for months, until the last few days."

Ben could hardly contain himself as he got hold of the camera and took it down to the living room.

"Good thing there's no sound on that tape," Corinne whispered to the others, as Ben loaded the tape into the only TV with a VCR in the house. "Let's let her sleep as long as possible," she mouthed, glancing over her shoulder as MaryAnn stirred.

Ben pressed Play and they saw the stilted motions of Corinne changing sheets and dusting furniture, preparing the unused room for Jake. They watched Jake help his father to bed and saw MaryAnn enter and exit twice. The third time, she set a drink on the nightstand and stood for several minutes, arms crossed, staring at Rob sleeping. They watched intently as they saw her rouse him and hand him the drink.

Ben was incredulous as he stared at the screen. "Why would she give him more alcohol?" he said loudly.

"What are you watching?" MaryAnn asked groggily.

They spun around and stared at her.

MaryAnn saw the accusation in their eyes. As she struggled to her feet her bag fell open on her lap, exposing the butt of a handgun. She pulled it out, turned it over in her hand, and aimed it toward the group.

"Whoa," said Jake raising his hands.

"MaryAnn! What are you doing?" Corinne took a deep breath and forced herself to speak calmly. "Just because you gave Rob another drink doesn't mean you killed him."

"You aren't going to pin this on me! I loved Rob. You and Grace hated him."

"No we didn't." Corinne started toward MaryAnn as Grace ejected the tape.

"Don't move!" MaryAnn yelled, waving the gun toward Ben and Jake. "And you boys didn't love him! You just wanted his money. He loved me!"

"What was in that drink?" Ben demanded

"Plain cranberry juice. He was thirsty so I gave him a drink. Tell them, Grace. You gave him a drink too." She turned toward Grace who had begun pulling the magnetic tape out of the cassette.

Corinne followed her eyes. "What are you doing, Grace?"

"We don't need this any more. We all saw her kill him."

"Grace!" Three voices shouted in unison.

"What? You saw it. She killed him. Case closed."

Jake leapt forward and grabbed the cassette, as Grace pulled away from him

MaryAnn trained the gun on the moving pair. "Stop!"

Taking advantage of the distraction, Ben lunged, knocking MaryAnn down, sending the gun skittering across the floor. Grace dove and grabbed it, pointing it at MaryAnn as she got to her feet.

"You murderer!" Grace screamed, pulling the trigger.

For a moment they stood in stunned silence, then MaryAnn laughed maniacally. "It isn't loaded. It was a Christmas present. For Rob." She began to wail.

Corinne stared at her sister in disbelief. "You would have killed her."

"She's a lying, greedy witch…I overheard them arguing about the will. He was cutting the boys out. She was going to get everything! It should have been yours, Corinne; yours and the boys." She glared at MaryAnn "I did give him another drink. He was so thirsty he drank that antifreeze just like it was another cosmo. They would have thought you did it, you conniving witch! You should be going to prison for the rest of your life." Grace fell to her knees.

"Instead, you will." Corinne said softly.

Grace sobbed into her hands. She looked up, shaking her head. "No. I only have a few months at best. Fast-growing brain tumor. I didn't want Emme to be a financial burden on any of you. The money should have been yours anyway, Corinne. Not hers. I did it for all of you—my family, Emme's family..."

IT was after midnight when the ME's van finally left. MaryAnn's car followed, fishtailing down the slippery drive.

Corinne stood inside as the sheriff loaded a handcuffed Grace into the cruiser. She saw Grace strain to look out the back window, taking in the scene within the house. Their eyes met briefly. Blinking back tears as the car disappeared from view, Corinne took consolation in knowing Grace had seen her family gathered around the cradle, Corinne and her two sons gazing down at Grace's beloved child.

RONI OLSON, having spent most of the last four decades raising her four children, has recently altered her lifestyle to focus on her lifelong desire to write. Transplanted from the Pacific Northwest, Roni enjoys life in downtown Scottsdale, AZ with her dog, Jemima. She is the current president of the Desert Sleuths Chapter of Sisters in Crime.

A CHRISTMAS STALKING
JUDY STARBUCK

AT the crack of dawn I eased down the curving staircase and listened for the slightest sound that would indicate whether my husband, Neil, had returned home. For the past three months he had tried as hard to avoid me as I had to find him. On the few nights he slept at home, it wasn't in our bed. Instead, he sequestered himself in his home office with the door locked.

Tonight was the annual Christmas Tree Lighting Ceremony in Marion Square, followed by the Parade of Boats and fireworks. For the past ten years Neil and I had celebrated the holiday kickoff with hordes of other citizens of Charleston, but this year things had changed.

I heard footsteps and found Neil in the kitchen. "We haven't spoken for days. What's going on?" The tailored suit and crisp white shirt he wore gave the appearance of a confident executive, but his blotchy complexion and red-rimmed eyes diminished his image. The muscular physique he had attained through hours at the gym now showed the beginning of a paunch.

Neil glared at me, his eyes mere slits. "Just leave me alone Ashley Jane." He pulled a cup from the shelf, and slammed it on the counter. "Where's the coffee?"

"Make it yourself."

He threw the porcelain cup across the room, just missing me. Then he stepped forward and slapped my face with such force that I fell, landing on my left arm. Pain radiated from my wrist to my shoulder. Stunned, I lay there as Neil stormed out the door and drove away.

I moved my arm and wiggled my fingers. Nothing broken. No time to stop and worry about it. I needed to find out what had turned my handsome loving husband into a monster. Even in good times Neil stayed away for hours after we had a fight. I knew we wouldn't be attending the Lighting Ceremony tonight.

With the assistance of my Swiss army knife, I unlocked his office door. I gasped when I saw the disarray, and smelled the stench. Rotting food, dishes caked with leftovers, and dirty clothes were strewn everywhere. Wastebaskets overflowed with beer cans and papers littered the floor.

I glanced at the papers and realized they were financial statements from my personal bank accounts. The sale of my mystery novels generated a healthy sum as did the interest on the trust fund left me by my grandmother. Apparently Neil had gotten into my private files and made copies. Why was he suddenly so interested in my money?

I continued to search his wood-paneled office, pulling books from shelves, lifting the Persian carpet, and looking behind furniture. I found a small key taped to the bottom of a heavy potted plant when I knocked it over during my frantic search. I rushed to his desk and unlocked it. I spent an hour digesting the contents of his files, but realized that nothing appeared out of the ordinary.

When I moved to his closet, I heard a loose floorboard creak under my foot. I knelt down and pushed his gym bag to the side. Tool marks had scratched the wood. I opened my knife, pried up the panel, and discovered a black metal box. His secret safe.

Neil was so predictable it was easy to figure out the combination, his date of birth. I swung the safe open and froze. Nestled on top of a pile of papers sparkled the two-carat diamond ring my beloved grandmother had left me. It disappeared at about the same time Neil underwent his strange personality change. We had already collected the insurance. I held the ring to my chest for a moment before I allowed my anger to surface. How dare he take this priceless memento from me? I winced as I slipped my wedding ring from my injured hand, and flung it into his safe, sliding my grandmother's ring on my finger in its place.

I recognized the folder that held our wills, powers of

attorney, and living wills. Neil had gotten one of his partners to update them three months ago. We had named one another as our sole beneficiaries, but he stood to gain far more from my demise than I from his.

Next I noticed a thick tri-fold packet of papers that bore my name across the front. When I unfolded it I made another frightening discovery. Two months ago he had taken out a life insurance policy on me for five million dollars. My signature was forged on every page.

Now I knew that he wanted me dead. But why? I leafed through paper after paper in the safe and soon found the answer. His poker party nights had not been with some friendly neighborhood group. The papers showed he had gambling IOU's that amounted to an incredible amount of money. One had been marked "paid" in the exact amount we had received from the insurance company for the lost ring. Several others would come due next month.

I had to get away now and figure things out later. I'm a mystery writer, so I had plenty of fictional experience in disappearing acts, new identities, and alternate forms of transportation. I went and sat for a moment in my living room, staring wistfully at the beautifully decorated Christmas tree, and devised a plan.

First, I photographed the paperwork in the safe and closed it, slipping the gym bag back in place. Then I walked into my office and printed out several copies. Each set went in a different manila envelope. I planned to mail one to Neil on my way out of town and labeled the other three, "In case of emergency send to the CHARLESTON, SC POLICE DEPARTMENT." I figured they would be my life assurance policy.

Next I copied my important files and meaningful pictures onto several flash drives. I filled a hiking backpack with everything I would need for my escape and backed out of our driveway for the last time.

I emptied my personal bank accounts and notified my attorney that I wanted him to hold the money in my name alone until I contacted him. I added that if something should happen to me, the beneficiary of my estate should be changed to the local animal shelter. Following his instructions, I wrote a statement of intent, had it notarized at the bank, and mailed it to him along with one of the manila envelopes. I assured him that I would let him know how to reach me when I was settled. I sent a check from our joint account to the insurance company, telling them I had found the ring, then headed for Citadel Mall.

I walked into Dillard's as trim blond blue-eyed Ashley Jane Aldrich, and emerged through Sears as frumpy redheaded Ruby Johnson with money stuffed under oversized clothes. Ruby Johnson went as far as Wisconsin on the Greyhound, but moved on to San Antonio as a raven-haired Janis Mann attired in black with a Don't Mess With Me attitude. When she exited a bus in San Francisco, she was slender, brown-haired Sara Taylor.

FROM a college trip years before, I remembered Sea Rock, California as a beautiful community. With its breathtaking coastline and magnificent Victorian homes set against a forest of redwood giants, the town was blessed with a thriving tourist trade. In addition the town had recently passed legislation that made it legal for each adult to grow twenty-five organic "medical" marijuana plants. Now blocks of gardens yielded millions of dollars worth of pot and had created a nouveau welfare system. Everyone in town was dependent on the marijuana economy. I figured a stranger in Sea Rock would blend right in with the tourists and those who wanted a taste of the alternate lifestyle.

I found a little carriage house apartment above a garage on a private street with only redwoods for neighbors. The owners leased the furnished one bedroom, one bath to me on a reduced month-to-month basis with the agreement that I would tend the lawn and gardens of the unoccupied main house.

I began each day of my new life with an early morning nature walk. One day thick fog rolled in and blurred my path so I used a faint light in the distance as my target destination. It led me to a charming bookstore named Foghorn's Books and Brew.

Louise, the owner, greeted me with the warmth of a dear friend. She wore a soft coral caftan and a long brown skirt, her gray hair held back with a turquoise-studded clasp. Bracelets of various colored beads wrapped her wrist. "What can I get for you, dear?"

The smell of fresh coffee and warm pastries mesmerized me. I turned and looked over at the small eating area furnished with antique tables and chairs. Every table had been shined to a high gloss and smelled faintly of lemon oil. Fresh flowers in a glass vase had been placed on each one.

One glass case displayed a choice of fresh muffins, croissants and sweet rolls. There were bowls of fresh fruit in another. "Am I dreaming? This place is fabulous and I haven't even looked at the books yet. What do you recommend?"

"Everything." She patted me gently on the back. "All of our pastries were baked fresh this morning. Today's special is a blueberry-banana muffin, fresh fruit and coffee."

"I'll take that along with a glass of orange juice. I'd like to buy a newspaper, too."

"You find what you want, dear." She pointed to the vast array of papers and magazines in the section called The Newsstand. I didn't want to give away my previous residence so I selected a San Francisco Chronicle and the New York Times.

"Be sure to look at the paintings around the store. In our little alcove called Fibber Magee's Closet you'll find items designed by local artisans. Everything I'm wearing has been created by a member of our community."

When she brought my food, she asked, "Are you here for long?"

"I'm not sure, but I like the area quite a bit. Maybe."

"I'm glad you like it. If there's anything I can help you with please let me know."

I toured the bookstore and selected several books. While in the mystery section, I looked for my books and was pleased when I found several copies of the latest ones. With relief, I realized the pen name and southern glamour girl photo would do nothing to identify the new me as the author.

While Louise rang up my purchases, I asked, "Can you recommend any carpenters?"

"Well, yes. Harley and Earl are fine craftsmen. They did all the work for the bookstore. They're also good musicians and play over at Whitecaps on Friday and Saturday nights. I'll get you their card. They live back in the woods where there's no phone service. When they're in town, which is nearly every day, you can reach them on their cell. Where are you staying?"

"I rented a small apartment over on Gurley Lane. On a month-to-month basis." Anticipating more questions, I added, "I got the owners' okay to add some bookshelves." I also needed new locks, and a security system, but she didn't need to know that.

"That must be the Bergs' place. Lovely couple. Where are they off to now?"

"They rented a place somewhere in France and won't be back until August."

"Harley and Earl live in cabins not far behind you. If I see them can I give them your name?"

"Sure. I'm Sara Taylor." I wrote down my new cell phone number.

"They practice their music in the evening. Have you heard them?"

I shook my head and told her I would be back in the morning for breakfast.

MY bedroom window opened onto the forest. No matter how cold the temperature dipped, I kept the window cracked. Just a waft of fresh air drifting through the room relaxed me. Today had been my first good day in a long while. I met Louise, found a perfect morning breakfast spot, and came home with new books. I climbed into bed under a plump down comforter and soon fell into a deep sleep.

Sometime later, I was awakened by the twang of bluegrass music coming through my open window. I sat up with a jerk. Although at first annoyed that my sleep had been interrupted, I found that the sound took on an alluring appeal. Then I remembered Louise saying Harley and Earl practiced in the woods behind me.

I decided to check out my neighbors. I threw on warm pants, a heavy jacket, and pulled a wool ski cap down over my hair. I carried a flashlight and pepper spray just in case I ran into someone else.

The night was dark but the sky was filled with stars. A pale moon helped me find my footing. I hung back when I saw two men sitting on broken-down lawn chairs in front of a crackling fire. One played a fiddle and the other strummed a guitar. The men laughed loudly, and stopped for refreshments after each tune. Smoke wafted, jugs emptied, and the songs livened.

One of them said something and the music stopped abruptly. They stood and looked my way, then started toward me. I backed up.

What if these guys weren't Harley and Earl? One was short and slender with a dirty blond ponytail and a scar down his cheek. The other one, a giant, was barrel-chested and bushy-haired. The fire gave their faces a ruddy glow and as they drew closer I smelled sweet weed, strong moonshine, and smoke.

The short one said, "What're you doing out here?"

Although every system in my body churned, I managed to stand tall and sound fearless through my clenched jaw. "Hey guys, I heard your music and just came to listen."

The big one said, "Well how bout that, Earl. It's a woman."

Relieved, I said, "You must be Harley and Earl. I called you today. I live in the little apartment at the edge of the forest. Louise at the bookstore gave me your names."

Earl said, "You're crazy to go in the woods alone." He looked up at his buddy. "Ain't she, Harley? These woods ain't no place for a woman alone."

"I can see that." I backed up several steps. "Well, I'll be leaving now." I kept backing up faster and faster until I tripped over a raised root and fell sideways in an awkward heap. My left arm, which hadn't completely healed from the injury in Charleston, caught the full force of my landing and blinding pain shot through it once again. Fear, pain and bad memories merged and I couldn't hold back tears. I squeezed my eyes shut and gulped back a sob.

"Ahh, don't cry. We didn't mean to scare you." Harley and Earl looked down at me with what seemed like genuine concern, then gently pulled me to my feet. "We'll help you home."

Once at my back door, Harley said, "Wrap your arm, take some pills for the pain, and get back into bed. We'll shut down the music for tonight. And don't ever go back into the woods alone."

"Thanks, guys." I managed a weak smile. As I let myself in, I turned back to them. "By the way, I'm Sara Taylor, and I like your music. Louise has my number. Can you call me tomorrow about doing some work around here?"

They nodded then disappeared into the forest. The next morning I found a box of herbal tea, fresh bread, and a bag of their homegrown pain remedy on my back doorstep.

MY life soon fell into a routine. Every morning began with a long walk and breakfast at Foghorn's. I got to know the bookstore as if it were my own. I bought books and candles and restocked my wardrobe with locally made items. I came with so little that anything new was a nice change. All my transactions were in cash so I didn't leave any tracks.

One morning I overheard Louise speaking on the phone to one of the employees who apparently couldn't make it to work. She looked frustrated. I went over to her and said, "Excuse me. I overheard your conversation. I'd be happy to fill in. My day is free."

In truth, I welcomed a day surrounded by books and people with some actual work to do. I donned an apron and from then on I spent five days a week working there. I never filled out an employment form and received my payment in books. Louise seemed to understand my situation.

Through the bookstore I discovered other creative hobbies like beading and quilting and learned the art of tai chi. In addition, I led book talks and author signings at the store. Louise seemed surprised at my expertise because she hadn't recognized me as one of her authors.

ALMOST a year had passed, and I'd begun to relax, although not entirely. One bright morning while rearranging books in the travel section, I heard a voice behind me. "Ashley Jane! Is that you?" Elegantly jeweled and reeking of the Magnolia perfume that had always made me queasy, I recognized the woman, Cornelia Rice. She had been a social acquaintance from my old life.

Fear had turned me cold, sweat dotted my forehead, and bursts of lights flashed before my eyes. "I beg your pardon." I looked at her with conviction as I backed away from the cloying smell and gripped the counter. "You must be mistaken. My name is Sara."

She fanned her perfectly made-up face with a book in her hand. "Why, you surely took my breath away. You look just like Ashley Jane Aldrich from Charleston, or shall I say, previously from Charleston." She stood back and studied me from stem to stern. "Well, you must be right. Ashley Jane would never wear those, what do you call them?" She wrinkled her nose as she looked at my faded jeans, "Dungarees." She reached her hand out toward my hair then snapped it back. "And she had such lovely pale blond curls."

I feigned a laugh. "I must have a twin somewhere. Now is there something I can help you with? We have a wide selection of coffees and, as you can see, an endless selection of books."

She studied my blue-gray apron that bore the logo Foghorn Books & Brew, Sea Rock, CA on the front then eyed the thick brown hair that hung midway down my back. She remembered her southern manners long enough to respond, "No, thank you," and set the book back down on the table.

"Have a good day." I walked over to the coffee bar and waited on the next customer as if I didn't have a care. When I saw the southern belle exit the store and pull her cell phone out of her delicate purse, I dashed to the bathroom and got sick. I knew her message would get to Neil. I couldn't stay here.

I looked in the bathroom mirror at my face, all flushed

and puffy with dark streaks under my eyes, and it struck me with the impact of a mammoth redwood falling on my head. I didn't have to run. Neil Aldrich was not going to ruin my life again. He was the criminal, not me.

Louise knocked on the bathroom door. "Sara, dear, are you all right in there?"

I splashed my face with cold water and patted it dry. "Yes, I'll be right out." I opened the door and said, "I'm fine. I must have had something for dinner last night that hit me wrong."

AFTER work I left a message for Harley and Earl. "Why don't you come over tonight and bring your toolbox? I'll have soup and fresh bread for you." Our relationship was now based on respect and friendship and we'd spent many nights sharing a meal at my kitchen table after they had finished a project.

Over time, in addition to my bookshelves, they installed new locks, motion sensor lights, and stuck a decal for a security service on the window. As a finishing touch, I put a huge dog bowl on the back doorstep for my imaginary huge dog. All Harley ever said about my security measures was, "Someone's gotta be pretty mad for you to do all this."

I shrugged.

That night I asked them to add a spotlight at the roofline with an indoor switch. Without additional details, I asked if they would immediately notify the police if they saw it on, and I handed them one of my sealed manila envelopes for safekeeping. All I said was, "Thanks, guys, for everything."

Earl said, "I have a buddy who rigged up a remote alarm. The control fits in a pocket and works for about a mile around. If you push the button a silent signal would reach me and Harley."

"How do I get one?"

Earl said, "Leave it to us."

CHRISTMAS lights on the shops brightened the gray mornings as I walked to the store each day with my new remote alarm clutched firmly in my hand. Lively carols played over the bellow of the foghorns, but no amount of cheer could alleviate my anxiety.

I was always on guard now. I listened with animal alertness to every twig snap and cone thump to the ground. Even my skin was sensitive to any change in the air.

Before I left home each day, I vacuumed the carpet right up to the front door. When I returned at day's end, I checked every lock and latch, and scanned the windowpanes. I took a deep breath to see if I could pick up any unusual scent. Then I would kneel at the edge of the carpet to see if shoes had left an impression.

I used a different route to go to work every day and if anything seemed amiss, my plan was to run into the woods and use the remote device that alerted Harley and Earl. It was no coincidence that one of them just happened to be at the store at the end of each workday with the offer of a ride home.

The thirteenth of December kicked off the holiday festivities for the Sea Rock business community. At the bookstore we decorated a ten-foot spruce then hung our stockings on the stone fireplace. A local artist had embroidered five stockings with our names on them. Often friends and customers would slip cards in them. We drew names for a Secret Santa exchange that would be held at the Christmas party on December 23rd.

The night of the party we closed the doors an hour early. Everyone had brought an appetizer to share. Candles blazed as we drank cranberry-apple wassail and munched on our sumptuous feast. Music and laughter filled the main room of the oak-paneled bookstore and Louise passed out the stockings.

We took turns opening our gifts and I was delighted with my assortment of Foghorn's coffees. Everyone chatted about their Christmas plans and I received many invitations, and accepted one from Louise. What would my holiday hold?

As I prepared to leave, Louise handed me a small box wrapped in brown paper that had a Sea Rock postmark. Her eyes twinkled when she added, "I guess you have a secret admirer."

I shook my head as I opened the parcel. Inside the box was a puzzle with about twenty-five pieces. I went over to the fiction section and sat in one of the overstuffed chairs that had an end table to the side. As I pieced it together, it began to take shape as a picture of the tree I had decorated the previous Christmas in Charleston. In the center of the star at the top of the tree, our wedding photo had been superimposed.

My heart pounded as desperate thoughts raced through my brain. Neil was out there somewhere. Was he watching me right now? Where should I go?

I gave Louise a panicked look. "I have to leave. I'm going out the back door. Act like nothing is wrong." I went to my cabinet and pulled out one of the manila envelopes labeled, TO THE CHARLESTON, SC POLICE DEPARTMENT, and handed it to her. "If you don't hear from me in the morning, send this priority mail. And thanks, Louise, for absolutely everything."

"Sara, dear, you're scaring me. Why don't you come home with me tonight?" We stood eye to eye and she drew me to her in a warm hug. I allowed myself this brief moment of comfort. She pulled back and asked, "Do you want to talk about it?"

I shook my head. "Hopefully this will be over soon." When I saw the worry in her eyes, I added, "I plan to remain at Foghorn's into my retirement years."

WHEN I reached my front door, I slipped the key into the lock. It wouldn't turn. I tried the deadbolt lock. The key wouldn't slide in. The locks had been changed. Then I noticed a sliver of light coming through the door at the top of the stairs.

Frozen with confusion, I paused too long. An arm swung around and wedged itself under my chin. Someone several inches taller, reeking of alcohol, crushed me into his body. The bony part of his wrist pressed on my windpipe. I couldn't breathe.

It was Neil! While I gasped, he said, "Don't think you can get away from me, Ashley Jane. I haven't decided whether to strangle you here or drag you upstairs and take my time." His words slurred and he tightened the grip around my neck. "You ruined my life. People are after me now. I'll make you sorry you left."

With all my strength I kicked his ankle with the heel of my boot, then shot my elbow directly into his solar plexus. This broke his hold, and he doubled over with an *umph*. I turned and ran.

I looked back and saw him still buckled over. He gave me a look that made my throat tighten. Red-faced and panting, he rose to come after me. I raced as fast as I could to the back of the house and disappeared from his sight.

From my hiding place inside a vented opening at the base of the garage, I watched Neil fumble around with indecision, first looking one way, then another. I alerted Harley and Earl with my remote signal then climbed up the laundry chute that we had reinforced as part of my escape plan. The space was tight, but I could crawl up or down on the pegs pounded in to the sides. If Neil tried to follow me he would get stuck.

The top of the chute opened into my bathroom and I climbed out. Suddenly the apartment went dark and still. Neil had flipped the breakers. In the silence I heard footsteps on the stairs. Of course he could get in. He had the lock changed so he had the key.

One of my hands held a security flashlight and the other the pepper spray that I kept in the clothes hamper. I mentally rehearsed the martial arts techniques I had practiced since my arrival in Sea Rock. This was the moment I had prepared for. This was the moment I feared.

Neil was close. I felt motion in the air and smelled the liquor. He moved awkwardly from the living room to the kitchen and now toward the bathroom. I lowered myself into a crouch position. My eyes had adjusted and I saw the outline of his body as he entered the room. Rising up slowly, I turned, bent my right leg, and with full force, stomp-kicked the side of his leg at the kneecap. His knee popped and he fell to the floor, grasping his pain-addled knee.

He managed to drag himself with one arm toward me and grabbed my ankle. He jerked on it and I nearly lost my balance. His breaths came loud and fast as he tried to pull himself up by the handles on the cabinet drawers. As he got half way up, I slammed the side of his head with the flashlight and he dropped in silence.

By the time I ran down the stairs and out the front door, Harley and Earl were there and I heard the sound of sirens approaching. Medics went to work on Neil. They couldn't find a pulse and placed him on a gurney. Flashing lights in yellow, blue and red gave the brown redwoods an eerie look, like they were on fire.

I sat down on the ground and watched them load him into their vehicle. Neil had actually tried to kill me. As the ambulance pulled away, I covered my face and sobbed.

I spent a grueling night telling and retelling my story to various officers. Several hours into the questioning, Chief of Police Patterson came into the cramped interrogation room. He informed me that Neil had died. The nightmare was over.

THE following week I flew back to Charleston. Over time, I sold my house, changed my name, and transferred my accounts to Sea Rock. I was no longer the married southern socialite, Ashley Jane Aldrich, but now officially, bookseller Sara Taylor.

JUDY STARBUCK is a Scottsdale teacher, handwriting analyst, and mystery writer. Her short story, "The Sun Also Sets," is included in the award-winning anthology, *Map of Murder*, and "Neither Rare Nor Well Done" in another award-winning anthology, *Medium of Murder*. Her article "Books for Dinner" appeared in the Arts Section of the Arizona Republic and in the Northern California MWA Newsletter. She also contributed to the blog, Type M for Murder. She is involved in adoption search and support groups, is an Arizona-certified Confidential Intermediary and an active member of Sisters in Crime.

CHRISTMAS LIGHTS
SARAH PARKIN

MIKE Lindstrom pulled his red Ford F150 with the Mesquite Valley Landscaping logo into the driveway where he lived with his mom and brother. Many houses along the suburban street had Christmas lights up with trees and cacti decorated in the yards. One neighbor even put fake frost on the windows, but he wasn't fooling anyone. The forecast called for highs in the sixties all week in the small desert town of Mesquite Valley, Arizona.

He secured a tarp over the bed of his truck to protect his tools, then went to the back of the house and entered the kitchen. Sitting on the bench inside the door, he removed his boots, and noticed his mother staring out the kitchen window. Her hand held a plate just above the sink.

"Mom?"

She startled and the dish slipped into the sudsy water. "Oh, Michael! I didn't realize you'd come in."

"You okay?"

Mike worried about her since his father's death. His father struggled with drugs for decades, but had been clean for nearly twelve years. Eight months ago, he had overdosed and died in his art studio behind the house. She was apprehensive about finances without the income from his dad's artwork.

Nudging her over so he could wash his hands after a long day of planting trees, he gave her a kiss on the cheek. "Christmas is coming."

"I know." She sighed. "Eight more days. I just don't know what to do. It doesn't seem right to celebrate too much our first Christmas without him."

Mike tilted his head. "Let's talk about it at dinner.

Where's Gabe?" Gabriel was fifteen, born twelve years after Mike. A few years later, his dad got help with his drug abuse.

His mother looked at the clock. "Oh my! Time got away from me. Gabriel really should be home by now." She opened the oven door and checked the roasting pan filled with chicken surrounded by carrots, potatoes, and onions.

Mike breathed deeply. "Smells great, Mom."

Looking out the window, he saw a Mesquite Valley police car pull up to the house. Gabriel sat in the backseat. Detective Heather Martinson stepped from the car. She and Mike had dated on and off over the last six months, but he had called it off a few weeks earlier. They met when his father died and she worked the case to find the drug dealer. They had a suspect, "Buttons" Sinclair, but not enough evidence. Sinclair had done time in prison for selling drugs and had gotten out shortly before Mike's father overdosed. Sinclair had been seen with Mike's dad, but that wasn't enough grounds to press charges.

Shoving his feet back into his boots, Mike hustled out to the street. Heather opened the car door for Gabriel to climb out. Gabriel looked straight at Mike. "I didn't do anything."

Heather touched Mike's shoulder. "He's right. He didn't do anything. However, he was with some kids over at the Smoothie Hut. They had pills, Mike. Red and blue capsules, similar to the ones we found in your dad's studio. They're probably from Sinclair."

Mike glared at Gabriel. How could he be mixed up with kids like that?

Heather continued. "We're seeing a big increase in the pills recently. The Citizens for a Safe Mesquite Valley have set up a task force with a phone hotline and a reward."

Before he could ask Heather more, their mom came out the front door and rushed over to hug Gabriel. "Are you okay? What happened?"

"Nothing." Gabriel rolled his eyes and headed into the house.

"He's fine, Mom. We'll talk about it inside," Mike said.

"Won't you come in, Heather? I've got a chicken in the oven."

"Thanks for the offer, Angie, but I'm on duty."

His mother nodded and followed Gabriel.

"I don't think Gabe's taking the drugs, but I thought I'd better bring him home and let you know what's going on."

"I appreciate it." He began to step away.

"Plus I wanted a chance to see you," Heather said with a smile.

"Heather, we've been through this. I'm in the middle of starting a new business. I've moved back in with my mother. I'm in no position to settle down."

"I'm not asking you to settle down. I'm just asking to spend some time together."

Mike sighed. He liked Heather. Maybe even loved her. But he needed to remain with his grieving mother right now. And he really needed to get his business going. A relationship would only complicate things. "I can't right now, Heather. I'm sorry."

She smiled and nodded. "I won't give up that easy. I'll go for now. But I'll see you around."

He nodded, knowing they would keep running into each other. He was afraid he might fall totally in love with her at a time when he needed to focus on other priorities.

Once inside, Mike sat Gabriel down at the kitchen table. "Tell me."

"It's nothing. No big deal."

"No big deal?" Mike ran his fingers through his hair. "Pills, Gabe? After what happened to Dad?"

"It's not the same thing. I haven't tried any. Some of my friends have. They say they're just for fun. They aren't hooked or anything."

"Do they get them from Sinclair?"

Gabe shrugged. "I don't know."

His mom's chin trembled, "Gabriel, I won't have it. You will have nothing to do with drugs. If you do, I will put you in rehab so fast your head will spin."

"Mom, I told you. I'm not taking drugs."

"Fine," she said. "You were there. That's enough for me to ground you for two weeks."

"But that's over Christmas break!"

"Yes," she replied. "It is."

"But Mom," Gabriel whined.

"Mom's right," Mike agreed. "Even if you weren't doing anything wrong, you didn't do anything to stop something wrong. You've been raised to know better."

"That's not fair."

"Maybe. Maybe not. But that's the way it is." She opened the oven door and pulled the chicken dish out. "Now you boys wash up and get ready for supper."

As soon as everyone had food on their plates, she said, "This year is the first year we'll celebrate Christmas without your dad. It might be a good time to change some traditions. I was thinking we'll skip decorating the house. We don't have much money right now, and without your dad's income we need to cut back on the gifts. What do you think?"

Gabriel's fork clattered on his plate. "I think it's lousy. I need my own computer. All my friends have them. Are you are telling me I'm going to get a stupid basketball or something?"

Tears brimmed in his mother's eyes and Mike nudged his brother to cut the attitude, but it was too late.

"I'm doing the best I can." She set down her water glass, pushed back her chair, and left the room. Mike knew it was because she didn't want them to see her cry.

"It's not her fault, Gabe. She didn't want things this way."

"It isn't my fault either. I'm stuck here in a house where everyone's sad all the time. We don't have any money for anything and there's nothing to do," Gabriel's chair scraped across the floor as he jumped to his feet and began furiously pacing the kitchen. "I didn't make Dad overdose." He wrenched open a cupboard, yanked out a bag of sugar, ripping it open to empty it on the floor, followed by flour and macaroni.

Their mother rushed into the kitchen. "Gabriel! What are you doing?" Her panicked reaction encouraged him. He grabbed a box of salt and dumped it into the mix, kicking repeatedly and scattering it from wall to wall.

As she rushed toward Gabriel, Mike held her back. "Let him get the anger out."

Gabriel reached for a can of coffee from way in the back of the cupboard. His mother gasped. Appearing to know it would hurt her if he destroyed the last of Dad's special coffee, he slowly peeled off the lid, and then dumped out the contents.

The can clattered as red and blue pills scattered on the floor. For a moment, no one moved. Gabriel cried out. "I'm sorry, Mom...I'm...They're not mine."

Their mother approached the broom closet, but Mike stopped her. "Maybe we should call Heather."

Gabriel headed for his room. Mike knew he would climb in his bed with the blanket pulled over his head. The transition from fifteen-year-old child to grown-up sometimes took a little time.

"Leave him alone," she said. "He's frustrated and confused." She held her hand to her chest as if to slow down the heartbeat. "I'm so angry your father brought drugs inside this house. Out in the studio, well, that was his space, but in here...What if we weren't home when Gabe found them?"

An hour later, Heather arrived in one of the squad cars. The officers carefully bagged the pills and coffee can. "Maybe we'll get lucky and find Sinclair's print on the can," Heather said.

"Would it be enough to nail him?" Mike asked.

"He's been tough to tie down. But we keep trying."

The officers separately asked each member of the family some questions about how the drugs might have gotten into the coffee can. No one knew. They searched the rest of the house but found no other drugs. They had searched the studio back when his dad died and found pills in several hiding places, including in a plastic bag inside a paint can, and in a jar tucked in with the framing tools. As far as Mike knew, no one had been in the studio since then.

After Heather left, they cleaned up the kitchen and Gabriel went back to his room.

"How's Gabe doing?" Mike asked his mother.

"He'll fall asleep." She sunk into a chair and sighed. "He's like you at that age."

"Yeah, well, I didn't hang out with kids who took pills,

Mom."

"No, but you saw what drugs did to your father. He doesn't remember your father strung out, throwing paint and breaking glass. Gabe was just three when your dad got clean. We never saw another sign until the overdose." She shook her head. "All those years. I really thought he'd kicked it. I feel angry and betrayed, and I'm still so sad. I feel like a fool all over again."

"Oh, Mom. None of us knew."

She was quiet a long moment. "We need to watch Gabe."

"I will. I'll check on his friends, too. I'll pull out his yearbook and page through it."

"Thank you, Michael. I'm glad you're back home. I know you moved in so you would have the money for the business, but it's been a comfort having you here."

Mike shrugged, embarrassed. "I don't really do anything, Mom."

"You do more than you think." She patted his hand. "You know, Heather really cares for you, and I see how you care for her."

"Mom," he warned.

"All right. But you're throwing away a good thing."

"I hear you, Mom."

OVER the next few days, Gabriel helped Mike landscape. Mike showed him how to run irrigation lines and place mulch around tender plants. Neither one mentioned the pills. They came home dirty and worn-out, but it was a good tired. Several people called Gabriel to go out at night. He didn't tell them he was grounded, only that he had other plans.

On Friday night, after a lively debate over which holiday DVD to watch, they made popcorn and settled in. Everyone seemed to calm down and return to normal. Afterward, their mother said, "The movie perked me up. How about if we get the Christmas lights out of storage and put them up tomorrow?"

"Okay," Mike said. "As long as you're ready."

She shrugged. "I can't change the past. I want to work on moving forward."

"I'll drive over first thing tomorrow."

THE next morning, Mike was the first one up. He poured a bowl of cereal and clicked on the local news. The announcer stated that four kids in Mesquite Valley had overdosed last night. Mike dropped his spoon in the bowl. Two were in the hospital. Two had not survived, including the police chief's daughter. They didn't release the names of the students because they were minors.

Mike heard a noise. Gabriel stood behind him, staring at the television, before bolting to the bathroom to throw up. When he returned to the kitchen he sat with his phone texting friends. After twenty minutes, he had learned the names of the students. They weren't kids he knew well, but he did know them. In a town the size of Mesquite Valley, everyone knows everybody. No one mentioned that Gabriel would have been at the same party if he hadn't been grounded.

When his mom came in, they told her the news. She sat down with a paper and pencil and began a grocery list. "I need to take casseroles to those poor parents. When your father died, I couldn't even make macaroni and cheese." Gabriel asked if he could make something, too. They worked on the list together.

Mike wasn't interested in food preparation. He wanted to do something physical. He remembered his promise to get the Christmas decorations. It wasn't backbreaking labor, but it would keep his hands and mind busy. He drove to the storage unit two miles down the road.

He thought about Heather. His mom probably had her on the casserole list, too. She might have been the one to notify the parents of the children who overdosed. Her boss had to be grieving. He wondered how the whole department was doing.

Several rows of single car garages within a security fence made up the storage units. Mike punched in his code and the gate opened. At the family's unit, Mike pulled on work gloves and scanned the area. There was no one around. Inside he moved boxes around until he found the lights, fake pre-lit tree and boxes of ornaments. Everything fit neatly in the bed of the pick-up. As he closed the garage door, a car came down the driveway. "Buttons" Sinclair's Honda CRV rolled past him. Mike was convinced this man was responsible for the overdoses in Mesquite Valley.

Mike squeezed his fists, feeling the loss of his father all over again. He took several deep breaths and waited for Sinclair to stop at his own storage unit and open the door. Without thinking, he quietly eased closer and looked inside. His eyes locked on a scale, plastic gloves, zip-top bags, and a box of throwaway cell phones. Everything necessary for a drug operation. Four wooden chairs surrounded a square table covered with red and blue pills.

If Mike had thought about it first, he wouldn't have done it. But he didn't think. He grabbed a chair and smashed it down on Sinclair's head. Hard. Sinclair leaned left and slumped over the table.

Mike's heart thudded in his ears as he raced to his truck, grabbed the Christmas lights out of the box, and used the cords to hogtie Sinclair's hands and feet. Sinclair groaned, but didn't stir. Mike's mind wavered between fear and exhilaration that he had actually apprehended the drug dealer. He knew he should call Heather, or maybe even the main police station, but he wanted to talk to Sinclair alone.

Pulling his work gloves taut over his hands, he lowered the garage door only allowing enough light so he could look around. Mike saw dozens of boxes. Some held empty red and blue capsules. Others contained zip top bags, plastic gloves, cleaning powder. Then, on the table, next to the scale, he saw the local high school yearbook open to pages with student photos. The margins next to some photos were filled with notes along with stars and checkmarks.

Sinclair began to stir. "Hey," he growled, struggling against his Christmas light bindings. He looked around, eyes landing on Mike. "Frank's kid?"

"That's right. Frank was my dad. And he was a great dad for a lot of years...until he ran into you."

"Oh, your dad and I go way back."

"I never knew about you until right before he died."

"Really? He never talked about old Buttons Sinclair?"

"Nope."

"Musta felt guilty."

Mike frowned. "Guilty of what?"

"Sending me to prison." Sinclair gave Mike a sideways look. "You really don't know, do you? Then why do you have me all tied up?"

Mike wondered what he should know. The memories began to fit together as Mike remembered his dad going to rehab. He wanted to know more.

Sinclair struggled to sit up straight. "Come on. Untie me."

Mike shook his head. "Those kids are dead because of you. My father was an adult. He could make his own decisions. But those kids were—"

"Now wait," Sinclair said. "All I did was give those kids what they wanted. I was providing a service. Don't you see?"

"I'm sure the police chief will see it differently when he comes back from making funeral arrangements for his only daughter."

"You're not gonna turn me in, are you?" Sinclair looked around wildly. "You're a rat. Just like your father."

"Looks to me like you're the rat. You get people hooked on this stuff!" Mike pounded the table, causing the pills to jump around.

"Your father sent me to prison. I'm not goin' back there."

Mike leaned back and crossed his arms. "Actually, it looks like you might. The evidence here seems pretty strong." They both looked around at the drug paraphernalia.

Sinclair shook his head. "I'm not goin' back to prison."

Mike pulled out one of the chairs and sat down in front of Sinclair. "Tell me about my dad."

"Why?"

"Because I'll call the police if you don't."

Sinclair tilted his face sideways, conceding the point. "Okay," Sinclair narrowed his eyes. "After you untie my hands."

Mike shook his head. "Tell me about what happened with my father."

"When? Last spring? Or years ago?"

"Both."

"Pick one."

Mike wanted to hear about his dad, but he was in no mood to bargain. He took his cell phone from his pocket and punched the "9" button.

"Okay," Sinclair said. "Okay. I'll tell you about Frank."

Mike flipped his cell phone closed.

"Frank was a great customer in the old days," he began. He told about his father being a regular customer. The amounts he would need would increase as he came closer to completion of an art project. He was a steady client. Then, nearly thirteen years ago, the police caught them making a deal. Both were taken to the police station. Sinclair refused to talk. But Mike's dad, afraid to be taken away from the family, agreed to testify against Sinclair in exchange for a probationary sentence which involved an in-house treatment program.

Mike's mind buzzed as he remembered the police coming to the house, and his dad being gone for a long time, followed by his sober return, and a long stretch of happy family times. "So why, after all this time, did you feel the need to get him hooked again?"

"Ya gotta understand. This is business. He had to expect some payback. I did hard time while Frank had a soft life at home."

"So you got him to take drugs again?" asked Mike. "After twelve years of sobriety?"

"No," Sinclair said regretfully. "I tried to get him hooked again. I left his favorite pills in all sorts of places for him to find. He told me he flushed them down the toilet. Perfectly good pills. Not even cut with cleaning powder yet."

"So how did you finally reel him in?"

"I was gonna get him going on the pills again, then get to know his kid and his kid's friends. But I couldn't get him to take any. So I broke into that studio and put powder into the orange juice in the fridge."

Mike remembered how his dad would finish a painting and then down an entire sixteen-ounce bottle of juice in celebration.

His dad hadn't gone back to drugs. He had overdosed, but he didn't know it. Sinclair seemed to relish the storytelling, enjoyed the revenge in killing Mike's father.

"I'll deny everything I said if you try to tell it to the cops," Sinclair said. "Remember, your dad had a drug history. They won't believe you."

Mike had heard enough. He felt a strong urge to bash Sinclair in the head again and keep bashing until his strength ran out. The feeling repulsed him and he didn't want to be near Sinclair any longer. He realized he needed to leave and stepped toward the door.

"Hey! You can't just leave me here! Those kids chose to take those drugs. You can't pin their death on me."

Mike ducked under the garage door, and slid it closed. Then, worried that Sinclair could get out even if he was tied up, slid the lock on, securing the storage unit. He heard Sinclair's yells, but he didn't care.

Unsure of what to do next, he got in his truck and drove toward home. Sinclair's words sunk in. Sobs wracked his body as he pulled over to the side of the road. His father had held onto sobriety after all, and this man had killed him. After a few moments, he began to think rationally. He had wanted to hurt Sinclair. It scared him to think he might have the capability to kill someone. Mike just wanted him to go away. He certainly didn't want him to keep on supplying drugs. There had been enough overdosing, enough people hurt from the long-term damage this man brought to the community.

He called Heather. She answered on the first ring.

"Hi there, what's up?" she said.

"I...I did something. I found someone you're looking for...I have him tied up."

"What do you mean, tied up?"

"Well, I used our Christmas lights. My mom won't be too thrilled."

He explained everything.

"You've told us what we need to know," Heather said. "Go home. We'll take care of it. Don't say anything to anyone until we know what's going on."

He drove home and hauled the tree into the house.

Gabriel helped him place ornaments on all the limbs.

They were just finishing when his mother came in with groceries. "What about the lights, Michael? We should get those up on the house."

Mike merely shrugged. "I couldn't find them, Mom." He didn't feel good about lying to her. In fact, he didn't know how he felt about the whole day. He told his mother he was going out for the evening, even though he didn't have plans. Then he took a shower, washing away all he'd seen and heard that day. He stayed under the hot spray a long time.

He went to the local bar where he was surprised to overhear rumors about Sinclair being found dead.

"Someone found him in that storage place on Briar-wood!"

"I heard he overdosed on the same stuff as those kids."

"Swallowed a bunch of his own pills."

"I always knew he was worthless."

Mike listened as he drank several beers and stared at the television even though he couldn't focus. He thought of all the pills he had left right in front of Sinclair. Did he do it subconsciously? No. He didn't think so. He couldn't do to Sinclair what Sinclair did to others.

He wasn't sure how much time had passed when Heather showed up at his side. "You okay?" she asked.

"I don't know."

"You eat anything?"

"Nope."

"Come home with me. I'll fix some spaghetti."

Any escape sounded like a good idea. She grabbed his hand, led him to her car, and drove him to her apartment. As she boiled pasta, she told him how Sinclair was already dead when the police arrived. It appeared that he had leaned over and gobbled up as many pills off the table as he could.

"Why would he kill himself?"

She strained the noodles. "With so many previous offenses, and the wrath of the police chief, he was going to serve a long sentence."

Mike wondered out loud if he was responsible. "I really wanted him dead, but I never thought he would take his own pills. I didn't think I left him in a dangerous situation."

"Sinclair made his own choice." She dished up the pasta. "A lot of people want other people dead. Wanting and actually killing someone are two separate things. We are allowed to think and feel whatever we want. It's our actions that make the difference."

The spaghetti was good. So was what happened afterward. Mike knew he loved her.

IN the morning, Mike tried to sneak into the house before his mother woke up, but ended up handing her the newspaper as she opened the front door.

"Good Morning," they both said to one another.

She smiled. "I hope you were where I think you were."

"Probably," he replied.

"Breakfast?"

"Sure."

His mother had already heard the news reports about Sinclair, but didn't know the details. Mike explained that he had been there and used the Christmas lights to tie him up. He carefully told her that his dad hadn't overdosed.

"I knew it," she sobbed. "I knew he wasn't using drugs again."

He held her while she cried.

Gabriel had just joined them for pancakes when the doorbell rang. His mother opened the door to Heather.

"Won't you come in?" his mother asked hopefully.

"Oh, no," said Heather. "I just need Michael for a minute."

Mike followed Heather to the cruiser parked at the curb. "The Captain wants you to know you'll be receiving a reward check from the Citizens for a Safe Mesquite Valley."

"I don't want it. I just want to forget about the whole thing."

"Give it some thought. Think about your family. You can't just wish everything away."

"Okay. Thanks, I guess."

Mike gave Heather a kiss, even though he was certain his mother watched from the window.

ON Christmas Eve, their mother prepared a beef roast dinner while Mike and Gabriel played video games. Under the Christmas tree were some large packages Mike had placed there the day before. He felt satisfied with himself. The house smelled wonderful as the roast cooked. They ate cookies and laughed for the first time in a while.

At four o'clock, the doorbell rang. Mike answered it, and Heather came in, a pie in each hand. Mike looked from Heather to his mother.

"Oh, Michael," his mother said with a smile. "Did I mention I invited Heather for Christmas Eve Dinner?"

"Why no, Mother, you didn't." He grinned, reaching out to take the pies. "But I'm glad she's here."

Heather smiled, too. "I confess I didn't make them myself, but I got them from my favorite bakery."

"I'm sure they're wonderful," said his mother.

Gabriel came into the kitchen. "Hey Mom, since we're starting new traditions this year, can we open presents on Christmas Eve instead of waiting until Christmas morning?"

"Okay," she said. "We can try it and see."

Heather spoke up, "I'd like to give my gift to you first, Angie."

They all gathered around the tree.

Heather took a deep breath. "This may not seem Christmas-like, but I think it's important. It isn't an actual present. It's information."

"Information?" his mother asked.

"Yes, and I hope it brings you peace of mind. They've changed Frank's records to indicate there was no suicide. His death has been ruled a homicide by Sinclair with an intentional overdose. You were right all along. Frank didn't go back to drugs."

His mother nodded as a single tear rolled down her face. Mike kissed Heather on the cheek, then went to his mother and wrapped his arms around her.

"I know you already told me," she said. "But now it's official."

After a bit of nose-blowing and dabbing of eyes, his

mother told Heather how proud she was to have someone on the police force so close to the family. Heather blushed.

They passed around presents. Gabriel couldn't resist and opened the one he thought was the right size and shape first. "Yes," he shouted, beaming at the newest model laptop. "I got one. I got one."

Then, his mom opened a small box, which held a credit card, and a checkbook showing a generous balance.

"Michael? How can you do all this?"

Mike smiled. "I found a good use for the Christmas lights."

SARAH PARKIN, a freelance writer since 1999, has provided articles and essays to *The Arizona Republic, Newsmakers, Contemporary Musicians, The Texas Project, Encyclopedia of World Biography, Women Etcetera, View Highlife, Eat Fresh AZ, Southern Traveler,* and *Highroads.* Her short story, "Quick Draw," was published in *Medium of Murder* (Red Coyote Press, 2008). She travels extensively, writing about "destinations with character." She also covers the Phoenix Farmer's Market column for Examiner.com. More information is available at SParkinProductions.com.

THE GIFT
JoAnne Zeterberg

MY name is Samantha Gaines and I see dead people. It started when I was little, well before movies and TV made seeing dead people cool. The main difference was that my spirits were really nice to me; so nice, in fact, that I didn't realize talking to them was abnormal until I overheard my parents arguing about it when I was five.

Mom had tucked me into bed, but I'd wanted another cookie, so down the stairs I crept. I reached the bottom step and peeked through the banister, trying to figure out how to sneak past my parents and into the kitchen. Then Mom spoke, raising her voice to be heard over the basketball game Dad was watching on television.

"She's always talking to them, Bob," she said, her hands working the knitting needles at a brisk pace. They were in their usual spots—Mom on the couch and Dad making the most of his Lazy Boy in full recline. "What happens when she starts grade school next year and walks around talking to people no one else can see?"

"Every kid has imaginary friends, Fran. I don't see what you're getting so upset about," said my dad, always the voice of reason.

"Yes, kids have imaginary friends, but they're like Tinker Bell or Fluffy the rabbit." The clacking of the needles stopped as Mom's eyes focused on Dad like a laser. "Do you know what Samantha said when I asked her what she was laughing at during lunch today?"

A sigh. "No, but I'm sure you'll tell me."

"Vito. That's what she said. Vito." Mom's hands fussed with the frothy orange yarn that filled her lap. "Not Tinker Bell, not Fluffy. Vito. What child has an imaginary friend named Vito?"

129

I watched my dad shrug. Apparently there was no good answer to that one.

The knitting resumed. "So I asked her to describe him, and do you know what she said then? She said he was fat, with a shiny head, one big eyebrow and a cigar. Sound familiar?"

"Yeah," Dad said with a chuckle. "It sounds like your uncle from Queens."

"Exactly!" Mom stabbed her knitting needles in Dad's direction. "Uncle Vito from Queens who died over ten years ago."

"Come on, Fran. You don't really think Sam's talking to your dead uncle Vito, do you? "

When Mom replied, her voice was hardly more than a whisper. "My mother had The Gift," she said. "I think Sam has it, too."

So there it was. The Gift. That's what they called it then. Over time, I learned not to talk to the dead when the living were within earshot. Eventually, they stopped coming to me, presumably because the dead really dislike being ignored. They stopped, that is until recently, when I took a header off a ladder while hanging Christmas lights in front of my gift shop. Now they were back. And one of them seemed very angry.

I squinted against the fluorescent glare and cast a glance around the ER waiting room. More than a dozen people in various states of illness and injury sat in plastic chairs, clearly absorbed in their own misery.

"Let's go. I'm fine," I insisted. "It's just a little bump on the head."

"You're not fine," countered Ben Davis, my boyfriend of three years and Sheriff of our Arizona mountain town of Eagle Falls. "It's the size of a goose egg and I can see it from here."

I was about to argue with him until I saw the concern in his hazel eyes. He draped his arm across my shoulders and gently drew me toward him. With a resigned sigh, I rested my head on his shoulder and couldn't help smiling as a lock of his chestnut curls tickled my forehead.

I'd just started to doze off when the sliding doors to the ER's inner sanctum opened and the duty nurse called my name. As we followed her inside, Ben steadied me against a wave of dizziness that threatened to put me horizontal for the second time that night. Once in the exam room, he helped me change into a drafty hospital gown and got me settled on the gurney. The short walk and effort of changing clothes increased the pounding in my head to rock-concert level. Moments later, the doctor, a grandfatherly man with wire-rimmed glasses, breezed through the curtains.

"Ms. Gaines, I'm Doctor Perkins." He glanced at my chart. "Says here you fell off a ladder. Did you lose consciousness?"

"No," I said at the same time Ben said, "Yes."

The doctor looked over the rim of his glasses at each of us in turn then settled on Ben. "How long was she out?"

"About a minute," he said. "But it was a long minute."

Dr. Perkins nodded and returned his attention to me. "Well, your vitals look good now, but I want an X-ray and CT scan before I let you go. Unless I see something I don't like, we'll have you on your way home shortly."

True to Doc Perkins's word, Ben and I walked out of the ER less than two hours later with a prescription for pain medicine and instructions for Ben to awaken me every few hours for the rest of the night.

"Thanks for staying here with me," I said to Ben as we walked down the long corridor toward the exit.

"Anytime, hon." Ben took my hand. "I'll finish hanging the Christmas lights for you tomorrow night."

We rounded the final corner just in time for me to nearly collide with a woman in a hospital gown pushing an IV pole. Her brown hair was tousled and streaked with gray. Her dull blue eyes regarded me curiously.

"Oh, I'm sorry," I said as I crowded into Ben to let the woman pass.

"Don't worry about it," Ben said with a smile. "I'm great at hanging lights. Your store will be the best on the block."

"No, I meant..." I turned to point out the woman to

Ben, but the hallway behind us was empty.

SERENDIPITY is my dream-come-true, a cozy New Age store offering everything from crystals and essential oils to books and handmade gifts. Bamboo flooring and butter-cream yellow walls impart a warm cozy feel, while generous front windows let in plenty of natural light. I designed the interior with the principles of Feng Shui in mind and have arranged the merchandise accordingly. Books and two overstuffed chairs extend an invitation to sit and read in the Knowledge & Spirituality corner. Candles and scented lotions tempt customers in Romance. Crystals sparkle in Creativity, and the cash register rings up purchases in Serendipity's Wealth corner. To complete the ambience, candles and oils burn during business hours, their aromas dictated by the time of day—invigorating blends of citrus or eucalyptus in the morning, calming lavender and sage in the afternoon.

"I can't believe you fell off the ladder," Amanda said as she unlocked the door and flipped the sign on Serendipity's front window from Shut to Open. My best friend and only employee, Amanda has worked with me since I opened the store five years ago.

I swept a feather duster over a display of hand-poured candles that were artfully embellished with dried wildflowers and sprigs of herbs. "Well, Grace is my middle name." My duster and I moved on to another shelf, this one holding fist-sized crystals of amethyst, fluorite and smoky quartz.

Amanda laughed, her blue eyes twinkling. "I know, but you really should be more careful."

"Geez, Amanda. I'm thirty-three not eighty, and I'm fine." I gently ran a hand over the back of my head feeling the lump that made my short auburn hair stick out.

"Speaking of eighty," Amanda said glancing out the window, "here comes Miss Lillie."

I stowed the feather duster behind the check-out counter and glanced out the front window.

At eighty years young, Lillian Beechler was the oldest-living descendent of Maxwell Beechler, the founding father of Eagle Falls. She was a well-loved member of the community, active in local charities and, until recently, a member of the town council. On this cold mid-December morning, she rivaled the cardinals in a red wool coat and matching hat. As she crossed Main Street, a man whom I guessed to be in his late twenties followed closely behind. A scowl marred his otherwise handsome face.

I went to the small kitchenette at the back of the store to pour a cup of the apple-cinnamon tea Miss Lillie favored. A moment later, the bell above our front door announced her arrival. She was alone, apparently the man following her had continued on his way.

"Good morning, Miss Lillie," Amanda said a bit too loudly. "How are you today?"

"My ears and I are just fine, Amanda," Miss Lillie replied with a smile. "Good morning, Sam." She kissed me on the cheek, her lips cold from the brisk air outside.

"It's good to see you, Miss Lillie. How about some tea to warm you up?"

"Oh, that would be lovely. Thank you, dear."

I took her coat and led her to one of the chairs in the reading nook. On the table next to her I placed the tea and a plate of oatmeal cookies from the bakery next door, and sat down to visit for a few minutes. When we'd covered the latest town gossip and my trip to the ER the night before, Miss Lillie set down her cup and her voice took on a serious tone.

"I've been meaning to ask you, dear, if you ever fill mail orders."

"Of course," I replied. "But, if you can't get into town, I'd be happy to bring your order to you at home."

Miss Lillie shifted slightly in her chair. "Actually, I'll be leaving Eagle Falls next week. Arthur has decided it's time I moved into one of those, what do you call them...assisted living homes in Phoenix." Arthur Finkle was Miss Lillie's nephew, a forceful man in his fifties who managed the only bank in town. He had a reputation as a brilliant businessman, but always struck me as being a little on the slick side.

"I don't understand, you seem to be doing so well here."

"I thought so, too. But after that little fall I took in September, Arthur is worried about me living on my own."

She glanced around the store. "It makes me sad to leave Eagle Falls and all my friends. I was hoping to spend one more Christmas here, but…"

I could see the wistfulness in her eyes. "Christmas is only a week away. Surely it could wait until after the holidays."

"No, Arthur has everything set up and he's already met with the Historical Society about the house." She smiled at this. "I was born in that house, you know. Grandfather built it with his own hands and a good portion of his heart, when he founded this town. I'm donating it to the Society so that the community can enjoy it after I'm gone." She hesitated a moment. "Everything just seems to be moving so quickly."

She waived her hand as if brushing away an unpleasant insect. "Once Arthur sets his mind to something, he's like a hound with a bone. I guess I should just be grateful I have him to look after me. Now, I'd best be on my way. Arthur's coming over for coffee this afternoon so I can sign the papers on the house, and I still have to get to the market."

I helped her into her coat, then she took my arm and we walked to the front door. "I'll be back in a couple of days for the oils I ordered," she said, patting me on the cheek. "Don't be sad, dear. It's for the best. I'll see you soon." With a final wave, she walked out into the morning chill.

"What was that about?" Amanda asked.

I told her about Miss Lillie's impending move.

"It's so sad." We both turned to watch Miss Lillie cross Main Street.

"I wonder who that is?" I said, noticing that the same young man was following her once again.

"Who?" Amanda said.

"The man following Miss Lillie."

Amanda's brows came together as she scanned the street. "I don't see anybody."

Just then, the man turned and looked directly at me with eyes as dark as ink wells. The hairs on the back of my neck rose.

"You're right," I said, my eyes still locked on the man only I could see. "It must have been a reflection."

BEN came by Serendipity that evening after work to help me finish hanging the Christmas lights. When we'd hung the last strand and the store was aglow in holiday cheer, we headed across the street and settled into a window booth at Moretti's Taste of Italy to admire our handiwork. I told him about my visit with Miss Lillie over plates of Papa Nick's spicy Shrimp Arrabiata.

"It was strange," I said as Ben poured the last of a bottle of Merlot into our glasses. "She just seemed completely resigned to the move. Like all the fight had gone out of her."

"Well, she is getting up there in age and I'm sure her fall down the porch steps shook her up. She's lucky she didn't break a hip." Ben set the wine bottle aside and snagged a piece of garlic bread from the basket on the table between us.

"I know, but it just seems like Arthur's pushing her too fast. I mean this town's her whole life. He's already got her house donated, so she won't even get to spend Christmas there or see the holiday parade or—"

"Honey, try not to worry about it so much. She'll be fine. Arthur's a bit of a windbag, but I'm sure he'll take good care of her."

"I guess you're right. She just seemed so sad about it all." I glanced out at Serendipity and all the other stores decorated in their holiday best. "She won't even get to come to the Christmas Eve open house at the store."

Ben reached out and took my hand in his. "Tell you what. After she gets settled, we'll drive down to Phoenix and visit her. We can make a weekend out of it and stay in one of those ritzy resorts. What do you say?"

I gave his hand a squeeze. "Deal. But if she's not happy in the old folks' home, we're breaking her out, okay?"

Ben laughed. "Sure, I can see the headline now. 'Local Sheriff Arrested in Granny-napping Case.' That'll look really good on my resume."

We'd just finished our spumoni and were debating who was going to carry who home, when Ben's cell phone rang.

"Davis." He listened for a moment, then pulled a pen and notebook from his shirt pocket and began jotting notes.

"Again? Is he there now? Yeah, okay. Tell Barnes to secure the scene. I'll be there in five." He snapped his phone shut and looked at me. "Someone broke into Arthur Finkle's house and trashed his home office for the third time in a week. Finkle's pitchin' a royal fit right now, so I've got to go over there." Ben put some money down for our tab and we slid out of the booth.

"Mind if I tag along?"

"Nope. Just promise you'll stay in the car and not deck Finkle for moving Miss Lillie?"

"Don't ask for the impossible, Sheriff."

THE moon cast a cool glow over the neighborhood as we pulled up to the gray and white Victorian. Deputy Sandford "Sandy" Barnes stood under the porch light with Arthur Finkle. They were a study in contrasts. Sandy was athletic and tall, Finkle portly and short; Sandy emitted calm reserve, while Finkle was rigid with emotion.

As Ben parked the Blazer behind Sandy's cruiser, I rolled down my window and could hear Arthur Finkle's voice rising in anger, his pudgy finger jabbing dangerously close to Sandy's chest.

"I'll be right back." Ben got out and strode up to the porch joining his deputy and Finkle. Though I couldn't hear what Ben said, it seemed to calm Finkle and, after another moment, the three of them went into the house.

Feeling too full from dinner to sit comfortably, I got out of the truck and stretched, then leaned back against the door. I pulled my sweater tight around me to ward off the night's chill.

"You can see me, can't you?"

Startled, I whirled around toward the voice. Standing in the street on the other side of the truck was the spirit who had followed Miss Lillie that morning outside Serendipity.

"Yes," I said catching my breath. "Who are you?"

"We have to stop him. What he's doing isn't right and I won't let him hurt her."

The ghost vanished momentarily then reappeared on the sidewalk next to me. Up close I could appreciate how attractive he must have been in life—tall and rangy with a mane of sandy blonde hair and kind brown eyes that now sparked with intensity. His clothing, khaki pants, button-down shirt and leather jacket, was classic, but of an older style than similar fashions of today.

"What do you mean hurt her? You have to help me understand what's going on here."

He glanced over my shoulder then faded away. A second later, an elderly woman walking a tiny dog strolled up the sidewalk.

"I'm sorry, did you say something?" As she spoke, her dog sniffed at the air and let out a growl, the hair on its hackles rising.

"No," I said quickly and gave a nervous laugh. "No, no. I was just talking to myself. You know, just wondering what's going on here with the police and all." Geez, I sounded like an idiot.

The woman gave me a polite nod and a wide berth, then went on her way, pulling the growling ankle-biter behind her.

"He's an evil man," said the ghost as he reappeared on the sidewalk before me.

Conscious of the fact that I was standing under a street light in plain view of anyone in the houses or on the street, I pulled out my cell phone and pretended to make a call. At least I wouldn't look like a lunatic talking to myself in the dark.

"Tell me your name," I said looking directly at the ghost.

"David," he said and glanced toward the house. "Nothing I do seems to stop him."

"Have you been doing this, David? Setting off Arthur's alarm and messing up his office?"

"Yes. Someone needs to get the papers from him before he hurts her."

"Papers? How is he going to hurt—" David was gone before I finished the question. A moment later the front door opened and Ben walked down the porch steps toward me. I closed my phone and dropped it back into my purse.

"How'd it go?" I asked.

He rubbed a hand over his face. "Well, Finkle's office

sure is a mess, but nothing seems to be missing that he can tell. He's noticed some kids hanging around the area lately and thinks they're breaking in looking for money to buy drugs. We'll step up the patrol around the neighborhood and see if anything shakes out."

As we got into the Blazer to head home, I wondered how I would tell the man I loved that what he had on his hands wasn't teenagers with a drug problem; it was a middle-aged banker with a ghost problem.

OVER breakfast the next morning, I wanted to tell Ben about David and my Gift, but couldn't quite find the right words. I knew Ben loved me and was a very open-minded man, but somehow *Morning, honey. How'd you sleep? By the way, Arthur's being haunted by a ghost that I can talk to. Would you pass the syrup?* didn't seem like the best way to break it to him. This kind of confession needed a little more finesse.

After seeing Ben off to the station, I hopped into my VW Bug and headed to Serendipity. When the store opened, I left Amanda in charge, picked up some blueberry scones from the bakery next door and drove to Miss Lillie's house to deliver her essential oils and do a little detective work.

Miss Lillie's two-story Victorian on the outskirts of town was as bright and cheerful as Arthur's was gray and dreary. Painted canary yellow with emerald shutters and trim, the house and its manicured grounds stood in happy testament to Miss Lillie's pride in her history and community.

I rapped on the door and wasn't surprised when it opened quickly and Miss Lillie welcomed me in with a hug. "It's so nice of you to drive out here, dear. Are those blueberry scones I smell?"

I pushed the door closed behind me and followed her into a living room impeccably decorated with period furnishings.

"They sure are, fresh out of the oven from Hot Cross Buns. When I decided to bring your oils over, I thought we deserved a treat."

"What a wonderful idea." Miss Lillie took the bakery box from me. "Please, sit down and make yourself comfortable.

I'll put these on a plate and bring some tea."

"Can I help you?"

"No, no, dear. It's not often I have guests to spoil. I'll be right back."

I placed the small bag with Miss Lillie's essential oils on the coffee table, then looked around the living room. I could hear Miss Lillie humming in the kitchen as I zeroed in on a collection of framed photos on the mantle. I didn't have to look far to find a photo of David with a much younger and strikingly beautiful Miss Lillie. In the picture, his arms wrapped around her from behind in a warm embrace and she seemed to be laughing at something he'd said. I was so engrossed in the picture that I didn't hear Miss Lillie come into the room.

"I see you've found my David," she said as she placed a tea tray on the coffee table.

"He's so handsome and you both look so happy."

"We were, then." She walked over and took the photo from me. For a moment she seemed lost in bittersweet memory, then she sighed and placed the frame back on the mantle. We sat together on the couch and she poured us each a cup of tea.

"If you don't mind my being forward, were you and David married?"

"It's not forward at all. It's always good to talk about love, as you and our fine Sheriff must know." She smiled and took a sip of tea. "David and I met shortly after the war. He was just out of the service and was hitchhiking through Arizona on his way to find work in California. My father gave him a ride into town and invited him to stay for supper. He was so good-looking and so sweet." Miss Lillie laughed, her cheeks blushing pink. "It feels silly to say it, but we fell in love over mother's brisket and potatoes that night. David stayed on in town and took a job at the local hardware store. We courted all summer and were engaged to be married on Christmas Eve." Her gaze drifted to David's picture on the mantle. When she looked back at me, there were tears in her eyes. "But, he was killed a week before our wedding when he tried to break up a fight between two drunken men in town.

One of the men pulled out a gun and fired. My David was gone."

I wiped away a tear from under my eye. "I'm so sorry. You must have been devastated."

"I was. And in all the years since, there just hasn't been anyone who could take David's place in my heart or my life." At this mention of his name, David appeared at Miss Lillie's side, hardly more than a glimmer at first, then with more form and presence.

"It's odd. Even though he's been gone for so long, I still find myself talking to him." She paused then added in a whisper, "And sometimes I swear he answers me."

As I watched, David placed an ethereal hand on her shoulder and she ever so subtly leaned into it. "But that probably makes me sound like a crazy old lady."

I glanced at David. "Not at all. I believe the people we love are always with us, watching over us."

"You've got to warn her about Arthur," David said. "I've seen the papers. He's cheating her."

I cleared my throat. "Miss Lillie, how's everything going with Arthur and your move?"

She straightened at the change of subject. "Oh, just fine I guess. He told me at coffee yesterday that I didn't need to sign the donation papers because he'd already taken care of it. I'd given him my power of attorney last fall, so he could help me with my business affairs. It makes it easier that way."

"Those were sale papers he signed," David said angrily. "He's not donating her home. He's selling it out from under her so he can steal the money."

Now things made sense. With his aunt's power of attorney and his own knowledge of banking and finances, Arthur could easily sell Miss Lillie's home and hide the money away for himself.

"Miss Lillie, will you come with me right now to see Arthur?"

"Arthur? But I don't understand, dear. Why?"

Think quick, Sam. "Well, there was a break-in at his house last night and Ben told me some papers were stolen," I fibbed. "I think we should just go make sure everything's okay with the donation of your house."

She looked confused, but after a little more cajoling agreed to go with me. Ten minutes later, we were seated in front of Arthur's mahogany desk at the bank.

"Aunt Lillie, it's good to see you." If Arthur was surprised by our unexpected arrival at his office, he covered it well. He looked at me. "And who's this young lady? You look familiar, but I can't place you."

"Sam Gaines, Mr. Finkle. I'm a friend of your aunt's and I was with the Sheriff at your house last night."

"Oh, yes, of course. What can I do for you lovely ladies?"

"Sam told me about the break-in at your house, Arthur. I was so sorry to hear some things were stolen."

Arthur shot me a glance. "Nothing was taken. I told the Sheriff that last night."

"I must have misunderstood," I said quickly. "I thought Ben mentioned that some papers pertaining to the donation of your aunt's home had been taken."

Beads of sweat popped out on Arthur's forehead. "No, that's absolutely wrong. Everything's fine. In fact, I'm storing the papers in a safe deposit box here at the bank until I deliver them to the Historical Society. Now, if you ladies will excuse me, I'm a very busy man."

Miss Lillie seemed to pick up on Arthur's bluff. "Well, since they're here and safe, I'd like to see them and take a copy for my files."

Arthur went apoplectic and a flush crept up his neck. "Surely, that's not necessary, Aunt Lillie. I have everything in order. Don't you trust me?" He pointed at me. "This woman's just trying to scare you."

Miss Lillie stood and glared at her nephew. "My papers, Arthur. Now."

Next to her, David appeared and smiled.

I'VE always loved Christmas Eve in Eagle Falls, and this year was better than ever. Like Serendipity, all the stores along Main Street stayed open late and bustled with last-minute holiday shoppers. Serendipity glowed on this night, the air scented with the spiced cider and gingerbread I'd prepared for the carolers and townsfolk who strolled the sidewalks. From my perch behind the check-out counter, I watched as Miss Lillie held court in Serendipity's reading nook, David's glowing presence always beside her.

"You're looking a bit smug, Ms. Gaines," Ben whispered as he came up behind me and wrapped me in a hug.

"Not smug, just happy. She belongs in that house, not in a nursing home. Besides, since she's sort of adopted us now that Arthur's out of the picture, we can keep an eye on her."

Ben nuzzled my ear. "I still haven't figured out just how you knew Arthur was deceiving her."

David and I glanced at each other and he tipped his fingers in salute.

I smiled. "It's just a gift I have."

JOANNE ZETERBERG is a professional writer, editor and creative director working in the Scottsdale, Arizona, tourism industry. Her work is published regularly in *Experience Scottsdale*, the city's official visitors' guide. She also has several freelance clients and through them has had articles published in *Business Week* and *The Business Journal*. JoAnne has studied at developmental workshops with internationally known psychic mediums James Van Praagh and John Holland, is an active member of Sisters in Crime, and is currently at work on a mystery novel set in Alaska.

THE PRICE OF DIAMONDS
ANNE MARISKY

"REJECTED? What do you mean rejected? And what are you doing to my card?" Michael heard a loud click as the clerk sliced the small rectangle of plastic cleanly in half.

"I'm sorry, sir, but the credit card company dictates that we do this." She handed back the dismembered remains.

He pointed them at her. "But I can't be over my limit. This is a platinum card. Plat-in-um. Do you know what that means?"

The clerk glared at him and tapped long red fingernails against the glass counter.

Michael looked down at his intended purchase, a white gold necklace with a single perfect diamond pendant. The jewel was nestled against black velvet inside a small box. His wife, Cynthia, had fallen in love with it a month ago and had been dropping hints ever since. He knew she wanted it because her friend had received a diamond necklace from her husband last Christmas. Apparently, this one was much nicer. Unfortunately, in Cynthia's vocabulary, "nicer" usually meant "more expensive." He studied the necklace. It was beautiful. Michael reached out to touch the glittering stone, but the clerk snatched it first and snapped the box shut.

"Do you have another card?"

Michael felt heat rising in his face. "Not at the moment." Every other card in his wallet was similarly maxed out, thanks to Cynthia. He slid the shards deep into his pocket. "Now what am I going to do?"

"We have a nice selection of cubic zirconia pendants." She gestured to another part of the case. "They don't cost as much."

"I can't give her a cubic zirconia. I need a real diamond. I

143

need *that* diamond. My wife loves it." He would have happily gone further into debt to buy the necklace, if only not to hear another word about it.

"I'm sorry, sir, but I can't just give you the necklace. We need some form of payment. We accept cash."

He glanced down from her face to read her nametag. "Wendy. You seem like a sensitive person. I do have a little cash, but it's not quite enough. It's just temporary, though." He leaned forward a little. "Does the store offer a payment plan?"

"Not really." Wendy examined her nails. They extended almost a full inch past the tips of her fingers. "You know, we're not supposed to tell customers things like this, but my uncle is a pawnbroker. That watch you're wearing might..."

"This watch?" Michael straightened up and covered his watch with his hand. "I can't pawn this watch. My father gave it to me after my first promotion. I love this watch."

"You must be pretty important, then. What about an advance on your job?"

He cleared his throat. "My company's going through a little rough patch right now." That is, if laying off him and his entire department qualified as a "rough patch." It certainly did for him. He still hadn't figured out how he was going to tell Cynthia. He had been hoping the necklace would make her happy long enough for him to find a new job on his own before she insisted he take a job at her father's bank.

"That's a shame. What about a second job, then?" She tapped a fingernail on the counter again. "I happen to know of one."

"What kind of job?"

"There's a problem with the store Santa and they need to hire someone at the last minute. My cousin is in charge of finding a new one. If you show up and tell him Wendy sent you, you might get it."

Was she kidding? Him a department store Santa? "I don't know."

"Well, as a store employee, you'd get a discount. And..." She glanced over her shoulder then leaned forward. "I also happen to know that the store is going to have a screaming sale right before Christmas."

Employee discount, plus a sale, plus the little bit of cash he had, plus….No. No way. "It's only a week until Christmas. I couldn't possibly make enough as a Santa to pay for that necklace. And what if someone I know sees me?" That would thrill Cynthia.

"All anyone will see is a guy in a Santa suit. They all look alike. Trust me. No one will know it's you." She shrugged. "If you're not interested—"

"I didn't say that. I just…"

Wendy opened the box to let him see the diamond again. The facets caught the light from the fluorescents above and sparkled. He swallowed. He already knew his chances of getting a better opportunity only a week before Christmas were nonexistent. He looked at the necklace again. It would soften the blow about his job considerably. And it would be paid for. He took a deep breath.

"What's your cousin's name?"

"I cannot believe I'm doing this." As he studied himself in the mirror, Michael brushed away strands of fake white facial hair scratching his upper lip. He had to admit, Wendy had been right. The costume completely obliterated his individuality. Only his eyes and hands were visible. If his mother walked up to him right now, he doubted even she would recognize him.

"You look great." Chris, Wendy's cousin, didn't look up as he reached into a box to grab a pointed red hat with fluffy white trim. "Very authentic. The kids'll love you." The hat was too small, but Chris pulled it down hard over the white wig covering Michael's head. He felt a little lightheaded. The puffball at the tip drooped limply into his eyes. He pushed it aside.

"So what do I do again?"

"Just hold the kids. Ask 'em what they want. Tell 'em they'll get it. Smile when they take the pic. Hand the darlings back. Nothin' to it."

"How much is the employee discount again?"

"Yeah, your diamond. Listen. You do the job, I promise

you'll be fine. Course, there is that small costume cleaning fee. And one or two other small charges. Ah, don't worry, it'll be enough."

He suddenly felt queasy. This had better not be a waste of time. He checked himself in the mirror again and tried to adjust the hat to a comfortable angle. "So what happened to the last Santa? Wendy didn't say."

"Oh, that guy. He had another gig come up. Really left us in the lurch. Lucky for us that you happened by. Hard to find replacements at the last minute."

"Well, I guess it was lucky for me, too. You know, I do appreciate the job."

"Your wife is gonna be thrilled Christmas morning. Wendy says she stops by at least once a week just to try the thing on."

"How does she know it's my wife?"

"Apparently your wife likes to talk. Wendy realized you were the husband from your name on your credit card." He grinned. "Boy, I bet that was embarrassing when she cut that up."

"Yeah, a bit."

"Why didn't you just get a loan from your wife's dad? Wendy says he's president of his own bank."

Right. A loan from the guy who had been telling him how inadequate he was to take care of his precious Cindy since the day Michael had picked her up for their first date. "I prefer to work things out on my own."

Chris smiled at Michael and gave him a little shove toward the door. "You'll be great. Go get 'em."

THE toddler on his lap slapped him in the eye, opened her mouth wide, and let out a bloodcurdling howl. The elf behind the camera snapped the picture just as Michael winced. The toddler's parents frowned.

"Smile, Santa," the elf said. She snapped again. Michael flinched as the flash assaulted his eyes for the thousandth time that day. The parents walked up to reclaim their offspring and check their proofs. Michael thankfully handed back the child.

The elf, whose name was Dorrie, took their order and handed them a receipt. They were still frowning as they bundled their child into her stroller and headed off toward house wares. Dorrie snapped her gum as she started to pack up the camera. Michael looked around.

"Where's the next one?"

"That was it. Last one. Shift's over. Congratulations, you survived."

Michael slumped back into the Santa chair. "How many more days until Christmas?"

She laughed. "It only gets worse from here on."

"I was afraid of that." As he sank deeper into the chair, the beard pushed up further on his face and threatened to smother him.

"Don't worry, you did great."

"I wish someone would tell that to the parents."

She examined the camera lenses as she slid them into their compartments one by one. "So why'd you take this job?"

He shrugged. "I'm trying to buy my wife a Christmas gift. Seemed like a good idea at the time."

"What are you getting her?"

He pushed himself out of the chair and stretched his shoulders a little. "Diamond necklace."

"Sweet. I wish I had a Santa like you." She stopped packing and looked up. "Wait a minute. How are you going to afford something like that with the pay from here?"

"With the extra sale right before Christmas and the employee discount, Chris said I'll make enough. I also have a little bit of cash."

She shook her head. "Santas must be worth a lot more than elves." She returned to packing. "Why didn't you just charge it? That's what everybody else does."

He cracked his knuckles. "So why are you here?"

"Me? Oh, I'm a student. You know, always in the market for extra cash."

"I know the feeling."

Dorrie zipped up the camera case. "What happened to the last Santa?"

"You don't know?"

She laughed. "I'm not exactly on the 'need to know' list."

"Chris said he had another job. He didn't really go into detail."

"Probably more like he just went nuts and ran off."

"I can understand that."

"See you tomorrow, Santa. Unless you go nuts, too." She slung the camera bag over her shoulder and walked away.

Michael let out a breath he had been holding. "Feels like I'm already there."

"HOW was work today?" Cynthia called from the kitchen as Michael walked through the front door.

Michael dropped his keys on the table in the entryway. "Wonderful." If you liked being bit, kicked, and screamed at. And that was just the parents. He walked to the liquor cabinet in the dining room and poured a scotch. The first slow burn down his throat did nothing for the knot in his stomach. He clenched the glass and took another drink. He walked into the kitchen. "How was your day?"

Cynthia was preparing dinner. "Great. I had lunch with Janie. I showed her the necklace at the store afterwards. She thinks it's much nicer than Laura's too. Janie's planning a trip to France this summer. Did you know that..." Cynthia continued to talk, but Michael's awareness of her words faded. If he told her about losing his job now, he wondered, would she volunteer to help out, look for a job too, or just demand he take the job at the bank? Would she only be worried about the loss of all the little extras like the diamond? He watched her place a tomato on a wooden cutting board and start to slice it. The blade of the knife was dull and couldn't cut cleanly. Juice oozed from the tomato onto the cutting board. He knew what she would choose.

"Michael!"

"What?"

"You're not listening to me."

"Yes, I am. Janie had lunch in France."

She shook her head and attacked the tomato again. "I told you to sharpen all these knives a month ago. I'm going to end up cutting myself on one of them."

Michael stared into his glass at the amber liquid and took another sip. "I'll do it after Christmas."

He heard a loud *thunk* as stainless steel broke through tomato flesh and connected with wood. She put down the knife. "I left a message on your cell phone but you didn't call back."

He looked back up at her. He'd forgotten to check his cell. "I've told you I'm busy with a big project. You didn't try my office, did you?"

"No, you told me not to. I still don't understand why."

"It's this project. We're all very busy and I don't want any distractions."

Cynthia picked up the cutting board and pushed the watery chunks into a bowl with the knife. She set the board down and lined up another tomato. "I've been really worried about you since this project started. You're so tense now. You know you don't have to work there. Daddy has always said you should be working for him at the bank."

Michael slammed his glass down on the counter. Scotch splashed everywhere as the glass shattered. She jumped at the sound. *That finally got her quiet*, he thought. They stared at each other for a long minute.

"Did you cut yourself?"

He looked at his hand. It was wet with liquor, but not blood. "No."

She stared at him a moment longer before turning back to the tomato. "You're covered in booze. I'll have to get that suit cleaned now."

He reached for a towel and started to clean up the liquid and glass.

Cynthia sawed the knife back and forth. "This is exactly what I'm talking about."

"I don't need help from your father."

"He'd be so happy to help."

And to get a chance to catalog my faults on a daily basis. "I don't need his help. I can take care of things myself. Work will be fine. Everything will be fine."

"If you say so." She slid the remains of the second

tomato into the bowl.

Michael cleaned up the last of the broken glass and walked back to the dining room to pour himself another drink.

A week later, Michael stood in a room off the store's delivery dock where he had gone to return the Santa suit and pick up his paycheck. He stared at the check, feeling his mouth go dry. "This is it?" One week's work, one miserable week filled with screaming kids and angry parents, and this was it? He tightened his grip on the check, almost tearing it. They misprinted it. They must have. Shouldn't there be one more number on the end?

"Yeah, but remember we had to charge you to clean the suit an' all."

Michael glared at him. "Yes, I remember. The cleaning fee." He looked at the check again, hoping the numbers had changed. They hadn't. "You lied to me. You said it would be enough. It's not." He shook the check at him. "I can't buy that necklace with this."

Chris shrugged.

"It's Christmas Eve. How am I going to get enough to pay for the necklace now? You have ruined everything!" His only chance of postponing the inevitable meltdown about his job, of not hearing about what a complete failure he was from both Cynthia and her father, was gone. Totally gone. He stared at Chris.

Chris started to turn away, then stopped and snapped his fingers. "You know, if you still want to make a little extra, you could run an errand for me. You'd have to wear the suit, but it would make you enough to buy that diamond you're wanting."

I can't believe he thinks I'd ever take another job from him. Michael closed his eyes and started to count backwards from 100, but the sound of his father-in-law's voice in his head drowned out his own. He looked at Chris again. "What kind of errand?"

"Oh, one of our big customers wants to surprise his kids with a visit from Santa on Christmas Eve. You'd drive over the presents he bought, give 'em to his kids, say ho, ho, ho, whatever, and come back to pick up the extra green. Easy."

Easy. Nothing about this had been easy. "I can earn enough money from that to buy the necklace? What's the catch?"

"No catch. The guy's rich. Loves his kids. I was gonna do it myself, but I'm stuck at the store. And I'm feeling bad. You're disappointed. I can see that. I want to make it up to you." He stood. "What do you say? Wanna do it? You'll have plenty of time to come back before the store closes and still get your rock. Wendy showed it to me. It's real pretty. I can see why your wife loves it."

Michael pictured the diamond, glittering against its black backdrop. The few extra days of peace it would buy. He'd put so much into this already. He swallowed. "Yeah, okay, I'll do it."

"Great. Get the suit back on."

His hand shook a little as he picked up the red coat. "Where do I go?"

"Here's the address and the goodies." Chris handed him a piece of paper and gestured to three bulging black cloth bags lined against the back wall. He clapped Michael on the arm. "You'll do great. Just do what you've been doing all week."

Michael finished dressing and picked up one of the sacks. He adjusted his grip. It was heavier than he expected.

"You look great in that getup. Just like the real Santa. Better than the last guy." Chris picked up one of the other bags. "Come on, I'll help you carry them to your car."

MICHAEL stepped up to the door and adjusted the bag on his shoulder. He checked the address again. This couldn't be the right place. Everything about it screamed warehouse district. Maybe it was one of those trendy loft conversion things. He took a deep breath and knocked. Nothing. He watched the small fog that took shape and then disappeared as he breathed. He knocked again and stomped his feet. Red fuzzy suits were not as warm as one might imagine. At last a man answered. He was tall and lean, and his short dark hair came together over his forehead in a distinct widow's peak.

"Hi, Chris sent me. I'm from the store."

"Yes, I know. Come in. You have the bags?"

"Right here. I have the other two in my trunk." Michael stepped over the threshold and passed him the bag. He looked around. Okay, not a loft conversion. In fact, not a residence of any sort. The large ill-lit room was empty save for an old tub and a plastic tarp. A couple of canisters were lined up next to the tub. It was no warmer inside. His breathing quickened, leaving no time for the cloud from his breath to dissipate. "What's going on here?"

The man opened the bag and looked inside. "Just disposing of some garbage."

Michael watched him take out the packages and place them in the tub. Three of them. Each was about the size of a frozen turkey. Each wrapped securely in plastic. As the man moved, Michael could see a gun under his jacket. He felt tingling in his limbs. *I've got to get out of here.* He started toward the door, but the man was quicker and grabbed his arm.

"Not just yet. We've got a lot of work to do."

Michael tried to pull away, but the man only tightened his grip. Michael looked at him. Eyes the same color as the concrete floor stared back. His intestines twisted. "Please let me go."

"I will, after we take care of business."

Michael felt as if his throat were being squeezed instead of his arm. "You will?"

The man seemed to smile, but his cheek muscles pulled the corners of his mouth back instead of up. "It must be your lucky day, because if it was up to me, you'd be dead already, but Chris said I'm to let you go after. Stop panicking and pull yourself together." He let go of Michael's arm and patted the gun under his jacket. "Just do what I say or I'll kill you anyway, okay?"

Michael couldn't remember seeing any other people in the area. No one would ever hear him. He nodded.

"Great. Let's get the other bags in."

WHEN it was over, Michael got back in his car and started to drive. He was on the other side of town when the car sputtered and rolled to a stop. He realized the gauge was on empty but he couldn't remember what he was supposed to do about it. He glanced around. Darkened storefronts stared back.

Headlights shone in his rearview mirror as a car turned a corner behind him. He didn't move as the headlights stopped behind him instead of going around. The passenger door opened and Chris slid in next to him.

"So how did it go?"

Michael continued to stare forward. On the inside, did Chris look like those same horrible bundles too? No, maybe more like Cynthia's tomatoes. Red, pulpy, bloody tomatoes. "You lied to me. You used me."

"Hey, hold on." Chris closed the car door. "I needed some help. You needed some money. We each got somethin' outta this. You got to quit this drivin' around now and get a hold of yourself."

"I'm going to the police."

"You don't want to do that."

"I didn't know what was going on."

Chris frowned and shook his head. He put his hand on Michael's shoulder and dug his fingers into the muscle. Michael winced and took his hands off the wheel. "I like you, Mike, so I'm going to give you a chance here. You really think I'd let you go to the police?"

Michael met his eyes. He couldn't speak.

"I don't believe you would go anyway." He leaned close to Michael's ear. "You still want your little rock, don't you?"

Michael swallowed. "I don't care about that anymore. I just want out of this."

"Well, I bet you do care about going home in one piece."

The pain increased from his shoulder. Michael felt his chest tighten. "Why me?"

"You think I'm nuts? Somethin' goes wrong, you think I'm gettin' pulled over with all that in my back seat? No way. But a guy like you? We checked you out. You're perfect. Who's gonna believe you? No job. Maxed out on credit. Trying to buy jewelry you can't afford. Can't even tell your wife you've got money problems. Rich daddy-in-law hates you. Guy like you'd never be able to prove he didn't do it." Chris released his shoulder. The pain as the blood rushed back in was worse.

"Is that why you told that guy to let me go? Take the fall for the murder?"

"Not unless we have to. It was a beautiful plan. The tricky part was keepin' that guy on ice for a week 'til the loading dock was quiet enough we could move him outta there. Actually movin' him was the easy part."

Easy for him, he meant. "You don't think someone's going to remember seeing Santa?"

"On Christmas Eve? It's a perfect disguise. You know how many Santas must be running around today? Going in and out of stores? Hundreds. Well, dozens anyway. If anyone did happen to see you, they're not gonna be able to identify you." Chris reached into his jacket pocket and pulled out a small box in shiny silver paper. He waved it at him. "I went ahead and picked it up. I had an idea you might not come back to the store. I even had Wendy wrap it for you."

Michael looked at the box. Looked back at Chris. "Why did you kill him?"

"Who says I'm the one who killed him? I didn't hear anybody say that. Let's just say he turned out to be the kind of guy who didn't know his place. Wanted a bigger piece than he deserved. No room in this business for guys like that."

Michael just stared at him. He couldn't move.

"Why did you tell that guy to let me go?"

"That's the best part." Chris grinned. "I got another job for you."

Another job. Hysterical laughter threatened to explode. "What, murder someone?"

"No, no. I got a different guy for that. What I want is for you to take that job at your daddy-in-law's bank."

Michael shook his head. He couldn't have heard right. "Why?"

"Let's just say for now that we could use somebody who was able to help us out with certain transactions from time to time. And, hey, you need a job anyway, so I think this is a real win-win."

"You're joking."

"No, I'm not. And you're not in a position to refuse. We've got enough evidence on you now to make sure you cooperate. The alternative is not pleasant for either of us. I'd really rather not kill you on Christmas Eve. What kind of a guy do you think I am?" He offered the box again. "Come on. Take it. You earned it."

Michael looked at the small silver box again. He closed his eyes. *I should just let him kill me now and be done with it. At least it would be quicker.* He opened his eyes and took a deep breath before reaching out to take the box.

"This is goin' to be great. I've really enjoyed workin' with you. But time to get you home now. Your wife's probably wonderin' what's happened to you."

Michael looked at the box in his hand. "I can't go home. I'm out of gas."

Chris smiled. "I'll take care of you. Don't worry about a thing. We'll get you started on that well-deserved holiday."

CHRISTMAS morning, Michael was sitting in the living room, waiting for Cynthia. She came down as the clock struck nine. She yawned and plopped next to him on their sofa in front of the tree.

"You should have gotten me up. I didn't hear you come in last night."

"Work ran late."

She rubbed her hands together. "Well, come on, let's do presents. Where's mine?"

He reached into the pocket of his robe and brought out the small box. Cynthia quickly ripped off the silver paper and opened the box. "Oh, Michael, it's beautiful. I was afraid you hadn't bought it. It was still in the store yesterday morning." She took it out of the box and let the chain dangle from her fingers. The diamond glittered in the multicolored light from the tree. "Help me put it on."

She held her hair off the back of her neck so he could fasten the clasp. His hands shook as he tried to open the tiny claw, but he finally managed to join the two ends. She turned around and sat back so he could admire the effect. It was beautiful on her, but all he could think when he looked at her was how much she looked like her father.

"This is so much nicer than the one Laura got last year. I love it. Thanks so much." She gave him a quick kiss.

"You're welcome. Merry Christmas."

Cynthia jumped up and went over to the tree to get a small green box. "Open mine now."

Michael took it and started to tear the paper.

She sat down next to him and giggled. "I think I maxed out the credit card when I bought it. I hope you're not mad."

The tearing stopped. He felt the blood drain from his face, and his fingers on the paper felt suddenly numb. He heard again the loud click as Wendy sliced his card in two, but then he thought he heard stainless steel hitting wood. Why was Cynthia cutting tomatoes on Christmas morning? They didn't need tomatoes now. She should be sitting down and enjoying the tree and the morning and her new necklace.

She put her hand on his arm. "Michael?" He blinked and looked at her sitting next to him. The diamond sparkled in the base of her throat. He heard the thunk of the knife again. She shouldn't be cutting anything with that knife. It was dull and she was going to cut herself on it. He'd promised her he would sharpen all of them. *Thunk*. He stood and walked to the kitchen.

MUCH later, after the detectives had questioned him for hours and his wife's blood had long since dried on his clothes and his skin and his hair, all they could get him to say was, "I should have pawned the watch."

ANNE MARISKY is the pen name of an Arizona native who has also lived in Wyoming, Colorado, and California. She has worked at her current job, an editor in the health care industry, for the past twelve years. She also spent a year and a half writing articles for a hospital employee newsletter. She has no immediate plans to leave her day job. "The Price of Diamonds" is her first published work of fiction.

THE 12 DAYS OF CHRISTMAS
SUZANNE FLAIG

1

THE radio was playing "The Twelve Days of Christmas."

"You know, today's the first day of Christmas," Maureen said.

Joe scratched his head. "What do you mean? It's only December 14th."

"No, silly, the first day of Christmas, like in the song. You should give your true love a partridge in a pear tree."

He gave her a disapproving look. They had been married for over twenty years, and she knew that look. The one that said, "You're acting crazy again."

She bit her lip and started washing the breakfast dishes.

Joe glanced at his watch. "I've got to get to work. See you later."

2

THE next evening, they attended a Christmas party at Maureen's best friend Kim's house. Maureen agonized over what to wear, and finally settled on a red blouse with the black pants that minimized her ample hips. She added her red and silver candy cane earrings for a festive touch.

Joe wore dress pants and a sports coat, a rare occurrence.

"You look nice," she said.

"Thought I'd dress up for the holiday," he said. "We don't go out very often."

When they arrived, Kim said, "Do you mind if I borrow Joe for awhile? I need someone who knows how to make a pitcher of margaritas."

"Sure," Maureen said. She wandered over to the buffet table to grab a plateful of snacks.

Joe emerged from the kitchen and handed her a frozen

margarita. "Try this."

"Mmm, that's good."

"Great. I'll make some more, and catch up with you later."

Maureen wandered around, chatting and drinking, feeling a pleasant buzz, until she realized she hadn't seen Joe in quite a while. She knew she was drinking too much, but so what? 'Tis the season, and all that. She stumbled into the kitchen. A few people stood around shooting the breeze, but she didn't see Joe or Kim, so she returned to the living room.

"Have you seen Joe?" she asked no one in particular.

"Not lately," someone replied.

Maureen felt dizzy, so she sat in the nearest chair and closed her eyes. *Where are you, Joe? I want to go home.*

3

MAUREEN awoke the next morning with a splitting headache. Rummaging around in the night stand for the bottle of aspirin she kept there, her hand bumped against the cold metal of Joe's gun. I hate that thing, she thought. He had bought it for protection after a rash of burglaries in the neighborhood, but they'd caught the guy, and Maureen had forgotten all about it. She found the aspirin, popped three in her mouth, and trudged downstairs.

Joe was in the kitchen, making coffee. "You look awful," he said. "Why'd you have so much to drink?"

"I didn't have anything better to do," she shot back. "You spent the entire time with Kim."

"What's your problem? You told me to help her."

"So how come you weren't in the kitchen when I came looking for you?"

"What now? You checking up on me?"

"I didn't think you'd disappear for the entire night." She sat down, propped her elbows on the table, and held her throbbing head in both hands. "Can you please get me a cup of coffee?"

Joe turned around slowly, poured a cup of black coffee, and set it in front of her. "You really shouldn't drink so much."

She raised her head and stared at him. "That's the first time I've had anything to drink in years." After a beat, she added, "You were mixing the drinks. What'd you put in those margaritas? Straight tequila?"

"Yeah, now it's my fault you got drunk." He turned his back on her.

"Well, where *were* you all night? Both you and Kim were missing for awhile. Explain that."

"I don't have to explain anything. You're delusional. Why don't you explain why I found you passed out on a chair in the living room."

He grabbed his jacket and slammed out the door.

4

THE following day ensued in stony silence. Joe hid behind the Sunday paper in the morning, then spent the afternoon glued to the TV. Maureen read the latest Sue Grafton mystery, daydreaming about methods of murder.

She seethed, replaying yesterday's argument. Just one of many that had flared up over the last few years of their marriage. *He's so damn critical lately. And as soon as I complain to him, he turns it around to make it all my fault.*

When had it all gone bad? They spent less time together these days; he always had an excuse to work overtime, or go out without telling her where he was going.

They went to bed angry, without the customary goodnight kiss. Tossing and turning, Maureen began to feel remorse about the argument. Maybe she *was* at fault. She shouldn't have had so much to drink. She had overreacted. She would apologize in the morning.

5

AFTER Joe left for work on Monday morning, Maureen decided to clean the bedroom closets. Dusting the top shelf of Joe's closet, she accidentally knocked down a long, thin box. Curiosity won out over guilt, and she opened the box. Tears welled up when she saw the breathtaking gold filigree necklace. This must be my Christmas present, she thought, spirits soaring. She returned the box to its hiding place in anticipation of Christmas morning.

The music was playing again. The Holiday Radio Station. All Christmas, All the Time. Today's the fifth day of Christmas, she thought, as she hummed along. *It's not five golden rings, but it is gold, and it's jewelry. How could I have doubted him?* After twenty years of marriage, she knew about the ups and downs. For better or worse. That morning, after she apologized, he had told her he loved her. Joe was right. She was imagining things. Maureen shook her head. She didn't know what had gotten into her.

She'd go shopping tomorrow and prepare Joe's favorite meal for dinner.

6

SHE hummed as she put away the groceries. Tonight, Joe would enjoy pot roast, homemade gravy, red potatoes and asparagus. Maureen cooked and cleaned, set the table with her best china, and waited for Joe to come home from work.

At six o'clock, his usual time to arrive home, the oven timer went off. Maureen was dressed in her little black dress and wearing Joe's favorite perfume. She waited, anticipation becoming concern, and just as she was getting frantic with worry, the phone rang. I knew it! He's been in an accident. But when she answered the phone, it was Joe on the other end.

"I'm sorry, honey, but I had to work late. It'll be a few more hours, but I'll be home as soon as I can."

Maureen sighed. Suddenly, she didn't feel like eating. She wrapped the food up and put it in the refrigerator. Joe could heat it up in the microwave when he got home. She changed into her flannel pajamas, made herself a sandwich, and curled up in front of the TV.

To reassure herself, Maureen reached up to the top shelf of Joe's closet to admire the necklace. She felt around the area where she had found it yesterday, but it was gone.

At nine o'clock, Joe still hadn't made it home, so she went to bed.

7

MAUREEN met Kim for lunch the next day. "I'm so disappointed," she told her friend. "I prepared a special meal for Joe last night, and he didn't come home until after ten o'clock."

"I'm sure he had a good reason," Kim replied.

"He *said* he had to work late."

"Well, there you go. Did he know about the dinner?"

Maureen hesitated before answering. "No, it was a surprise."

"See? You're upset with him for no reason."

"I guess," Maureen said. "But I'm not so sure. Something doesn't feel right."

They asked the waiter for their checks. Kim's napkin slid onto the floor and as she bent down to retrieve it, a dainty gold necklace that had been hidden under her blouse dangled from her neck. Maureen's heart skipped a beat as she recognized the same gold filigree necklace she had found in Joe's closet. Taking a deep breath, she managed to ask, "Where'd you get that beautiful necklace, Kim?"

Kim looked down and quickly tucked it back inside her blouse. "Umm. Ah. I'm not sure. I've had it a long time."

Maureen left the restaurant confused, trying to block out the accusations that kept niggling at her brain.

8

EMOTIONS churning like a Ferris wheel, Maureen spent the next day in turmoil. *They say the wife is the last to know.* She found no solace in that trite cliché. *Is this all my fault?* Maureen's self-doubt rose up. *Maybe I am crazy. I should give him a chance to explain.* Anger took over. *He'll just make up some excuse, pull the wool over my eyes again.*

And when Joe came home that night, he went straight to his workshop in the basement. Maureen stayed upstairs, wondering what to do.

She finally went downstairs to have it out.

"What's wrong, Maureen?"

"Joe, do you love me?"

"What kind of question is that?"

"The kind that needs an answer."

"Of course I love you. I've stayed with you for twenty years, haven't I?"

161

"That's not an answer."

He stood in front of her, arms crossed. "What the hell's wrong with you lately?"

Maureen bit back her tears. "I know where you went the night before last."

"What are you talking about? I told you I had to work late."

"You're lying. You were with Kim."

Joe's eyes narrowed. "Where did you get that idea?"

"I saw the necklace."

"What are you talking about?"

"The necklace that was in your closet. The one you gave to Kim. How long has it been going on, Joe? My best friend, for God's sake. How could you?"

"I swear, you're going nuts, Maureen. I didn't give Kim any necklace. I don't know where you got such a stupid idea, but I'm telling you, there's nothing going on between Kim and me."

"You say!"

Maureen stomped out of the room and went back upstairs.

She picked up the phone, an innocent act, planning to call her sister for advice, listening for a dial tone but instead recognizing the whispered voices. Realization hit her like a runaway freight train.

"Yes, I'll be there. What time tomorrow?"

"Eight o'clock. Does she suspect anything?"

"She saw the necklace."

Maureen gently replaced the receiver, tears spilling down her cheeks. She didn't want to hear any more. How could he do this to her? How could they do this? Anger flooded back with renewed vigor. Twenty years of love turned to hatred like the sudden jerk of whiplash.

9

THE next night, she greeted him at the door. On the surface, all was back to normal. "Dinner's ready."

"Great," he said.

They sat at the table, making small talk, avoiding the

arguments of the past few days.

"I have a meeting tonight," he said, "but I should be home by ten."

"I'll wait up." The words stuck in her throat, as dry as dead leaves, as dry as her dead emotions. She will follow him. She knows where to go.

He parked across the street from Kim's house; Maureen circled the block and found a spot around the corner. She had wanted to be wrong. The affirmation of her fears left her devastated. She sat in the dark, tears flowing freely, groping at the box of tissues by her side. Finally, she put the car into gear and drove slowly home. She was in bed when he returned. Silent tears drifted down her cheeks as she faced the wall, feigning sleep.

10

THE next morning, Joe asked, "How come you didn't wait up for me last night?"

Maureen looked at the floor. "I had a headache."

She really did have a headache. A sick headache from the thought of her husband cheating on her with her best friend.

All day, she ran the scenarios through her mind. She faced her choices: confront him, leave him, plead with him, ignore him, punish him. The answer came to her as she cleaned the bedroom.

11

CHRISTMAS Eve. The Eleventh Day of Christmas. *On the eleventh day of Christmas, my true love gave to me—*

There was no true love. There would be no twelfth day. Maureen went to the bedroom nightstand, then walked slowly down the stairs and waited for Joe to return. Her tunnel vision focused on the door; she ignored the holiday trappings, refused to look at the gaily decorated Christmas tree in the corner.

When Joe walked in the front door, Maureen was waiting. She fired off three shots and sank to the floor, both hands still clutching the gun. It was only then that she noticed the long, thin box wrapped in silver paper that lay under the Christmas tree.

Maureen refused to speak when the police came and led her away.

12

ON Christmas Day, the truth came out.

Kim pushed her fingers through her hair, tears sliding down her cheeks. "It was supposed to be a surprise for you, Maureen. I was learning jewelry-making. Joe admired my necklace and wanted one like it for you as a Christmas present. All the secret meetings…" Kim's voice stuck in her throat. "It was all for you, Maureen. All for you," she whispered.

Maureen thought about the long, thin box wrapped in silver paper under the Christmas tree, and cried as the matron led her back to her cell.

SUZANNE FLAIG is a freelance writer, editor and publisher. Her short stories have been published in several anthologies, the most recent in *Medium of Murder* (Red Coyote Press, 2008). Other publishing credits include articles in *Mystery Readers Journal, Arizona Senior World, KidsToday,* and *Music For the Love of It.* She has completed a mystery novel featuring piano teacher and amateur sleuth Missy Jenkins, and is currently working on the second book in the series. Suzanne is a past president of the Desert Sleuths Chapter of Sisters in Crime.

A HORSE OF HER OWN
MARY E. BURT

ERNIE Holbrook pushed up his dark glasses to better scan the crowd pouring into the main entrance to The Downs, the largest venue for harness racing in Michigan. Laughter with a familiar ring to it peeled out over the noise of the holiday throng, and he quickly stepped behind a pillar. It made the perfect hiding place, swathed in artificial greenery and Italian lights. Peeking out from under fake evergreen sprigs, he spied a knot of women deep in excited conversation. His wife Claudia's back was to him, but he recognized her silvery blonde hair flowing down her shoulders from under a dark green tam.

Ernie pounded the pillar, crushing one of the lights under his gloved fist. The woman actually believed her damned horse, Trevarian, was going to win!

Claudia and her friends took their turns at one of the betting windows, probably placing considerable sums of money on that loser, he thought bitterly.

Ernie waited until they finished before he got in line. He followed their progress and noted the section of grandstand they entered, keeping his face averted. "One thousand on Sundance." Sundance was the other favorite. And a sure thing.

He climbed into the stands, making sure they weren't looking in his direction, and chose an inconspicuous spot on one of the cold risers, far away from their blanket. Why hadn't Claudia taken her guests to the owners' box? Probably too many to fit. Three of those lousy women: Janice, Maria, and that stupid Phyllis, had been over to the house any number of times. And none of them ever mentioned

165

Trevarian.

Ernie had been suspicious for at least three months before he'd known for a certainty; the little signs that she was keeping a secret were there. The kicker had been that feed bill, sent to the house instead of the stables. After he opened that envelope, it felt like someone was beating him around the ears; his pulse thudded so loud he could hear it. The four hundred dollar bill was for a couple months of feed. Who, or what, were they feeding? He'd sat down heavily, sighed, and scanned the offending evidence, noting the address and name printed at the top—Paul Grunfeld, Trainer, Selwyn Horse Farms. Ernie shot up from the couch and rushed outside. Slamming the door behind him, he sprinted out to the truck, leapt in, and sped along familiar back roads. He knew those stables. Sam Selwyn had started them right next door to where he and Claudia had had their mushroom farm.

That feed bill confirmed his suspicions; Claudia was hiding something from him. Actually, he'd been afraid she was having an affair. It amazed him he'd managed to contain his anger this long. She'd been so distant, living in a world where he was not welcome. Their evenings together had become a charade of happier times. He passed her the salt for her baked potato; she politely requested the sugar for her tea. "It's bad for your teeth," was all he had said as he shoved the sugar bowl across to her.

They'd been married eleven years, but God, it seemed so much longer. He hadn't shared her passion for horses; in the beginning it made no difference, but eventually he wondered why on earth she had married him. Claudia telling her friends that his red vest attracted her to him didn't help matters much. His red vest and red beard reminded her of the devil— not a very propitious consideration on which to base a marriage, come to think of it. At first he'd been amused, but now that he had proof she'd been hiding something from him, he was humiliated.

"REMEMBER where we had the mushroom farm?" she'd asked over coffee one dreary Christmas morning two years ago.

"Yeah, sure." Oh God, not that place. Was she going to remind him of his wasted time and effort? That barn, the site of his failure, his downfall, the disgrace that led to his being rescued by her dad, the formidable Al Dutten, at whose garden store he now worked. Daily he compared his situation to Claudia's, whose position as a community college chemistry professor had won her respect from family and friends.

"I dreamed about it night after night," she was saying, "so finally I made myself go there."

"You didn't want to?" Finally, something they had in common.

"No, not really. But the country around there is beautiful as ever. Remember?"

Yeah, he remembered, all right. "We used to take that road out from campus," he said noncommittally.

"Blyth Road. I had a hard time finding it from the Interstate. Car almost slid into the ditch. The road was so icy." She picked up her coffee mug with both hands, but they shook so badly she placed the mug back on the table.

"Oh, Babe, really?" He reached over to touch her hand, but she jerked it away, slopping coffee.

"Don't call me Babe, Ernie. You know I don't like it."

Ernie raised both hands, palms facing her, mocking a genuflection. "Your wish, my darling, is my command." He drawled the darling; at her frown, he settled back in the chair. Jeez, he still jumped when she snapped her fingers! "You were saying?"

Claudia stared at him a long, full minute. Those light eyes of hers, bright as a cat's. He'd never be able to figure out why she told him she had visited the barn, but left out the critical detail.

"I parked by the roadside," Claudia said. "All the landmarks I remembered were gone. I got out of the car because I couldn't stop shaking. But oh, it's beautiful there when it snows."

The place was clear in his head, as if some jerk had taken a photograph of it and pasted the damn thing on his brain. Ernie envisioned the fields rolling away, fences outlining a patchwork pattern against the white. An errant wind would stir up the snow and blow flakes around in bright circles, tiny stars reflecting back winter sunlight.

"The house is as dilapidated as ever," Claudia said.

"Always was kinda scary, wasn't it?" Ernie clutched his own coffee cup. No one within memory had lived in that farmhouse. "Did you go into the barn?"

"At first I was afraid to, but it looked solid. Most of the red paint has worn away."

Back when they rented the barn, no rays of sunlight slid through untended chinks; its sides had been carefully caulked and the roof mended. In the winter, they kept a heater going and, in the summer, a fan blew in outside air from the loft because mushrooms demand even temperatures summer and winter. The summers must have been too hot or the winters too cold because the mushrooms never really grew. Oh, they started out all right, little bits of naked white flesh glowing softly in the grow lights that ran over the beds, but then they stopped developing. Their caps and stems remained so small they could never be marketed.

Moisture welled at the bottoms of Claudia's eyes.

Ernie stretched a hand out to her again. Memories flew at him like bats.

"Do you remember how you used to beg them to grow?"

He drew back his hand. That scene was something he'd rather forget. "I guess you blame me."

"No, of course not."

But he didn't believe her. After all, the entire enterprise had been his idea.

"They built stables the next farm over," he said then. "I'm surprised you didn't notice. Sam Selwyn somehow got enough money together to buy some high-priced stock. Your dad told me Selwyn horses win lots of races. The stables are nationally famous."

She turned and sat staring out the window, at grey skies and ice-covered trees and a neighboring field; they lived on a paved road that dwindled into dirt only a block down, where the city dispersed itself into the countryside.

NOT then, nor since, had she ever admitted she knew anything about Selwyn Farms, and here they'd gotten a bill from that outfit, with Grunfeld's name on it yet. Ernie had spent enough time around Claudia's dad to know that Grunfeld trained only the best of the Selwyn herd.

On the way to the stables he passed the mushroom farm. He gritted his teeth. He was ashamed to remember how he'd begged those suckers to grow. Once, Claudia had overheard him. "Damn it. Please grow. Grow!" he had sobbed. When he noticed her presence, he rushed past her, out of the barn.

Still angry, Ernie turned from Blythe onto Sycamore. A purple and white sign advertised Selwyn Horse Farms. Even from here he could tell it was a huge operation. He took a left onto a long drive lined with fir trees and located the office in the front of the main barn. As luck would have it, Sam happened to be in. The younger man had just been one of the Selwyn boys when Ernie was agonizing over dead and dying mushrooms. Now he and Sam were the same height. Maybe Sam was a little taller.

"Mr. Holbrook. What a surprise! We were wondering when you'd be coming around to see Trevarian."

"Trevarian?"

"Your horse, Mr. Holbrook." Sam frowned a little. "Of course Claudia's told you about him." He hesitated, perhaps confused by the look on Ernie's face.

Ernie was having a hard time controlling himself. He forgot he still held the bill, now crushed as his hands balled into fists, again and again.

"Look, I'll go get Mr. Grunfeld. He'll show you the horse." Pointing to the wadded-up paper Ernie was holding, he asked "Is that one of our statements, Mr. Holbrook?"

Ernie nodded.

"There isn't a problem with it, is there?"

Ernie shook his head.

"Look, just let me track down Grunfeld for you." Sam escaped quickly, leaving his secretary to stare at Ernie, who sat in a corner chair, still crumpling up the bill with one hand and shading his red face with the other.

In contrast to Sam, Ernie suspected Paul Grunfeld had

been in on Claudia's deception from the beginning. Paul's face confirmed his suspicions, and he didn't offer to shake hands. They walked without speaking to the paddock where Trevarian had been let out for his morning exercise. The gray stallion trotted round and round the enclosure, neighing and tossing its head. This is an expensive piece of horseflesh, Ernie thought; very expensive.

The two men leaned against the white railing, watching. "How old is he?" Ernie finally asked.

"Two going on three," the older man said. "Your wife's had him since he was a colt."

"Jesus!" he muttered. Over two years. She'd kept this to herself for over two years!

"They met in a strange way," Grunfeld continued. He seemed unaware of Ernie's consternation.

"Why was it strange?" Ernie asked. It was as though Grunfeld was talking about a person. Ernie supposed that to Grunfeld horses were people. Most likely the trainer's diminutive stature meant that he'd started life as a driver, so he'd probably spent more time with them than with humans.

"Well, when he was a colt he bolted, and I followed him over to the barn where you and Claudia used to have a business. She said she had visited the old haunt on a whim. Usually nobody ever goes there."

"Yeah, I guess no one else wanted to try it."

"Try what?"

"Mushrooms," Ernie muttered. "Look, would you please not tell Claudia I came by? I'm sure it would only upset her."

Grunfeld nodded. "Of course. I'll let Sam know as well." He sounded relieved.

"By the way, I think you usually get these." Ernie handed the feed bill to Grunfeld. "Came to us by mistake."

Grunfeld took the wrinkled slip of paper, not bothering to check the amount before he pocketed it.

"Pays you when she comes here, doesn't she?"

"Yes, that's how we've been handling it."

No paper trail that way, Ernie thought bitterly. "I might be coming by every so often to check on Trevarian's progress," he said aloud.

They shook hands. He'd keep up the charade, Ernie thought, as he politely took his leave. When he turned around, the trainer still stood there, staring after him.

On the drive back into town, one thought chased another like horses around a track, and he hardly noticed what road he took. Why had Claudia bought a horse? Why Trevarian? She'd come out here around Christmas. Did she think of him as a Christmas gift to herself?

Well, for God's sake, what about those pearl earrings he'd given her that same Christmas? No way they'd cost as much as a horse from Selwyn Farms, that's for sure. She'd gone and bought a horse of her own—a very expensive horse—most likely financed by Daddy Dutton. Where else could the money have come from? What about the costs of training and stabling, let alone feeding? He felt like stopping the car along the isolated road and screaming in frustration. Somehow, he managed to appear calm when he strode through their front door.

He mentioned nothing about his visit to Selwyn Farms to his wife. Since she hadn't admitted she owned the horse, why should he tell her he knew about it? Maybe eventually they would have it out, but he'd take his own sweet time and do things his way, for a change.

THAT night Claudia was extremely affectionate, almost as if she knew he'd discovered her secret and was trying to make it up to him, show him she loved him. She lit candles around their bed, the way she used to. They had a huge antique bed frame with a canopy top Claudia had draped in pink chiffon. It had been her habit to light candles placed on the dresser and on stands near the bed so a pink glow surrounded them while they made love. She hasn't done this for a very long time, Ernie thought, going along with her little game. When she wanted to cuddle after lovemaking, he pretended to be asleep, but he couldn't take his mind off Trevarian.

Trevarian. The sound of his name replayed over and over, jangling in his ears. In just a few hours, the stallion had taken on the emotional charge of a human rival. Ernie imagined the meeting between woman and colt almost as if he were seeing an encounter between a woman and her lover.

Grunfeld had told him the horse went into the old mushroom barn while Claudia had been inside. Did the intrusion frighten her at first? The colt's moving shadow would have shut out much of the setting sun's light filtering through the open doorway. Had the sudden darkness made her draw in her breath? Had she been startled by the soft snorting noises? He imagined Claudia turning slowly, discerning reddish curves and a tossing mane and tail that looked like flames in the dim light. The figure standing there might have been white or gray in the daytime. It stamped the hardened earth in a staccato rhythm. Maybe she was scared until she discovered it was only a colt. He damn well wished she had been scared. But had it been love at first sight? Ernie snorted, hoping he sounded like he was snoring. Love. Ha! Yeah, he could just see it. Slowly she begins walking toward the animal, a colt, almost grown. She can tell from his lines he's a purebred. He stands staring at her, pawing the ground. His eyes shine in the barn's semidarkness.

ON his next visit to Selwyn Stables, Ernie discovered his wife had spent $19,500 on the progeny of Sultan and Anastasia, a pair that'd made it big on the harness circuit. Sam Selwyn had bought them for breeding. Sultan was kept in a far pasture, but Anastasia had a stall up a bit from her son's, her name etched onto a bronze plaque to the side of the enclosure. The mare nickered softly, but continued feeding when Ernie and Grunfeld stopped to take a closer look. Trevarian, ready for a treat, came to them immediately. Grunfeld held out his palm and the colt blew softly into it and licked the trainer's fingers.

"Friendly horse," Ernie commented. Inside he was reeling at the five-figure price the trainer had just revealed.

"This horse has known nothing but love and affection his entire life, Mr. Holbrook," Grunfeld said. "That's how we train them here. No whipping. Sometimes the drivers crack whips over their heads to speed them up, but the lash never touches their hides. They race because it's in their blood. Your wife wouldn't have it any other way." He reached into his shirt pocket for a sugar cube that Trevarian gobbled up.

While he spoke, the trainer turned to face Ernie. The stallion playfully nudged his shoulder.

"He wants more," Ernie said.

Grunfeld grinned. "Our horses are loved, not spoiled, Mr. Holbrook."

"Please, call me Ernie. Has my wife ever ridden him?"

"No one but the trainer rides a trotter. She'll probably get to drive him around the track a couple of times, though."

On the way home from that visit, Ernie tried to imagine Claudia driving one of those racing carts—a sulky, he reminded himself. On Saturdays, when Claudia could get away, she came to watch the colt's progress, Grunfeld told him. Often with one or two friends. Yes, those same friends who conspired with her to keep Trevarian secret from Ernie.

Grunfeld had said that working carefully and slowly made racing play to the colt. He usually drove the cart, but sometimes he mounted the stallion or stood in the middle of the circle and cracked his whip to guide him around the turns. The horse finally graduated to pulling a real sulky on the regular track, with Grunfeld driving. Eventually Grunfeld would be replaced by a younger, lighter rein handler who would race Trevarian.

CLAUDIA wandered around the house like she was holding something to herself, some wonderful package or gift that she was unwrapping at her leisure. Once, she said to him, "You never look me in the face anymore. You seem to be always glancing at me sideways, like you have a secret. Do you have a secret?" She giggled.

Ernie almost slapped her. She sounded like one of those girls who'd turned high school into a torture chamber—the popular ones who thought their poop didn't smell. He hated her even more when she and those friends of hers got together. They'd come over, one at a time or in pairs, or sometimes all three, and congregate in the living room, where they would dissolve into fits of giggling. And they talked about Trevarian.

He knew they did because one time he hid in the front closet, its door cracked open just enough to listen to their conversation, to satisfy himself they were all part of the scheme. The girls were aahing and oohing because Grunfeld, bless his heart, had allowed Claudia to take the reins and drive Trevarian around the stretch.

"Only this one time," Claudia said to her friends, "he said I could do it only this one time."

"But Claudia, you're an experienced horsewoman."

"Just wait 'til I tell you what happened," Claudia said. "I never imagined how close to the ground the drivers really are. I thought being nearer the earth made driving safer than riding, but you should experience speeding along only inches from the track!"

"I guess you were dead wrong," one of the friends said. Maybe it was Maria, whom he could barely see through the crack. Claudia bobbed around just outside his line of vision. Maria laughed and shook those black curls.

Claudia continued with her story: "I knew Trevarian could run faster, so I urged him on."

"How?" the friends chimed in like a chorus.

"Well, you make clucking noises and flick the whip. The whip never really touches him, but of course he knows it's there. Kind of a motivator, you could say." Claudia chuckled. Ernie hadn't heard her laugh like that for years.

"Did he know it was you driving?" someone asked.

"He kept on turning his ears back, like he was asking, 'What're you doing back there?' "

At this everyone laughed. "Weren't you afraid?" another of the friends asked, her voice full of admiration.

"I wouldn't allow myself to think about it," Claudia said, "although there was this one little incident."

"What?" they all squealed.

"On the outside stretch he ran full out. At the far turn the sulky tilted. There I was, riding along on one wheel. I was sure we would crash, but Trevarian slowed down. I was back on two wheels again, and we were okay!"

"Phew," Phyllis said. "What a relief it must have been to stop!"

"You better believe it! But Paul thought I'd done well. I told him that I'd almost tipped over out there, and you know what he said?"

"No, what!" they cried in unison.

"He said that the horse was going slowly. I couldn't believe it. It seemed like we were flying. But he assured me that Trevarian is fast, very fast. Trevarian may be one of the best horses he's ever trained!"

"God, Claudia, I can't believe the luck you've had with that horse," Janice said. "We'll all be at his first race, won't we ladies?"

"Yes, to watch Trevarian win!"

Ernie waited until they repaired to the dining room before he slipped out of the closet and through the front door. He trod down the grass on the other side of the garage with his pacing. Trevarian, Trevarian. That name jarred him deep down. It's only a horse, he thought. Not really. Not at all. It's a betrayal.

HE began to dream about the animal. In the dream, he held a knife in his hand, a very sharp knife that would slice two ways. It was the kind of weapon no one would want raised against them on a dark night. He entered Trevarian's stall, knife in hand, and slashed, and slashed. Sometimes he woke up in the middle of the night after one of those dreams, drenched in sweat. He held his hand to his forehead, and the sweat poured off it and down his hand. The sweat reminded him of the blood in the dream. He sobbed, making dry husky sounds, because no tears would come.

His wife slept beside him, peacefully, oblivious to his torment. He wanted to shake her awake and scream at her: "I know you've lied to me for years." But he stopped himself. Yes, he slyly stopped himself. Claudia would learn her lesson, and she would learn it the hard way. Both of us can keep secrets, he told himself. Just you wait, Claudia.

Months slipped by; the weather turned clear and crisp. Trevarian was entered in his first contest after he turned three—right at Christmastime, Grunfeld informed Ernie. Frank, the driver who would race the stallion, arrived. He reminded Ernie of a Chihuahua: completely bald, with sweeping mustaches like dog's whiskers. Frank acted fierce with the horse, constantly snapping the whip over his head, but the stallion knew better. Trevarian would come behind the diminutive driver and nudge him while he stood conferring with Grunfeld; once or twice, the young horse almost succeeded in knocking him over. When that didn't work, Trevarian would nibble at Frank's shoulder until he fed the horse a few sugar cubes.

Ernie visited the stables when Claudia was at work. Sam and Paul accepted his involvement without any apparent qualms. When the two stood around conferring about a horse, they always included him in their conversation. Ernie picked up bits and pieces about horse racing, so he didn't think his time ill-spent. Somehow, somewhere all this stuff would come in handy. He asked his father-in-law judicious questions, worded so as not to arouse the older man's suspicions. Sometimes, Al Dutton did eye him strangely. Ernie had never shared the Dutton family's passion for horses. But if the older man was amazed at his son-in-law's newfound interest, he said nothing. Ernie was curious as hell to know whether Al knew about Claudia's $19,500 purchase, but, of course he never asked.

Ernie wasn't exactly sure how he would use his new knowledge. As the day of the race drew closer, his ideas began to jell. Late at night or when Claudia was out of the house, Ernie would sneak into her office and read bits and pieces of her chemistry texts. He did some research at the library on drugs used to rig a horse race. Finally, he ordered a concoction off the Internet. A clear, colorless liquid arrived, wrapped securely in a plain padded package. Sugar cubes absorbed it quite well.

The thing was, he'd have to switch out Frank's sugar cube supply, which might prove difficult right before the race, when everyone was around the horses. The driver had never accepted Ernie. Whenever he joined the driver, the trainer, and the stable owner as they stood in the stable yard reciting Trevarian's strengths and speculating on his chances for winning, Frank always made an excuse and left. He fended off Ernie's attempts to initiate an exchange between the two of them. Soon Ernie hated him almost as much as he hated

Trevarian.

Ernie visited the race track with Paul Grunfeld a couple of days before the race. The trainer introduced Ernie as one of the owners, and he got the royal treatment and a tour; including the sulky drivers' changing room, where each had a locker and access to showers.

Ernie glanced idly into the room and happened to see Frank at his locker. The little man glared at him. Ernie high-fived the driver and continued on his tour. His mind raced. Now he knew what he had to do.

THE gold and green Selwyn Horse Farm colors sparkled in the sun as Trevarian trotted toward the starting gate. Ernie watched Claudia and her friends clapping and holding up their fingers in the V-sign. The horses took off, the crowd yelling in pure excitement. Trevarian, the second favorite, just might win after all. The green and gold silks were coming up fast on the outside. The crowd rose, screaming, and the lucky few who had placed their bets on Trevarian danced for joy.

Trevarian drew even with the leader, Sundance. The crowd roared, and Trevarian passed Sundance. Suddenly, he slowed down. Frank cracked his whip over the stallion's head. No response! The other horses plunged ahead. Trevarian trotted slower and slower, until he was barely walking, then he stood still, his head down.

Ernie gazed at his rival through his binoculars, pleased to note that the horse was actually drooling. Frank leapt out of the racing cart and ran to the horse's head. Very gently, he took hold of the bridle, slowly turning the horse around, leading him toward the infield, the shortest way to the stables.

The rest of the horses and the drivers surged around the far curve of the track as Frank led Trevarian away.

Ernie trained his opera glasses on his wife. Her shoulders were shaking. One of the other women wrapped her arm around her. The group began to make their way out of the stands. Claudia stumbled toward the exit with a friend at each elbow.

The track stable stood silent and dark when Ernie slipped inside, staying hidden in the shadows. Only a few of the stalls were occupied. Trevarian was outside his stall, his handler soothing and steadying him, while the track vet examined him. Claudia, her friends, and Paul and Frank surrounded the trio in a silent circle. The stallion's head hung low, his legs trembling. He's definitely drooling, Ernie thought. Fear and shame made his triumph less satisfying than he had imagined it would be.

Ernie overheard the vet announce, "This animal's been drugged!"

Frank spoke up. "Claudia, did you know your husband was here only yesterday? He's been hanging around the Selwyn place too."

"My God!" Claudia's tone was venomous. "He did it, he did it then! Otherwise he would've told me he knew about Trevarian!"

She glared at each one in the group; no one seemed to want to meet her furious gaze.

As they spoke, the sick horse sank onto his forelegs. Claudia sobbed, and the other women murmured comforting words.

The race had ended, and the handlers were leading their horses into the stable. Several of the other men helped Frank, Grunfeld and the vet move the unsteady horse into his stall.

Ernie slipped from his place in the shadows and took a seat in the stands. The image of the defeated Trevarian rose in his mind. The three-year-old had appeared beaten down, even old. Maybe ruined forever. He pounded his hand into his fist. "It's all your fault, Claudia. Spending thousands of dollars behind my back!" he muttered, wiping away tears.

He saw his wife at the far end of the track, standing between two cops. She was pointing up at him.

✝ ✝ ✝

MARY E. BURT, from a very early age, wondered how writers worked their magic. Workshops on the "journal method" for teaching creative writing demystified the process. Eventually Mary wrote two mystery novels. She has also written numerous short stories, including "A Horse of Her Own." Two other short pieces, "The Carriage House" and "The Black Virgin of Guadalupe," have been published. Mary also has been both an editor and a teacher.

CHRISTMAS CAME LATE
HOWARD B. CARRON

March 1942

I was at Clark Air Field, December 8, 1941, when the Japanese attacked. The Army Air Force had left its only wing of bombers parked, wing to wing, in the open and they were quickly destroyed by Japanese bombers. I was at work as a guest chef at the Officer's Club, training kitchen staff and creating a Christmas menu when the concussion of the bombs knocked me down. My assistant, Luis, and a small group of Filipinos carried me out, half unconscious, from the burning building. We managed to escape through the deserted Sapanbatog Gate into the countryside.

There I was, Barney Aaron, a middle-aged, slightly over-weight American hotel restaurant chef fleeing from the Japanese attack in the company of men as frightened as I was. I spent the next few months moving from *baranggay* to *baranggay*, town to town, ending up in the vicinity of Mount Arayat and the neighboring Candaba Swamp where we were protected by dense mountain jungles and vast swamps. We were met by Crisanto Evangelista and his band of guerilla fighters who had been harassing the Japanese on their drive to Bataan and Corregidor.

"Hoy, Luis," Evangelista shouted. "You bring me more mouths to feed, no guns and a gringo."

"*Pare*, we don't eat much, and Barney is a first-class cook. He can make even weeds taste good."

"*Bahala na*. Whatever. We will have to train him to do something besides cooking. Barney, can you shoot a gun?"

"I was on the rifle team in high school. I probably remember how to do it without shooting myself in the foot."

"Luis, he has a sense of humor. We are making a trip to

181

the valley tomorrow for food. Perhaps we'll find some Japanese who want to share their guns with us." Laughing at his own joke, Evangelista wandered off and left us to fend for ourselves.

I was pretty beat up from my experiences and travel and I guess I looked pretty weak because I was placed under the care of Maritess, the daughter of the *baranggay* Captain. For the next few weeks, I was the object of her ministrations and I found myself responding not only to her expert care but becoming more and more attracted to her. This last did not go unnoticed by my compadres and was the source of much amusement for them. Luis told me to be careful about visiting with Maritess at night because that was when the *aswang* was about. I guess I looked confused because he continued.

"*Aswangs* can take the form of women by day and vampires by night," he said. "They are merciless and murderous shape-shifters that hunt small children and the frail elderly. They may also take the form of bloodsucking females who seduce and kill."

What struck me was the significant amount of superstition that pervaded this culture. The contrast between the sophisticated political motivations and their skill with guerilla warfare made this even more implausible. While there were many types of mythical creatures in their culture, the *aswang,* was the one with which I was becoming personally acquainted.

During those weeks, I also discovered that the encampment was the headquarters for the Huks, a short form of *Hukbalahap,* itself the abbreviated form of the Tagalog name for the guerrilla force known as the People's Anti-Japanese Army (*Hukbong Bayan Laban sa Hapon*). I learned there was no love lost on the American forces either, due mostly to the American occupation after the Spanish American War. However, the Americans were the lesser of the two evils in the eyes of Crisanto Evangelista, a dedicated disciple of Marxism, which drew its strength from the mostly agrarian peasants of Central Luzon. The goal, as Crisanto pointed out in our many discussions, was to lead the Philippines toward freedom from outsiders and not to take over the Philippine government. I am pretty apolitical, but I could understand their concerns.

Most of the Japanese guards were discards from the front-line soldiers, vicious and generally not too bright. It should be noted, however, that many of the soldiers who accompanied the prisoners of war were not only Japanese, but Korean. Since they were not trusted by the Japanese to fight on the battlefield, most Koreans in the Japanese army were forbidden to participate in combat roles and delegated to such service duties as guarding prisoners. One Filipino prisoner, of the more than one thousand released into the jungle by Colonel Takeo Imai for humanitarian reasons, who had joined with Crisanto, disclosed, "The Korean guards were the most abusive...the Koreans were anxious to get blood on their bayonets, and then they thought they were veterans." Honesto, the barrio spy who *helped* the Japanese and reported back to Crisanto, shared the local superstitions with the guards.

One night the last soldier in the local patrol disappeared. When the patrol returned to look for the missing man, they found their comrade hanging from his heels from a tree with two puncture holes in his neck. Every member of the patrol believed that the *aswang*, in their eternal search for human flesh and blood, had gotten him and that one of them would be next if they remained in the vicinity… and I wasn't so sure I didn't agree with them. This probably explained why the Huk encampment was rarely bothered in their home territory.

As a chef, I could prepare just about any meal, but out in the *baranggay* I was a bit handicapped. Maritess taught me how to set snares to catch wild chickens, which are smaller than American chickens. She also showed me how to catch birds at night by throwing a fish seine over their roosting places in the tall *kogon* grass, and to catch fish from the river with the same nets. Eventually, I became acquainted with the considerable array of foods eaten by my *baranggay* mates.

Sun and rest restored my health, slimmed me down, and turned me as brown as my Filipino friends. Except for my beard, which I shaved regularly with a straight razor, and my western nose, I fit in with my neighbors quite well. My language skills were good enough for the *barrio* but not for traveling elsewhere. Crisanto approved of my cooking and growing expertise in hunting. About a year passed before any serious demands were made on my skills as a soldier.

May 1943

MY friend Luis encouraged my association with Maritess despite my concerns that I was a good fifteen years older. Maritess spent a great deal of our time together teaching me *Kapampangan*, one of the dialects of the *Nueva Ecija* area. Mastery came slowly because of my confusion with the Tagalog and Spanish I had already learned. I laughingly mentioned to her the conversation with Luis about the *aswang*.

"*Too to oh*, it's true," she said very seriously. "You should not sleep with your belly exposed because an *aswang* might steal your intestines as you sleep. If it comes in when you are not asleep, the *aswang* would stand upside-down and then give off a strong odor which will make you stand still. The *aswang* will then drink your blood. People, who see at night what looks like a strand of cobweb hanging down from a tree, are warned not to reach for it, as it may be the tongue of an *aswang* waiting to catch an unsuspecting person. During the day, the *aswang* lives like a normal person. If you see your neighbor standing upside-down, then he or she is an *aswang*. An *aswang* can be spotted by looking into its eye. Your reflection would be upside-down."

As time passed, I found it harder to maintain a chaste relationship with Maritess. She was approaching her eighteenth birthday and, according to *barrio* mores, almost past the marriageable state. She was about five-feet tall, with typical long black hair, lithe and trimly built, a mixture of Malaysian, Chinese and Spanish. Her most outstanding feature was her large, dark eyes with impossibly long eyelashes set in an oval face just short of beautiful. When she laughed, I thought of wind chimes in a tropical breeze. Emilio, her father, genuinely liked me, but I was not sure what the future was going to bring.

Rice season, which runs from May through October, was upon us, and I was saved from making a decision, at least until the planting was done.

October 1943

BECAUSE of our location the constant presence of Japanese troops in the surrounding countryside did not impact on our *baranggay* life. This was not the case on our many forays into the valley. We regularly conducted supply-obtaining excursions usually attacking small Japanese outposts, and made frequent hit-and-run attacks on enemy stragglers and small garrisons. I was not often pressed into service on these expeditions, but rather was left in the barrio preparing food packages for the more able bodied members of Crisanto's forces.

My body had hardened into reasonable shape and so I occasionally joined the troops. My skills with the machete left much to be desired but I could still handle a rifle. Luis was an exceptional tracker as was Rodolfo, the *Negrito* from Mariveles. I was an adept student as we worked our way through the semi-jungle surrounding our encampment.

Stories of the brutal treatment of prisoners and villagers by the Japanese soldiers removed any doubts I had about taking a life. We were at war, and they were the enemy. Rodolfo told us of some of the atrocities his people encountered. He often accompanied us, acting as a forward scout.

When we raided an outpost, my job was to collect anything usable in the way of provisions while the rest of the group created a diversion. On occasion, a few souls were sent to their ancestors. On our last raid, I found a single natural pearl about the size of a marble in a simple gold setting with chain to match. I had no qualms about confiscating this jewelry as a present for Maritess.

It certainly turned into a nice gift and, as I discovered, was also a pledge of marriage! I'm not sure if giving such a token was really a traditional promise but everyone assured me that this was the case.

The Philippines is known as the "Land of Fiestas," and at Christmas time, this is especially true. Filipinos are proud to proclaim their Christmas celebration to be the longest and merriest in the world. It begins formally on December 16th with attendance at the first of nine pre-dawn or early morning masses and continues on nonstop until the first Sunday of January, Feast of the Three Kings, the official end of the season. The Philippines is the only Asian country where Christians predominate and the majority of its people are Roman Catholic. Christmas, therefore, is an extremely important and revered holiday for most Filipinos.

Despite their political agenda, Crisanto's *baranggay* still had time for family, for sharing, for giving, and a time for food, fun, and friendship. There are few pine trees in the valley so the bamboo *parol*, or star lantern, is the symbol of Christmas in the Philippines, representing the guiding light, the star of Bethlehem. Made of thin strips of wood or bamboo, tissue paper of different colors, or oiled and shellacked paper and some flexible wire, it is lit by a very small candle. The *Noche Buena* is very much like an open house celebration. Family, friends, relatives, and neighbors drop by to wish every family member *Maligayang Pasko*, Merry Christmas. Food is in abundance, often served buffet style.

Emilio, Maritess's father, decided to combine the festivities of the holiday and our marriage. I did not object very strongly, and a local priest was brought in for the ceremony. It didn't matter to anyone that I was Jewish. I'm not sure if they knew what that meant, and truthfully, it didn't matter to me. I don't know where they found the white dress or any of the other items that appeared at our wedding, but Maritess was absolutely radiant, her long black hair glistening with the sheen of coconut oil and a perfect white orchid tucked just above her ear. She wore the pearl, of course, and two simple gold bands, a gift from Crisanto, to complete the ceremony. Emilio gravely placed her hand in mine and closed his hands over both, squeezing them together while he looked deeply into my eyes for a long moment, smiled and released us to the shouts of the rest of the *barrio*. There was *Lechon* (roasted wild pig), *Kare-Kare* (Oxtail Stew in a peanut

186

based sauce) *Rellenong Manok* (baked stuffed chicken), *longaniza sisig* (sausage) and a few other roasted meats (of undetermined origin), lots of vegetables, rice, fruits and copious amounts of *Tuba*, Filipino *white lightning*. It was a wonderful evening.

October 1944

THE area surrounding our encampment was starting to host more and more Japanese troops although none of them made any attempts to attack us. Many attributed this to the troops' fear of the *aswang*.

There were two Japanese troopers who Honesto, our *barrio* spy, often used to garner information. Because they were basically outpost guards, their information was second hand at best. In the last few weeks, much of what Honesto gathered from them was confirmed by other sources. Crisanto was hungry for news and pushed Honesto to pump his sources a little harder. These guards, while not very bright, were also very nervous about the rumors. The day before we got the news that General MacArthur had landed at Leyte and the American troops were slowly working their way north, Honesto disappeared! Two days later we had a report that he had been seen at a satellite camp, thirteen kilometers northeast of Capas, a short distance from the main gate of Cabanatuan.

Every so often we would hear the sound of an American airplane flying overhead. News from the *baranggay* and villages closer to Cabanatuan brought tales of increased brutality in the prisons. Crisanto stepped up his hit and run tactics on small scouting parties and on the tail ends of convoys. More often than not I went also. I was becoming more adept at striking our objective and then melting into the jungle.

From time to time we met up with other guerilla groups. Once in a great while, I would find another American traveling with them and we would share some stateside stories. Most of the groups had little discipline and even less weaponry. They were always wary of Evangelista because of his reputation as a Huk.

One of the groups, however, led by Captain Juan Pajota, often had long conversations with Crisanto about tactics and especially about the prisoners in Cabanatuan. Later I discovered he was part of USAFFE (United States Army Forces - Far East). He was a small man, a natural leader and a brilliant tactician, who had observers in every village and *barrio* and knew the mayors and chiefs of all the *barrios* and *baranggays*. He also knew the terrain quite well which helped him keep out of the way of the Japanese.

Sometime in late December, Crisanto gathered most of us in the compound and said he had decided to help Captain Pajota in a mission. Apparently, there would be no Christmas festivities this year. We were going to Cabanatuan and, if successful, might have a celebration when we returned, that would be a Christmas remembrance to cherish for the rest of our lives. However, there was a slight problem that had to be taken care of first. The two guards that Honesto was *friendly* with had become suspicious of all the activity around our village. Luis had a suggestion he wanted to run by Crisanto. A short while later, Luis, Emilio and Rodolfo, who had followed captured family members from Mariveles and had a score to settle, quietly left.

The following morning one of the villagers reported to the Japanese patrol that the *aswang* had struck again. This time one of the troopers was missing his liver, and the other his heart. Another villager saw a large black bird walking with its feet facing backwards and toenails reversed. The frightened soldiers hurriedly buried their comrades nearby and, clearly agitated, abandoned the post.

Three days later I departed with Crisanto's small band, leaving behind a tearful Maritess. We joined Pajota's group not far from the Cabu River and in sight of the gates of Cabanatuan. There were about two hundred of us armed with Springfield's, BAR's and water-cooled .30 caliber machine guns mounted on tripods, that had been smuggled in by submarine, but many of the young men were armed only with machetes. Captain Pajota's spies and the Alamo Scouts (formally known as the U.S. Sixth Army Special Reconnaissance Unit) informed the American Commander that there were eight thousand Japanese troops inside the compound, and the rescue attempt had to be postponed twenty-four hours until the Japanese pulled out. We needed a better picture of the terrain because it was open rice land with no cover. Pajota reasoned that although it was impossible to get near the camp, they could spy on the camp from a higher outpost. He had spotted what appeared to be an abandoned shack that might be able to provide the vantage. Crisanto motioned for Emilio, Rodolfo and me to check it out.

As we approached the shack we heard laughter and moaning mingled together. Peering through the open window we could see someone tied to a post, head down, shirt cut into shreds. Sitting nearby with a jug of Tuba were two Japanese junior officers, with *tantos*, small swords under twelve inches, on the table next to them. Emilio gasped, stifling the sound by covering his mouth quickly. It was Honesto! We had to make a decision. We couldn't use our rifles. The likelihood that we could enter without alerting the guards and messing up the mission was too great. Rodolfo carefully placed one dart in the tube of his blowgun and another dart in the corner of his mouth, taking care not to touch the point. Two quick puffs of air, a split second apart, and the two torturers keeled over. Rodolfo jumped through the window. With a few swipes of his bolo, it was over.

The view from the shack was extraordinary; we could see right into the compound. We made notes, detailing the major features of the camp and the best routes for the Rangers. Meanwhile, Emilio cut Honesto free, and we made our way back to our staging area to give the information to Captain Pajota and the American Commander. None of Honesto's injuries were life threatening, but it was obvious from the festering wounds that he had been worked over for quite a while. An American medic treated his wounds and gave him a shot of morphine. We would have to wait for his story.

While we rested from our scouting trip, Luis and Rodolfo looked at me with raised eyebrows, a typical Filipino gesture. I waited while Rodolfo patiently cleaned his blowgun, lips twitching in an almost smile. Luis hacked the top off a young coconut and offered it to me. The fresh juice, called *buko*, was a welcome change from the tepid water we carried with us.

Luis began, "You remember the first *aswang* victim?"

"Well, yeah. Between you and Maritess and all the rumors, I think I have a handle on some weird stuff going on."

"Barney, we ambushed the last guy in that local patrol, knocked him out with one of Rodolfo's darts, and punctured his neck with two holes, vampire fashion."

I stared at the two of them, my mouth agape.

"Counting on the superstitions of the local Japanese patrol from the last *aswang* attack, we planned another. We still had the help of Rodolfo, an expert with the blowgun. We knew that we couldn't leave any marks on the bodies of the guards other than the puncture wounds from the *vampire*. With the skill of a jungle cat stalking his prey, Rodolfo approached the guardhouse the Japanese used. A gentle double puff of air, an unconcerned swat by the guards as if to wave away a fly or mosquito, and that was it. The bodies were strung up, darts removed and two puncture wounds placed strategically." Luis looked at me, smiling. "You were starting to believe, weren't you?"

I smiled sheepishly. "But what about the missing heart and liver?"

"Lots of loose dogs in the area."

MOST of the guerilla fighters had never directly confronted the enemy. We were used to hit-and-run tactics, stealing supplies, picking off stragglers, and then fading back into the jungle. Although I wasn't born in this country, I had lived here long enough to understand the pain and suffering and frustration of living under the thumb of the Japanese. Beneath the tension and nascent fear, there was a feeling of exultation, a promise of redemption for the years of subjugation.

An American explosives expert had placed a time bomb under the Cabu River Bridge, set to explode as the attack started, to keep the Japanese armored vehicles at bay. We had heard that an American Army Ranger company was prepared to attack the POW camp, although we had never heard of the existence of such a group.

It was still light out, the Japanese were eating their evening meal across the river and the Filipino and American troops were inching their way toward Cabanatuan. Crisanto, my friend, Luis, and Emilio, were lying beside me in the *kogon* grass. Rodolfo had moved closer to the area where the Filipino prisoners were enclosed, hopeful that some of his relatives might still be alive. The small growl of an approaching aircraft turned our attention skyward. At first I saw only the silhouette against the sun, black and sinister, with two tails and what looked like a stinger stuck in the nose. As it passed over us I realized that it was painted black. As it swooped over the encampment, the Japanese scattered for cover. This distraction had been suggested by Captain Pajota as a cover for our troops to move closer to the main gate of the prison camp. The strange plane made numerous passes over the Japanese but did not fire. Evening descended like a cloak thrown over the sun, and the plane left. The darkness before moonrise was so complete that I could not see my hand in front of my face.

Luis whispered, "Barney, the bridge is ready to blow at 7:45. The attack on the main gate is ready to start."

As the moon cast its silvery light upon the Imperial troops lounging around their dampened campfires, a hundred Filipinos picked out their individual targets. A barely audible shot from the prison a mile away was the signal for a barrage that wasted the troops caught in the open. Four years of anger and resentment poured through the barrels of the weapons as the Filipinos fired again and again. Just as the Japanese organized their first attempt to charge, the bridge was blown apart. When the smoke cleared, it was evident that only a portion of the bridge was destroyed. The Japanese charged, and the Filipinos fired, wiping out every man. Shouting *Banzai*, another sortie of Japanese attempted to cross the bridge only to meet the same fate. A third and fourth attempt was just as unsuccessful.

Forty minutes later, an eerie silence descended over the area and Captain Pajota signaled his troops to withdraw down the road slowly. We were now fighting a rear action as the freed and disoriented prisoners were being taken toward the carabao carts supplied and driven by the local farmers, an idea suggested and organized by Pajota to ferry the prisoners who were unable to walk toward Platero two miles away.

Around nine pm we saw two flares split the sky, the signal to withdraw from our positions and fall back to Platero. Our withdrawal was slow and hampered by attacks from different units of the Japanese army. Our force didn't seem to be particularly coordinated but the size of it was too large not to attract attention. It was several hours before we hit our rendezvous point near the Pampanga River. By this time, the rescued prisoners on the carabao carts extended almost two miles back from Platero. We might have that Christmas celebration after all.

Crisanto, Luis, Emilio, and I were assigned to scout out the next *baranggay* because it was another HUK encampment and it could be touchy if the Americans and the prisoners just walked through the area. As we approached, the Captain of the local guerilla force came out to meet us. Crisanto and he spoke briefly. Turning to us, Crisanto said, "*Walang problema*, there will be no problem going through, but there is a Japanese mortar emplacement just past the outskirts. We should check it out before moving such a large and slow group. Luis, you go back and tell Captain Pajota. Emilio, you and Barney circle around behind the last houses while the Captain and I move toward the mortar."

As Emilio and I circled around through the brush, the first of the Rangers broke cover. Just then, I heard the familiar thump of a mortar shell being dropped down the tube and then the whistle of the ordinance coming toward us. I seized Emilio and we rolled into the tangle of roots and grass as it exploded. I felt a hot, searing pain in my right thigh. Three or four shots came from the direction of the mortar emplacement, then silence. Suddenly, two Japanese soldiers came screaming from the emplacement brandishing their swords. They were about five yards from us before we could fire at them. At the same time, an American Ranger sprayed them with a Thompson sub-machine gun.

We never did find out if we had hit the Japanese, but the

192

shrapnel had hit my buttocks. I was bleeding from multiple wounds and starting to lose consciousness. Emilio was trying to stop the bleeding from the largest wound when a medic from the American Ranger company arrived. He cleaned out most of the pieces of shrapnel, dressed the smaller wounds and sutured the deep ones. He sprinkled penicillin over everything and said I could be moved. I would probably make it if I were lucky, although sitting would be a problem for many weeks.

It was thirty miles to the American lines and moving over five hundred freed prisoners would take time. We had to move slowly because of their condition. Honesto and I washed in and out of delirium, but at times he was conscious enough for me to get the gist of the torture he had undergone by his sadistic interrogators. He explained, "They mostly wanted to know what our plans were and if we were in contact with the Americans. Their English was terrible and their grasp of Tagalog so poor that the combination of the two languages got them nothing. Besides, they were more interested in drinking *Tuba* and cutting me for amusement."

The bulk of the convoy continued toward the advancing American forces while a small group consisting of one Ranger Medic, three Alamo Scouts, five wounded from Juan Pajota's group, and our band headed toward our *barrio*.

Crisanto had sent a messenger back to the *barrio*, and as we approached all the children flooded out carrying candles and singing:

"Joy to the world, the Lord is come! Let earth receive her King…"

There were parols hanging from the trees, and bamboo Christmas trees. Huge pots of steaming *Manok Nilaga*, chicken soup with *kang kong*, a kind of swamp cabbage, peppercorns and local ginger boiled away. Not much of a Christmas meal, but very welcome.

The Ranger was quite moved by the children's performance and then turned to Capt. Pajota and Crisanto. "I guess Christmas is a little late this year, but it's one we'll never forget. By the way, I've been meaning to ask. Who is this guy? He looks like an American."

"Yes, he is," said Crisanto. "A civilian from Clark Air Field."

"What's his name?" the Medic asked.

"His name is B—" Crisanto started.

"It is *Bayani*," Emilio said.

"*Bayani?*" Funny name for an American."

Capt. Pajota smiled broadly. "In our dialect, it means hero."

"Thank you, Emilio," I said, "but I'd like to think that the real heroes are Luis and Rodolfo and, of course, that very special ally, our friendly *aswang! Mabuhay,* long live."

"What we do for ourselves dies with us. What we do for others and the world remains and is immortal."

~Albert Pine

HOWARD "DOC" CARRON, born in Brooklyn, New York, is currently a Supervisor of Adult Services in the Queen Creek, Arizona library. His career includes: photographer, musician, teacher, ceramist, silversmith, sculptor, painter, wood block artist, writer, librarian and chef. Howard taught overseas from 1969 to 1993 at the elementary, secondary and college levels in Japan, Okinawa, Korea, Azores, Philippines and Germany. He is married and the father of three daughters.

THE LAST RESORT
NANCY NIELSON REDD

MINUTES before Big Richard Walker took his last breath, Dr. Clifford Shores, who'd just finished a friendly Scotch on the rocks with Big Richard, grabbed Billie Jo's hand. He gazed at her with exaggerated theatrics and said, "Goodnight, Sweetheart. I'll see you in my dreams." His twinkling eyes showed that he knew and loved being corny.

Billie Jo, aka BJ, managed Cactus Moon RV Park, in Candlewood, Arizona, fondly dubbed *The Last Resort* by its retired residents, and she catered to them in every possible way. With an indulgent smile, she hugged the widowed old physician as he left the New Year's Eve party, aware of the highball thermos bulging in his jacket pocket. Cactus Moon partygoers knew that if they wanted a drink, they had to bring it themselves. Dr. Shores and Richard Walker each brought drinks in a thermos, and they sometimes shared drinks.

A kind of silly goofiness pervaded the resort activities. Good-hearted tomfoolery, like the toilet races, kept the aging population of the resort laughing at themselves, at each other, and at life in general. The park, inside and out, still sparkled with Christmas lights and holiday greetings. Plans for the New Year's Eve party were a bit absurd, as usual. At midnight, Cactus Moon time, a grand prize for the favorite dessert made from Hostess Twinkies would be awarded.

On this one night, midnight arrived two and a half hours earlier than it did in the rest of the world. When the party began at 5:00 p.m., BJ called out, "The alarm clock is set forward so it will ring at midnight, but it will only be nine thirty our time. That is when we will count the votes for the grand prize winner. Everybody be sure to try the desserts and then vote."

The plans followed a familiar routine. First would be a potluck dinner with comfort foods from the time-tested recipes of the retirees in the park. All the latest online jokes culled from emails would be told while they ate. After dinner and clean-up, Las Vegas Night with games of chance would begin. Las Vegas Night functioned as a fund-raiser for park activities. The committee would print up play money to sell, and everyone would have a grand time. The festivities usually cleared three or four hundred dollars.

BJ circulated through the guests, making sure everyone felt included. Soon after Clifford left, she noticed Winnie Walker walk down the corridor to the Ladies Room. Beyond that room, another door led outside to the RV homes parked there for the winter.

When Winnie left the room, her husband, Big Richard Walker, pulled a king size sheet over his head through a hole cut in the center. He put on a Santa Claus beard and picked up a rusty scythe, thus becoming Father Time. On both the front and the back of the sheet, a hand-lettered sign read,

FORGIVE ME, WINNIE
I'M A BIG SHEET
XOXO

NO sooner had he costumed himself in his apology, than he trembled like a tree in a gust of wind and fell over with a bone-cracking *whump*. His thermos, with the dregs of the drink shared with Clifford, soared out of his hand into the nearest corner.

Little Richard happened to be passing behind him with a plate he had just filled with one piece each of the three finalists in the Twinkie contest, *Twinkie Tiramisu To Die For*, *Tropical Delight Twinkies*, and *RV Having Fun Yet, Cheri?* When Big Richard fell backwards, he mostly missed Little Richard, but his flailing right arm whacked Little in the back, knocking him face forward into the plate of cream-covered Twinkies. It was the last wacky joke he'd ever play on Little Richard, or anyone else.

A couple of guys saw the mishap and rushed to help. Big

Richard, with a groan rattling in his throat, stopped breathing.

"Lay him out!"

"Give him mouth-to-mouth!"

Each of the guys shouted instructions while Little Richard, his face a patchwork of chocolate, cherries and pineapple, stood up, pulled his cell phone out of his pants pocket and dialed 911, all the while running his tongue around his lips, and taking a couple of napkins out of his shirt pocket to wipe his face. A red cherry had landed on top of his shining silver hair.

"Where's Winnie?" someone asked.

"She went to the Ladies," a voice called from the crowd.

"That was thirty minutes ago," BJ said. "I'll run over to her RV to look for her."

BJ rarely went inside any of the residents' RVs, partly because they were small, but mostly because she was too busy to sit and chat. At the Walker's RV, the curtains were open. She could see the small couch with a fancy needlework pillow on it that said *Keep the Magic Alive,* with hearts and flowers intertwined around the embroidered sentiment. Her knock went unanswered.

BJ saw the sheriff's car drive in so she hurried back to the clubhouse. She and the sheriff, Jim Pierce, had gone to school together and had dated some. He still treated her like an old girlfriend, despite both being in their forties, she divorced with three grown kids, and he married to someone else.

The sheriff and one deputy, Dennis Wilkins, walked into the group of 'snow birds' recently arrived from points north to spend the winter in Arizona. As soon as they saw him, everyone stepped back to form a path leading to Big Richard's body. Nervous and unsettled at being part of important happenings, they shifted from group to group. Excited chit-chat burst out in all directions.

The sheriff said, "Don't anybody leave this room. Where's BJ?"

BJ stepped forward. "I'm here, Sheriff."

"Would you stand by, and make sure nobody leaves this room?"

"Yes, sir, but..."

"But what?"

"That man's wife," BJ said, pointing toward Big Richard, "left the party a while ago. She doesn't know he collapsed. Could I go look for her?"

Another deputy arrived. "No, I'll send Deputy Wilkins. Do you have any idea where she might be?"

Aware that inquisitive residents listened to every word, she said, "If he'll come to the office with me, I'll show him a park map." With that suggestion, she managed to keep any implications about Winnie's whereabouts from curious ears, knowing how gossip flew around the park.

In the office, she showed the deputy the map. "Try space thirty-nine first. One of her...umm...friends lives there. If she's not there, I don't know where she'd be."

A few minutes after the deputy went to look for her, Winnie ran in. "What happened?" she gasped, looking from face to face. Deputy Wilkins and Clifford Shores followed her in.

"Oh, Winnie. I'm glad you're back. Big just collapsed," BJ said.

"*What?* Where is he?"

BJ took her arm and started toward Big's body, and then turned to the resort residents to say, "You heard what the sheriff said, stay put." Out of managerial habit, she added, "Please."

The sheriff, squatting by the body, looked up when Winnie, Dr. Shores, BJ, and Deputy Wilkins surrounded him. He rose.

"You're this man's wife?" he asked. At her nod, he said, "I'm sorry, Ma'am. I'm afraid he's dead. Looks like he died before he hit the floor."

She stood a moment, her head down, apparently reading the apology on the costume she had not seen before. Everyone watched in silence until she lifted her head and said, "I'm a nurse. Do you mind if I take his pulse?"

"Sure. Go ahead." He stepped aside and said quietly to Wilkins, "Hefty guy. Probably a heart attack."

Wilkins nodded. He then motioned with his head, indicating he wanted a private word. He and the sheriff turned their backs for a whispered exchange.

"I knocked on the door at space thirty-nine. No answer, but then the old guy who lives there came up. He'd taken his garbage to the dumpster. I asked if he'd seen Mrs. Walker. He said he'd just been talking to her. She'd taken her garbage out, too, because tomorrow is pickup day. Probably won't come on New Year's Day, but they wanted to be prepared if it did." He paused. "So they said, anyway." The sheriff, while listening, noticed the thermos in the corner for the first time, and pointed it out to Wilkins before they turned back to the group around the body.

He jerked his thumb back over his shoulder and spoke to the crowd. "Who owns that thermos?"

"Belonged to Big Richard. Must have landed over there when he fell. He'd just had a drink with Dr. Shores."

"Bag it," the sheriff instructed Deputy Wilkins. "Just in case…"

BJ stood nearby as Winnie and Clifford knelt beside Big Richard. Winnie took his pulse, laid her head down to listen to his chest, and then sat back on her heels. She looked stunned as she shook her head. BJ thought she saw a couple of strange expressions fighting for dominance on Winnie's face: a fleeting look of triumph and satisfaction before shock and other more conventional expressions of grief replaced them. BJ chided herself for her uncharitable thoughts. Then, with tears glittering in her eyes, Winnie looked at the familiar faces surrounding her and said, "I…oh…it was quick?"

Little Richard said, "Yes, Winnie. He was gone in a flash."

She turned to the sheriff. "Will you have to do an autopsy?"

"In our little ol' county, Ma'am, we can't afford autopsies for every sudden death, unless suspicion stirs up our curiosity about a body."

Another couple of unreadable expressions crossed Winnie's face, but who'd think to question her charged emotions? Clifford's face showed nothing.

Sheriff Pierce helped Winnie to stand and then arranged Big's apologetic sheet costume to cover his face. Winnie blinked back tears. Clifford, his arm around her shoulder in an offering of sympathy and support, looked at her with his heart in his eyes.

The sheriff telephoned the Medical Examiner. When she arrived, Sheriff Pierce said to the gathered crowd, "While the ME examines the body, let's clear this room. BJ, will you take everybody to other rooms? Can we use your private office?" BJ nodded. The sheriff continued, "Will you take Mrs. Walker there and stay with her? I'll be a few more minutes." BJ nodded again.

"Deputy, come with me," Pierce said, leading him out of the clubhouse. "Does it strike you as a bit strange that Mrs. Walker would leave a party to take out her garbage?"

When Wilkins nodded, the sheriff continued, "Kinda strange, too, that almost her first comment concerned an autopsy." Wilkins nodded again.

"Call for a truck," the sheriff said. "Let's empty that Dumpster before the garbage collector comes, whenever that is. I want to take a look at the bags on top, so keep them separated."

After a short conference, the sheriff and the Medical Examiner agreed that the death appeared to be a heart attack, but the sheriff asked her to put off signing the death certificate until they'd examined the garbage bags. "Tomorrow should do it. I have some questions I want answered."

He went to BJ's office to tell Winnie they would not release Big's body for another few days, and that she could return to her RV, take care of telephone calls she needed to make, but not to set a funeral date yet.

The party was over before it got started and long before the alarm clock sounded. Somber residents waited in side rooms. When the sheriff talked to them, he heard a dozen different versions of the Walker's explosive anniversary party, which had been held a few days before Christmas. Some of them, remembering how hurt and angry Big Richard's behavior had made Winnie, wondered at his sudden death, but dismissed the thought, trusting the sheriff to do his job with the information he gathered.

Without a solid reason to suspect that anyone had committed murder, the sheriff released them, but asked them not to leave the area for a few days, and to be available should any questions arise.

BJ stopped the sheriff and his crew as they were leaving. "We've tons of fabulous Twinkie desserts if any of you want to sample them. You can even vote for the grand prize winner."

MOST of Big Richard Walker's jokes embarrassed his unfortunate victims. You'd think that after living for seventy-eight years, he'd have learned restraint, but being the jokester permeated his personality so deeply, it looked like he'd never change.

Richard Simpson had lived in Cactus Moon RV Park for the past five seasons. For four of those years, he'd been called Dick. Within six months of Dick and Winnie Walker moving into Cactus Moon a year ago, Dick Simpson had become Little Richard and Dick Walker had become Big Richard. In truth, the switch took just one day.

Dick Simpson, a 5'6", small-boned man, a born-again Christian, had an insensitivity that, almost without fail, hit folks the wrong way. He had a vain habit of telling people that, in their spiritual beliefs, they were now where he'd been twenty years ago. He was willing to bring them up to speed if they'd just listen to him. Though short, he had a glorious head of wavy, satiny silver hair; he kept it groomed and uncovered.

Dick Walker, a tall man, close to 6'4", and weighing in at 310 pounds, had a goofy personality to match his size. He lived to make people squirm. Coarse, crude, and just as insensitive as Dick Simpson, he seemed to have no idea how jarring he could be.

Dick Walker always wore a baseball cap covering his shiny bald head. A week after he and Winnie moved into the park, he arrived at early morning coffee wearing a new cap with *Big Richard* stitched across the front. When Dick Simpson came in a few minutes later, Big whipped out a similar cap with *Little Richard* across the front.

Before Dick Simpson could sit down, Big planted the new cap on his head.

"What's with this Richard stuff?" one of the guys asked. "Just plain Dick sounds fine to me."

"Well, think about it," Big said. "With two Dick's running around here, nobody will know who you mean unless we do something like this. I could hardly put *Big Dick* on my hat, now could I? Whadda ya think, *Little*...?"

Embarrassed laughter exploded, and the guys all turned to see what Dick Simpson would say. He took off the hat, laid it on the table, ran his fingers through his hair to fluff it up, and said, "Big or little, who cares? I don't have to cover my head like you do, *Dickie*. You keep this hat and alternate between wearing them—that way you'll keep us all guessin'."

Points for that round went to Dick Simpson, but the name stuck. Ever after, the guys called him *Little* and called Dick Walker *Big*.

ON December 16th, a month after the Walkers arrived for the winter, they invited everyone in the park to help them celebrate their fiftieth anniversary at an ice cream social in the clubhouse. Incorrigible as ever, Big embarrassed Winnie in front of all their guests, including six of their seven children who'd flown in for the occasion. Jovial park residents gathered to enjoy the party. The clubhouse rang with hearty congratulations. Before anyone left, Big stood up and called for attention.

"I want to thank you all for coming to help us celebrate, especially our kids, who have come so far. Our youngest son is in Iraq right now, or he'd be here, too. We have sixteen grandchildren and I've lost track of the great grands—how many is it now, Winnie?"

"Five, and two more on the way."

"I just want to make one little announcement. I think it's time you kids knew. Your mother and I never married. We're not legal, we've just been living together for all these years."

In the thud of sudden silence, Winnie's teary voice broke. "Will you sit down and be quiet?"

No one else spoke until Big said, "Well, aren't any of you

little bastards going to say a word?"

"Mom?" one son spoke.

"Is this true?" a daughter asked.

"How has she put up with you for fifty years?" Little Richard nailed him. "And why would she stay with you if she weren't married to you?"

Before bedlam could break out, Big went down on his knees in front of Winnie, and said, "Will you marry me, Sweetheart?"

"Richard, this is ridiculous. Will you stop? Every occasion is not all about *you*."

"But, Winnie, don't we have to get married, now that I've got you pregnant again?"

Silence cloaked the room.

With extreme dignity, tall white-haired Winnie, somewhere in her mid-seventies, followed by her daughters and some of the guests, walked out of the room. Just as she opened the door, a voice rang out from the crowd.

"Don't get mad, Winnie. *Get even!*"

The party died. Big, still on his knees, gasped as he tried to pull himself to his feet. His heavy body and bad knees made that look doubtful. Three of the guys and a couple of his sons who'd stayed behind out of pity, had to help him up.

ONE of them said, "Man, if I pulled that stunt on my wife, she'd kill me, and she'd make sure I died a slow and painful death."

"You'd better get home and apologize like you've never apologized before."

"I'm glad I'm not in your shoes. You probably can't even get in the house. My wife would lock the door and throw away the key."

The five men walked together to Big's RV space. No lights showed. They watched as Winnie's car and the rental car of their daughters drove out of the park. His king-sized SUV sat alone in the driveway. Big exhaled a whoosh of air and sat down in a specially built-for-his-size patio chair, his head in his hands. For the first time since they'd known him, he made no smart-ass remarks. In clumsy sympathy, they tried to console him.

"She'll come back. In fifty years, how many times has she forgiven you?"

"Yeah. She's not gonna dump ya now. If she'da wanted to do that, she'da done it long ago."

"I don't know. That was pretty strong stuff...I hate to think what my wife woulda done if I'da embarrassed her like that in fronta our kids."

WHEN Big went inside the motor home, he found a note propped against Winnie's Magic needlework pillow.

> *My hand is shaking so I can hardly write, Richard. You lied for a laugh, but no one thought it was funny. You made a mockery of our life and marriage. I just feel hollow, like I have a big hole in my heart. I don't know if I can process this into denial the way I've always done before. One of the girls will call you.*

AFTER she retired from nursing, Winnie immersed herself in holistic medicine and natural remedies. She had a container herb garden from which she made tinctures, salves, and healing concoctions. She also had flowering plants, including a bright pink azalea. Many of the women saved their face cream jars so she could fill them with *Winnie's Wonder Salve*, good for superficial cuts and scrapes. Within the first year of the Walker's presence in the park, residents came to rely on Winnie to help heal cuts, colds, and coughs. Through her natural medications, she and Clifford Shores, the retired doctor, became friends and often discussed how many medications were derived from plants.

She gathered all sorts of plants for her potions and lotions. She knew which were the most beneficial as well as which were the most poisonous. She knew the oleander bushes that surrounded the park were poisonous, as well as rhubarb leaves and the pretty azalea plant that bloomed in her kitchen.

WINNIE returned to Big and the RV Park ten days after she left, on December 26th, five days before the New Year's Eve party. No one said much, but they watched both Winnie and Big Richard with curiosity. Winnie's quietness was more obvious than ever. All the ladies knew she still needed time to bounce back. For a couple of days after her return, Big became more subdued, and seemed to walk on eggshells with Winnie and everybody else, but by the day of the New Year's Eve party, his exuberance had returned.

On Dec. 27th, the winter pruning and clean-up began. The men looked for any and all kinds of diversions and begged to help around the park. They mobilized once each season to trim the high oleander hedge. Park Management warned the cutters to use extreme caution because all parts of the oleander plant were toxic, especially the sap. BJ typed up a cautionary paper and Gabe, the park's maintenance man, kept a close eye on the proceedings.

"IF you want to help, please follow these guidelines:
Avoid scratches, check for snakes under the bushes, and never clown around with the cuttings."

BIG wore outsized, baggy shorts around the park. Despite his size, he had a natural rhythm and grace in his movements, but anyone can trip. On the day of the oleander trimming, he drove his golf cart to join the work party. When he stepped out of the cart, he slipped, but caught the edge of the cart so that his three hundred pounds didn't fall with full force. His weight pulled the cart over on top of him. The mishap knocked him to his bare knees, and he came up bleeding.

A couple of the men helped him to his RV. Winnie took him to the emergency room for X-rays and treatment for his scrapes, scratches, and bruises. The X-rays revealed no breaks. The doctor gave him a prescription for an expensive antibiotic but Big refused to have it filled. He wanted to be cared for by Winnie. She brought him home and, at his insistence, took off the bandages.

With new preparations brought back from her ten days in Colorado, she disinfected his wounds with a bottle of brownish liquid that had a strong smell and a sharp sting.

Then she slathered on one of her fresh new salves and told Big to lie down on the couch while she brewed one of her original herb teas.

"Winnie, my right heel is really sore. Could you take a look at it?"

Winnie discovered that blood had crusted around a deep crack in the coarse, dry edge of his heel. She disinfected it with more of her homemade remedy and coated it with salve. She measured dried leaves and twigs and seeds out of a plastic baggie labeled, *Winnie's Colorado Mountain Herb Tea*. She brought Big a cup of the steaming brew.

"You might not like the taste of this, but I want you to drink it all."

He took a big slurp and sputtered, "Good grief, woman. Are you trying to poison me?"

Winnie continued with her treatments, keeping Big settled in front of the TV, and serving him, nonstop, her special tea. In addition to being brought to his knees by a golf cart, he seemed to have caught the stomach flu. He complained of head and stomach aches, he felt nauseous and even vomited a couple of times, plus he was groggy and cranky.

In a private moment, when Gabe came to check on him, Big handed him some cash, and asked, "Will you go to Goodwill and see if you can find me a king size white sheet? And will you get me a big black Magic Marker?"

When Winnie went for groceries on the morning of the New Year's party, Big made his secret preparations. He still didn't feel at the top of his form, but he had a surprise for Winnie and insisted on going to the party. He finished making his costume and took it to the clubhouse where he hid it in the shuffleboard cupboard. He then spent a couple of hours baking for the dessert contest at the party.

Since her return from Colorado, Winnie had been edgy. Contrite and nervous, Big gave her time and space—well, as much space as was possible in an RV. He thought his Father Time surprise would say it all and she'd be her old self again, but he misjudged the damage he'd inflicted. He didn't know that Winnie was not the only one in the park who'd been offended by his behavior.

THE day after Big's death, Sheriff Pierce and Deputy Wilkins went through the garbage bags they'd retrieved and what they found caused the sheriff to order an autopsy. The day the ME's office received the autopsy report showing Prinivil and Diuril, Advil, elevated potassium levels, *Hypericum perforatum*, and *Valeriana officinalis* in Richard Walker's body, in addition to a liberal quantity of Scotch, Sheriff Pierce went to Cactus Moon RV Park to ask Winnie Walker if she or Richard took sleeping pills.

"Yes, Richard sometimes took Lunesta. I preferred that he take valerian root but it wasn't always strong enough. And he dosed himself with Advil for his headache just before we went to the party." He nodded and told her that he had released the body and she could make her funeral arrangements.

When Sheriff Pierce drove back by the office, he lifted his hand in a salute to BJ, standing outside her office. With a glance in his rearview mirrors, he noticed that she watched his car as it turned left and stopped at Dr. Shores' space, number thirty-nine. He also noticed that the water aerobics class had gathered to watch as well. After several minutes, when he emerged with Dr. Shores, helped him into the official car, and drove out of the park, curious eyes followed them. From that very moment, rumors and speculations flew.

The newspaper headline the following day read: "Septuagenarian Arrested in Retiree Park Murder." The first sentence read "Retired doctor confesses to poisoning Richard Walker."

A few days later, Sheriff Pierce stopped in the park office to chat with BJ. She told him they were having a memorial service for Big in the clubhouse the next day if he'd like to come.

"Can you tell me what you found in the garbage bags? Enquiring minds want to know."

"Just a lot of salve wiped up with paper towels in Mrs. Walker's bags. Looked like she'd dropped a jar and broke it and had to clean it up. Couldn't use the salve because of glass slivers."

"Is that all?"

"No. A baggie of her herbal tea with just a smidgen left in it. We had just enough suspicion that we had it analyzed."

"And?" she prodded him.

He read from a paper he took out of his pocket. "His insides were a combination pharmacy, health food store, and liquor cabinet. Massive amounts of *Hypericum perforatum* and *Valeriana officinalis* could have tipped the scale. That's St. John's wort and valerian root, but a substantial amount of potassium combined with his blood pressure medication killed him."

BJ lowered her head to look over her reading glasses. "Potassium?"

"Don't feel bad. I had to ask, too. Not many of us know that a delicate balance of potassium both inside and outside the cells is essential to good health. Too much or too little can be fatal. A medical doctor would know that. We found evidence of dissolved potassium in Richard Walker's thermos, and an empty bottle of potassium capsules in the doctor's garbage bag. When I went to Dr. Shores' RV, he told me to come on in, he'd been expecting me."

BJ looked at him in silence for a long moment. She chewed the inside of her lip, blinked a couple of times, and then shook her head.

"What?" he asked.

"Did he tell you he has lung cancer?"

"Yep. He sat there spitting blood while I talked to him. He might not live long enough to stand trial." The sheriff paused. "He told me he loves Winnie and just couldn't stand to see that big oaf abuse her ever again."

"Thanks, Jim, for coming to tell me." Tears welled in her eyes. "I guess we're never too old to be fools for love."

When the sheriff stood up to leave, BJ said, "Wanna hear something ironic? The New Year's Eve grand prize winner was Big Richard for his *Twinkie Tiramisu To Die For.*"

† † †

NANCY NIELSON REDD lives in Gilbert, Arizona. Her family owned and operated businesses: feeding livestock, mining, a trading post, a convenience store, and an RV park. She graduated from ASU with a BA in English. Her non-fiction credits include articles in the Page, Arizona *Chronicle,* and other newspapers, and articles in *Blue Mountain Shadows,* a historical quarterly. In fiction, her short story, "Still Life, With Snow" was included in *Map of Murder* (Red Coyote Press, 2007).

NEW YEAR'S EVE SURPRISE
KRIS NERI

Lefty Katz was jinxed. Others insisted he was just a screw-up, sure to wreck anything he put his scheming mind to. But Lefty knew better—he'd always been cursed. That he currently lived in poverty in Mexico, on the lam from the U.S. law, proved it. And why? Because he had the lousy luck to try to rob a convenience store—when the cash register was empty. See? Jinxed.

He had been traveling through California when he'd needed that infusion of convenience store cash, so he managed to slip across the border into Mexico before the cops caught him. Totally broke, though. And there, without the proper papers, he couldn't work legally. That meant taking low-end jobs that paid in cash, and barely enough of it to survive. Now it was just days before Christmas, and he was about to have his worst holiday ever.

But, finally, luck smiled on Lefty. And he had his latest dead-end job to thank for the chance. Months earlier he'd found work as a dishwasher in one of the posh Cabo San Lucas resorts. A lousy job, but it had its compensations. Since Lefty's washtub faced the cooks' station, he learned loads more about cooking than he ever expected.

By working nights, he could hang around the marina during the day, picking up odd jobs swabbing down yachts. Lefty would watch the elegant crafts sail out to sea, filled with rich tourists eager to fish for deep sea marlin, Cabo's prime and pricey recreational activity. Lefty always dreamed about working on a yacht, but he didn't see that happening with his bad luck.

Then Lefty spotted the sign that would change his life. "Chef needed for private yacht," the flyer in Spanish, which

211

he'd learned in school, said. "Paid daily in dollars. No English-speakers—Spanish-speaking only."

As a lifelong crook, even if not a good one, that last line tweaked Lefty's antennae. The yacht's owners had to be Americans. Why else would they pay in dollars? You'd think Americans would want an English-speaking employee. Unless they were making plans they didn't want their chef to understand. They were running some kind of scam, Lefty decided. To deal himself into it, he just had to pretend not to understand English, until the time was right.

The yacht proved to be a sleek antique beauty. Although it seemed too elegant for the tacky name, "Dolly Sue," which someone had painted badly on the stern, just above where the dinghy hung. The men aboard confirmed his suspicions about the operation. The guy in charge, Dick Ashcroft, was a gaunt, flinty man, with pale blue eyes so cold, Lefty thought they could freeze meat. Ashcroft might have dressed in the duds they sold in the high-priced shops, but Lefty knew this guy had clawed his way to the top. Unlike the other two, who looked like overage prep school boys. The plump one, Nick Kandensky, had soft moist hands that he kept wiping against his pants, until the creases disappeared. The last one was an obnoxious snob who introduced himself as "Brandon Chandler, the Third." He actually said that—"the Third"—as if a dishwasher barely eking out a living cared what his father and grandfather had been called.

To Lefty's astonishment, they expected him to demonstrate his cooking skills. While he figured he'd blow the audition, since he'd only watched chefs work, he took a chance. He told Ashcroft, the only one who spoke a little Spanish, that he'd make a special dish to honor the impending holiday, Christmas Surprise. The "surprise" part being if it actually worked.

The ship's galley looked as sleek and gleaming as he expected, with rich burl cabinets and shiny stainless steel counters, over aged teak floors. And they stocked it well with fresh and canned foods. But it was awfully small. A real chef might have been put off by its compact design or that its old-fashioned propane stove burned cooler than traditional gas or electric ranges. Fortunately, Lefty had nothing to compare it to, and he took to that efficient space like a flying marlin to the deep blue sea. Using no more utensils than fit in the small stainless steel sink, Lefty turned out a fabulous lunch of spicy marlin steaks with some tomato and chili concoction, in Christmas red and green, that he'd seen the chef at the resort make a few nights before. All three men cleaned their elegant china plates down to the pattern.

After they finished, Ashcroft asked Lefty in halting Spanish, "What's your name, boy?"

Name? Lefty hadn't come up with a Spanish name. It occurred to him that the Spanish word for "left" was *izquierda*. *"Soy Izzy,"* he said at last. I'm Izzy.

"Izzy? Izzy doesn't sound like a Spanish name to me," that Third guy said after Ashcroft translated.

But Lefty just used a technique that would work well for him in the days that followed and pretended he couldn't understand Ashcroft's Spanish. Ashcroft stomped off in anger, causing Lefty to conclude he wasn't a man who took criticism or failure well. He should try walking in Lefty's unlucky shoes. Still, Ashcroft hired Lefty and said they would set sail the following morning.

NOTHING much happened during their first few days at sea. They sent him to shore for a small Christmas tree for the salon. But the cheap so-and-so's didn't come across with any holiday bonus for Lefty. They didn't do anything special for the holiday, either, except to keep fishing, just like every other day. They caught a marlin, which didn't fit in the small refrigerator. Lefty had to empty the cupboard next to the stove and pack the extra fish in some ice from the freezer in the storage locker. The three passengers crewed the yacht themselves, but that still left time to fish. And lots of marlin ran in the waters off Mexico.

Lefty cooked loads of it in his small galley. He named it all in honor of the coming holidays: Christmas Surprise, Boxing Day Surprise and New Year's Eve Surprise—he was running out of names! New Year's Eve Surprise looked a lot like Christmas Surprise, only instead of the tomato-and-chili sauce, he topped with some fruity concoction he'd made with canned fruit cocktail and enough brandy to fill a small ocean. He felt too superstitious not to keep the "surprise" theme going, since it had worked so well for his cooking audition.

They paid Lefty daily as promised with a fifty-dollar bill. Fifty bucks! There were times when he hadn't made that much in a month.

At first, nothing obviously crooked appeared to be going on. But Lefty slept on a cot in the storage locker off the galley, too far from the salon, where the men gathered for after dinner drinks, to hear much conversation. Lefty did discover that the three were top executives of some bank, which apparently had lost a bundle under their guidance. He also learned the yacht itself belonged to the bank. He couldn't imagine a staid bank giving its yacht a name as hokey as "Dolly Sue." But Lefty began to believe he'd been wrong in thinking those guys were pulling a scam. If all they were doing was fishing, despite those fifty-dollar payments, Lefty was going to be disappointed.

Then, a few days after Christmas, things changed. Ashcroft dropped anchor well out in the Pacific and turned to Lefty. "Izzy, you're going to take the dinghy to Cabo and overnight a letter from the FedEx office there," he said in his halting Spanish. "Think you can do that?"

Could he? Sure. Did he want to? No way. The dinghy was motorized, but small. And marlin weren't the only fish in those waters—they'd also seen lots of sharks swim past. But the hard look in Ashcroft's pale blue eyes told Lefty the order wasn't subject to debate.

The round trip in the dinghy passed without trouble. That night, the murmuring voices coming from the salon seemed more frantic, but Lefty couldn't catch a word. Two days later, after they moved the yacht again, they sent him to a different village and another FedEx office. That night the trio seemed even edgier. But Lefty couldn't figure out why.

There had to be something crooked going on. Why had they taken the precaution of hiring a Spanish-speaking chef if they never said anything important in front of him? Life really had jinxed him, Lefty decided. The scam of the century could be going on under his nose, and he still couldn't pick up its scent.

But that night, while serving an increasing number of brandies, he overheard something interesting.

"Dick," Kandensky said. "You never told us how you found out the Board of Directors planned to fire us."

Ashcroft removed a fat fountain pen from his pocket. "Gentlemen, we have this to thank for the warning."

"A pen?" Third asked.

Turns out it wasn't a pen at all, Lefty discovered, but a listening device disguised as a pen, which Ashcroft purchased on the Internet. The pen part transmitted a signal to a tiny receiver that fit in the listener's ear. When Ashcroft thought his Board might have been planning some move against him and his cohorts, he excused himself from the meeting, leaving the pen behind. Then, outside the boardroom, he heard what they said behind his back.

"And that's how we're able to take action against those ungrateful jerks," Ashcroft said, slurring his words. "So we can get what's coming to us."

Yes! Lefty knew it. But how could he make this pay off for him?

His break didn't come until he made a trip to yet another FedEx office. The clerk there was busy, but someone had left a tattered copy of *USA Today* on the counter. Lefty had never been one to read newspapers, but the faces of his three employers jumped out at him. "Bank Executives Kidnapped in Mexico," the headline screamed. "Twenty Million Dollar Ransom Demanded by Abductors."

Lefty's mind reeled. Twenty million dollars! But what abductors? Those three were no more kidnap victims than he was. That was the scam! They'd faked their own kidnapping to extract a ransom from the bank, before the Board had a chance to fire them. Sweet.

Lefty kept reading. His assessment of the three was right. Ashcroft had been an explosives expert in the military, the article revealed, prior to working at the bank. The other two were spoiled brats who went through their families' money before they lost the bank's. More interesting, though, was the authorities' view of the kidnapping. Since ransom messages came from all over Mexico, the cops couldn't determine the victims' whereabouts. Neither, the paper said, had anyone spotted the bank's yacht, the "Dollar Sign."

"Dollar Sign?" That was a better name for a yacht owned by a bank than "Dolly Sue." But now Lefty understood the name's bad paintjob—his employers had painted a new name on the boat, so passing vessels wouldn't recognize it.

That evening, one night before New Year's Eve, after Lefty served New Year's Eve Surprise again, they moved the yacht once more. Then Ashcroft left in the dinghy, disguised by a hooded jacket and sunglasses, even though the sun had already set. He brought along a large backpack.

When he returned hours later, Ashcroft said to Lefty in his awful Spanish, "Izzy, you're going to shore tomorrow afternoon. But this time, we want you to pick up a couple of boxes from FedEx, rather than mailing anything. Come straight back here, mind you. Don't get caught up in the New Year's Eve frivolity." He turned a stern look on Lefty. "They're big on celebrating with firecrackers here, and we don't want anything to happen to that...equipment...we've ordered."

Equipment, my eye, Lefty thought. The boxes he'd pick up wouldn't be filled with equipment, but money! Ransom money. His chance had finally arrived.

But in the morning, Lefty couldn't decide who was more nervous, him or his employers. Him, definitely. He was the one taking the risk. It occurred to him that if the bank was simply shipping the ransom money to a FedEx office, as he gathered the notes he'd sent must have demanded, the Mexican *Federales* were going to close in on him when he picked up the shipment.

He thought about taking the dinghy to shore and just disappearing. But the money he'd made cooking wasn't enough to support him for long. And he couldn't go back to washing dishes. There had to be more to this scam than he knew.

His nervousness grew when he tied up the dinghy at the dock and took a cab into town. Though it was still only late afternoon, the New Year's Eve celebration had already begun. People staggered about with empty champagne bottles, while others set off so many firecrackers, the air smelled of gunpowder. But armed *Federales* also patrolled the area, especially around the Fed-Ex store.

When he told the cab driver to wait for him, his voice came out in a squeak. His knees trembled as he approached the FedEx store, when he counted how many armed guards surrounded it, all trying to act casual. Lefty hesitated, ready to turn away.

But just then an explosion went off down the street. That time it was no firecracker—a store burst into flames! Most of the *Federales* ran that way. Then another blast went off. On and on it went until much of the district had burst into flames.

Ashcroft! Lefty thought. The newspaper said he'd been an explosives expert. He must have been setting those charges when he left the yacht the night before. What a great diversion.

Within moments, the entire area was enveloped in absolute chaos. When the FedEx clerk ran through the doorway of one of the few storefronts untouched by the explosive charges, Lefty dashed in. He zipped around the counter only to stumble over two large boxes addressed to: "The captain of the Dollar Sign."

That was it! The ransom. Despite their hefty weight, Lefty scooped up the boxes and ran back to the cab. Briefly, he considered just escaping with more money than he would ever see. But he remembered Ashcroft's frosty eyes—he would hunt Lefty down. He'd have to find another way to steal a piece of it. At the dinghy, he loaded his cargo and raced back to the yacht.

Once he stepped on board, however, Ashcroft took charge of the packages. "Izzy, you've done a fine job. Here's an extra day's pay." He handed Lefty a fifty-dollar bill. "Now I'm going to take you back to shore in the dinghy."

No! Lefty really was jinxed. He couldn't get this close to a big score and walk away with a measly fifty bucks.

"I need to get my stuff," Lefty said, stalling for time.

"Oh. Well, hurry up," Ashcroft said with a frown.

While the three men, who'd just be made newly richer, huddled near the bow of the yacht with the packages, Lefty slipped through the salon. He spotted Ashcroft's transmitter-pen and receiver there. Suddenly, he knew how to change his bad luck. He snatched up the receiver-part an instant before Ashcroft appeared and put the pen in his pocket.

Lefty gathered his things and returned to the dinghy. With no more than an absent smile, Ashcroft dropped him on shore, before heading back to the yacht.

But Lefty had a plan. He would pay the captain of another vessel to take him back to the yacht, where he'd sneak on board and hide. Then, with the help of the receiver, he'd listen until he'd learned where they'd stored the money. Once they went to sleep, he'd take as much of it as he could carry and escape in the dinghy. When he hit shore again, he would have plenty of money to keep him going for a long time. Yet it wouldn't be so much that they'd care enough to find him.

The one flaw in his scheme was finding a captain to take him to the yacht. Most of the boats had been chartered for New Year's Eve cruises. The only one who agreed to take him demanded all the money he'd made cooking. But it was worth it. Besides, there was plenty more on board.

That evening, Lefty crept over the rear rail of the yacht. He kept a low profile, but he didn't see or hear the three passengers. Must be in their staterooms, Lefty thought, counting their money. He zipped to the tiny galley and crawled into one of the cabinets. It was a tight fit, especially with a container in there that held a large section of marlin on ice. Lefty would have liked that extra room. He could also have done without the fishy smell. But he couldn't afford to make too much noise.

He slipped the receiver into his ear. Ashcroft's voice came through quite clearly.

"Gentlemen, we did it. We took the bank for plenty. Soon they'll think we're dead, so they'll never come looking for us."

Dead? Lefty thought. Why would the bank directors think

that? It occurred to him that in addition to Ashcroft's voice, the sound of lapping water was coming through awfully strong. Never before had it sounded that pronounced on the yacht.

"You're a genius, Dick," Third's voice said.

And was that an outboard motor he heard? Another thought struck Lefty almost instantly—when he'd climbed on board, the dinghy hadn't been hanging from the stern as usual. Could they be off in it right now, with the money? Why would they?

That answer came through the receiver, as if they'd heard Lefty's thoughts.

"Yup," Third said, "They'll never even look for us, once the yacht blows."

Once the yacht blows...?

"They'll figure some New Year's Eve firecrackers ignited the propane stove, and it exploded," Third continued.

"Where did you put the bomb?" Kandensky's voice asked.

Bomb?

Ashcroft said, "Right next to the stove. I stuck it in a piece of fish Izzy left on ice in the galley."

Tentatively, Lefty opened the container and picked up that section of marlin, which seemed awfully heavy. He peered beneath the silver skin. Red LED numbers—of the sort you never see in fish, but often see on bombs—flashed before his eyes.

4...3...2...

Jinxed right to the end, Lefty's last thought was that *this* was the real New Year's Eve Surprise.

† † †

KRIS NERI is the author of the Agatha, Anthony and Macavity Award-nominated Tracy Eaton mysteries and the forthcoming Samantha Brennan/Annabelle Haggerty supernatural- mystery series, as well as a standalone suspense novel. She has published sixty short stories and is a two-time Derringer Award-winner and a two-time Pushcart Prize-nominee for her short mystery fiction. Readers can reach her through her website, www.krisneri.com.

Praise For Sisters in Crime Desert Sleuths Chapter Anthologies from DS Publishing

SO WEST: SO DEADLY

† 2016 International Book Awards Finalist - Best Anthology

"The Wild (South)West has never been so much wicked fun. This exceptional collection showcases new and exciting talent, while exploring the Southwest in all of its magnificence...and malfeasance."

~ HILARY DAVIDSON, Award-Winning author of *Blood Always Tells*

"What a constellation of talent there is amongst The Desert Sleuths! There are echoes of short story greats in this anthology—Stephen King, Lee Child, Laura Lippman—but with unique shadings that come deep from Arizona's dry, hot heart. There is something for everyone in this not-to-be-missed collection."

~ JENNY MILCHMAN, Mary Higgins Clark award-winning author of *Cover of Snow* and *Ruin Falls*

SOWEST: CRIME TIME

"Suspenseful, surprising and sometimes even hilarious! This twisty and entertaining collection of revenge, retaliation, and diabolical deeds not only showcases the gorgeous and unique southwest—but also the skill and originality of these incredibly talented sisters in crime. Loved it!"

~ HANK PHILLIPPI RYAN, Agatha, Anthony, Macavity, Mary Higgins Clark Award-Winning author

"From the desert to the mountains, from the grungiest cabin to the swankiest mansion, from the oldest native traditions to streets in Scottsdale where the stucco isn't dry—these stories bring the southwest to exuberant life. Heart swelling hero(in)es, dastardly villains, and a glorious rabblesome chorus of authentic folks jump off the pages. What a box of delights!"

~ CATRIONA McPHERSON, Anthony, Agatha, Macavity, Bruce Alexander Award-winning author

Praise For Sisters in Crime Desert Sleuths Chapter Anthologies from DS Publishing

SOWEST: DESERT JUSTICE
† *Suspense Magazine*'s Best Anthology of 2012 Finalist
† New Mexico-Arizona Book Awards Finalist –
Best Anthology 2012

"Arizonans and all who love their mountains and deserts spiced with danger are in for a treat. The Sisters in Crime Desert Sleuths have put together another anthology of stories that powerfully evoke all the beautiful (and deadly) aspects of their state: white water rivers, hidden caves, steep mountain trails, blast-furnace deserts and yes, diamondback rattlers. Visit at your own risk!"
~ MARGARET MARON, award-winning author of
Three-Day Town and *The Buzzard Table*

"Reading SoWest: Desert Justice is like smacking open a piñata and having 20 engaging, enticing and enthralling stories rain down in their brilliant jewel-toned wrappers for a reader to snatch up and savor.
~ JENN MCKINLAY, *New York Times* bestselling author

SOWEST, SO WILD
† *Suspense Magazine*'s Best Anthology of 2011 Finalist

"Arizona proves hot, dry, and deadly in this anthology. There's something for everyone to enjoy here, in tales of murder ranging from the humorous to the macabre."
~MEG GARDINER, Edgar Award winning author of
The Nightmare Thief

"An old time sheriff only had six bullets loaded into his gun to take care of the bad guys—with *SoWest So Wild*, twenty different authors take aim and each one hits the bulls-eye. You'll never look at the Wild West the same way again."
~ TONI L.P. KELNER, co-editor of the *New York Times* bestselling anthology *Death's Excellent Vacation*

www.ingramcontent.com/pod-product-compliance
Lightning Source LLC
Chambersburg PA
CBHW051458170626
46811CB00002B/539